GHOST OF SUMMER

Sally Berneathy

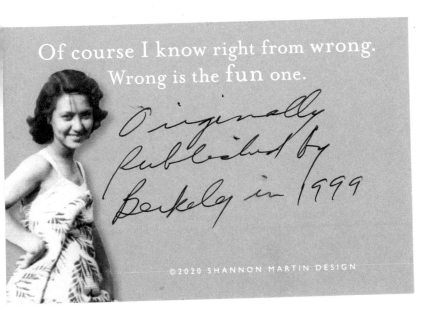

Of course I know right from wrong.
Wrong is the fun one.

Originally published by Berkeley in 1999

©2020 SHANNON MARTIN DESIGN

Books by Sally Berneathy

Death by Chocolate
(book 1 in the Death by Chocolate series)

Murder, Lies and Chocolate
(book 2 in the Death by Chocolate series)

The Great Chocolate Scam
(book 3 in the Death by Chocolate series)

The Ex Who Wouldn't Die
(book 1 in Charley's Ghost series)

The Ex Who Glowed in the Dark
(book 2 in Charley's Ghost series)

Ghost of Summer
Copyright ©2012 Sally Berneathy

ISBN-10: 1939551129
ISBN-13: 978-1-939551-12-2

Original cover art by Alicia Hope,
http://www.aliciahopeauthor.blogspot.com/

Prologue

"Mommy!" Two-year old Katie Fallon sobbed uncontrollably against her father's chest, soaking his best white shirt with her tears.

Jerome Fallon held his daughter close and tried to comfort her, but it was hard to offer comfort when he could find none for himself. "Mama's in heaven now, Katie-girl. She's an angel."

"No! Don't want her in heaven! Want her with me!"

That was exactly the way he felt about his wife's untimely death. He didn't want her to be an angel. He wanted her here with him, in his arms, in his life.

Tears streamed down his face as he patted Katie's small shoulder. Feeling helpless and lost, he looked around the big old house that had been filled with so much love and happiness only a week ago. Now it was empty.

Since he was the Sheriff of Briar Creek County, Texas, he'd been the one to investigate the accident up on the highway, the one with no survivors, the one where his wife, returning from a shopping trip to Tyler, had died instantly.

Every morning since then he'd awakened expecting to find Emma beside him, and every morning he'd found only the empty bed.

For Katie's sake, he had to carry on.

If he could just figure out how to do that.

Emma had been his rock, his soul-mate, his anchor in life. He had no idea how he was going to make it without her. Nor did he have any idea how he was going to be able to raise Katie without Emma.

"Don't cry, Katie-girl. Please don't cry. Papa's here."

Small wonder she couldn't stop crying when he couldn't either.

A knock came from the front door.

"Come on in!" He swiped a hand across his face, trying to wipe away some of the tears.

His and Emma's best friends, George and Francine Rodgers, came in with their son, Luke, a year older than Katie and already her best friend. George and Francine stood awkwardly just inside the door, but Luke ran over to Katie, rested one little hand on Jerome's knee and patted Katie's shoulder with the other.

"It was a nice funeral, Jerome," Francine said. "Very simple. Emma would have wanted that."

Jerome nodded. Emma would have wanted not to die, to stay with her family. But he didn't say that.

"Katie?" Luke said tentatively. "Don't cry."

To Jerome's surprise, Katie looked up at Luke, her sobs subsiding a little.

Luke reached into his jeans pocket. "I got gum." He handed her a piece.

She took it, unwrapped the stick and put it into her mouth, chewing in rhythm with her decreasing sobs and sniffles.

"Wanna play ball?" he asked.

She nodded, sniffed a couple of times and slid from her father's lap. Luke took her hand and led her across the room then out the front door.

Luke had only been a year old when Katie was born, but he'd immediately taken to her, and the two of them had been inseparable ever since.

"We came by to see if you wanted us to take Katie to our house for a while and give you a chance to rest," George said.

Jerome looked at his empty lap, at the empty room.

No, he didn't want them to take Katie away even for a

minute. She was all he had left.

But she had calmed when Luke came to her. Maybe he himself was responsible for some of her grief. He was sure at her age she didn't comprehend what was going on, but maybe she sensed his sorrow. Maybe he was transferring his anguish to her.

He nodded. "Thanks. That might be a good idea if you wouldn't mind taking her for a few hours."

Francine, her own eyes red from crying, came over and gave him a hug. George followed and gripped his shoulder silently.

"You try to get some rest, then come over to our house whenever you're ready and we'll have dinner," Francine said.

Jerome nodded again.

He walked to the door with them, then closed it and went upstairs, heading for the room he'd shared with Emma for nineteen years. He knew he wouldn't really rest, but he was bone-weary. He might as well lie down.

As he walked slowly down the hall, he noticed a faint glow coming from his room.

No, it wasn't really a glow.

Well, maybe it was, only he couldn't be sure if he actually saw it or only felt it.

He really was tired, so tired he couldn't see straight.

He turned into his room and was greeted by Emma's favorite scent, lilacs.

"Hello, Jerome." Emma stood by the window, smiling at him.

He blinked, rubbed his eyes then shook his head.

Emma was dead. He was having a hallucination.

"Dead is a relative term," she said as if she'd heard his thought. "My body has changed a bit. It's much lighter now. I'll never have to go on a diet again."

Jerome's mouth dropped. "Emma?"

"Yes, dear?"

He looked away, closed his eyes, pinched himself, then looked back again. She was still there, the same as always, a slim figure with auburn hair. She even wore her favorite blue dress.

Well, actually, she wasn't quite the same.

She was sort of...transparent.

And she sort of glowed.

She came to him—floated to him?—lifted a hand and touched his cheek. Her fingers were warm and cool at the same time and tingled pleasantly against his skin. "It's really me, Jerome. I just couldn't leave you and Katie. Heaven's quite nice, but I already had heaven down here with you. I missed you both so terribly much I got a kind of special dispensation to come back long enough to help you get our Katie raised, if that's all right with you."

Again tears streamed down Jerome's face, but this time they were tears of joy. "All right? Oh, Emma, my sweet Emma!"

If this was a hallucination, he wanted to go on having it.

He wrapped his arms around her...and through her. It was like reaching inside sunlight. Not unpleasant but a little odd.

"That's all right, dear," she said. "We'll have a lot of years to practice with all the peculiarities of this new body. I'll stay until our Katie is grown and finds her true love, the way you and I found each other."

Chapter One

"Papa, I have wonderful news!" Kate Fallon clutched the phone to her ear and smiled brightly across her living room at her fiancé who smiled back at her. "Spencer and I have decided to get married."

Kate chewed her lip, realized she was doing it and ordered herself to relax. Papa was always supportive of anything that made her happy, and the emotional stability she'd found with Spencer made her happy. Spencer was reliable, solid and dependable.

"Spencer," Papa repeated in his lazy, east Texas drawl. "Do I know Spencer?"

"Spencer Osborne. You met him at my company's awards banquet last winter. He was my escort."

"Oh, yeah. Tall, blond hair, navy blue suit without one speck of lint on it. Stands really straight. Walks like he had a yard stick stuck to his spine."

Kate noticed she was sitting—perching, really—on the edge of her chair in just such a stance. She made an effort to sit back, to relax, but it was a futile effort.

Papa hadn't said anything negative about Spencer. He was actually dead-on in his description. Spencer was meticulous, and his posture was excellent. However, she sensed her father didn't like her fiancé.

"We've decided on Labor Day weekend for our wedding," she continued and wondered if she sounded as nervous to Papa and Spencer as she did to herself.

Well, every woman was nervous about getting married. That was normal.

"That'll give us three months to get all the legalities taken care of. The ceremony will be very informal, at the office of the Justice of the Peace with only family then a small reception afterward. You're the sum total of my family and Spencer's an only child, too, so it will be really small."

"Good idea. Spend the money on a bang-up honeymoon. Go to Hawaii or something."

Kate lifted a hand to blot the dampness of perspiration from her upper lip. Was something wrong with the air conditioner? Her open, spacious condo that always seemed cool with its off-white carpet, white furniture and glass-topped tables, had suddenly become almost as warm as the June day outside—and June in Dallas could get pretty warm.

"Actually, we're not going on a honeymoon. We plan to invest the money we'll save."

Spencer smiled and nodded approval.

"I see. Well, that sounds real sensible, sweetheart."

Papa was saying the right words, but Kate still perched tensely on the edge of her chair, worried about his approval.

What was the matter with her? Papa had never objected to any of her decisions. She still wasn't sure why she'd been reluctant to tell him about her impending marriage. However, he seemed...well, maybe *pleased* wasn't the right word. *Okay.* He seemed okay with it.

"So you'll come?" she said.

"Of course I will. I wouldn't miss my little girl's wedding for anything. Your mother and I have been looking forward to that day. We did kind of want to see you walk down the aisle of the Grand Avenue Methodist Church here in Briar Creek where we got married, but whatever you want is fine with us. I know you said the ceremony would be informal, but you will want to wear your mother's dress, won't you? That would mean so much to her, and it won't cost you anything except the cleaning bill. It's probably a mite dusty from being stored in that trunk in the attic."

Kate frowned, then quickly erased the expression so

Spencer wouldn't think anything was wrong.

Had she heard right? Was Papa talking as if Mama was still alive?

Though she'd didn't really remember the mother who had died when she was two, Papa had raised her with her mother's presence. *Your mother would want you to brush your teeth. Your mother and I decided when you were a baby...*

But he hadn't been talking in the past tense just now. He'd used the present. *Your mother and I have been looking forward to that day...whatever you want is fine with us.*

She noticed she was biting her lip again.

She was really letting her nerves get the best of her. What difference did it make if Papa didn't get his verb tenses quite right all the time? He was the County Sheriff. The job didn't require a PhD in English grammar.

"Katie-girl? Are you there?"

"Oh, yes! I'm sorry. I was just thinking about Mama's dress. It's so...so elegant. I don't know if it will be appropriate. I'll have to talk to Spencer. See what he's planning to wear."

When she'd been a little girl, she'd dreamed about walking down the aisle of the Grand Avenue Methodist Church in that dress, Mama beside her in spirit. But those were the dreams of a little girl, not a grown, practical woman who no longer had stars in her eyes.

"Whatever you want to do is fine with us. Are you planning to come visit before the wedding?"

Us? Whatever you want to do is fine with us?

"Of course I'm coming to visit. I couldn't stay away from you for three months. I've got some vacation time at work, and I thought I'd try to get down there for a couple of days next month, maybe make the Fourth of July weekend. We could take Spencer to the big barbecue."

"We could do that. Does Spencer like barbecue?"

The room became even warmer. The air conditioner was broken. No doubt about it. Where was she going to find a repairman on Sunday afternoon?

"No, uh, maybe he does. Actually, not really." He'd said it was fine for people who couldn't buy a decent cut of meat and had to add artificial flavor. "But there's other food, it's a great festival, and the fireworks are incredible."

"I'd really like for you to come down sooner."

That wasn't like Papa to push her on anything.

"I don't know. There's so much to do. We've got to see the lawyer about a prenuptial agreement. I've got to—" She hesitated, unsure why she didn't want to tell Papa about the sensible decision she and Spencer had reached concerning not bringing any more children into an already overpopulated, over-polluted world...children Kate wasn't at all sure she'd be able to care for. The idea of having children frightened her on a personal as well as a social level.

She knew Papa wanted grandchildren, knew he and Mama had wanted a dozen kids. However, he'd always encouraged her to make her own decisions and had never criticized those decisions.

She lifted her chin and stared out the glass doors at the tree that grew half over her third-floor balcony. That tree always seemed reassuring to her. She'd chosen this condo for its view of trees and the creek below.

"I'm having a tubal ligation in two weeks." There. She'd said it.

In spite of her reassurances to herself, her knowledge she was doing the right thing, she held her breath waiting for Papa's response, and the temperature in the room rose a few more degrees. Maybe she'd accidentally turned on the heat instead of the air conditioning.

"I've heard they can do that and send you home in

one day," Papa said. "Modern science sure is great."

He hadn't said one word against her decision. So why did she still feel so nervous?

"You know I've never really been able to relate to babies and small children." That was an understatement. They terrified her with their softness and fragility. "Who knows if I could have children anyway?" she rushed on. "Look how many years it took you and Mama to have me. Something like that could be hereditary."

"You know whatever you choose to do is fine with your mother and me."

He'd done it again, made it sound as if he'd been talking to Mama recently. Was something wrong?

Stop that! she ordered herself. *Papa's fine. Don't look for problems.*

"Well, I'd better go and get started on some of these projects or I'll never get finished in time for the wedding. I love you, Papa."

"I love you, too, Katie-girl. Oh, could you hold on just a minute? Your mother wants to talk to you."

"What? Papa? Papa! Hello?" Katie shot out of her chair, unable to maintain her perch any longer. She clutched the phone more tightly to her ear as if she could thereby hear something other than silence.

From the corner of her eye, she saw Spencer rise from his chair and cross the room to her...walking like he had a yardstick stuck to his spine, some small part of her panic-stricken brain noted. The scent of his expensive, sophisticated cologne reached her just before he did, and suddenly it became cloying rather than comforting. He laid a firm, supportive hand on her arm.

And on the other end of the phone, silence.

"Kate?" Spencer said softly. "Is there a problem?"

"No, no, of course not." She pressed the phone even more tightly to her ear as if in fear Spencer would hear the silence and know that her father—no, she wouldn't, couldn't think that. "Everything's fine. My father, uh, dropped the phone a minute, but he's back now. Are you there, Papa?" Silence. She laughed in a high-pitched tone she'd never heard before. "You are? Good. Great. Listen, Papa, maybe I can get down there soon after all and help you get those, uh, tax problems all straightened out. Don't you worry, Papa. I'll be there. Very soon. And everything will be fine. I promise. I love you, Papa."

She disconnected the call, smoothed her sweaty palms down the sides of her beige slacks and gave Spencer what she hoped was a reassuring smile. "I have to go see Papa. Next weekend."

Spencer frowned in disbelief. No surprise. Her smile hadn't felt very reassuring from her end, and her voice had sounded distinctly desperate. "Are you sure you're all right?" he asked.

"Of course! Absolutely. I'll just run down there and get things taken care of then run right back. One weekend. That's all it'll take."

"You know I'm playing golf with Gordon Bennett, our company CEO, next Saturday so I won't be able to go with you."

"I know." *Thank goodness!* She didn't want Spencer to see her father like this. Papa had always been such a strong, proud man. "This will be a good time for a father-daughter visit. I'm sure it's a shock to him that his little girl's getting married." Maybe that was it. The shock had temporarily scattered his wits. He'd be okay once he had a chance to get used to the idea of her getting married.

But Papa had never been the type to be shocked by anything.

Spencer nodded. "Of course. Well, are you ready to go shopping for rings?"

She wasn't. Not now. She needed to be alone for a

little while, to replay Papa's conversation in her head, to see if she could make any sense of it. "Actually, I seem to have developed a bit of a headache. Maybe we could reschedule for next weekend. No, that won't work. I'll be at Papa's. Weekend after next, then."

Spencer's lips tightened slightly. He hated having his schedules changed, but there was no way she could focus on wedding rings right now when her head was filled with chaos and fear.

"I really don't feel well," she added. "Let me lie down for a couple of hours. Maybe we can squeeze in some shopping before dinner."

"All right. I'll pick you up about six." He leaned over and gave her a quick, dry kiss. She could count on him not to pry, to give her privacy, not insist on getting too close. It was one of the things she valued about Spencer, one of the reasons she'd agreed to marry him.

"I'll be ready then."

But as she closed the front door behind him, she wondered if she would be ready.

Was Papa losing his grip on reality? Had he taken the first step toward senility? The fear of that possibility pushed everything else out of her head.

She went into the kitchen and poured a glass of wine then returned to her chair. She took a sip, set the glass on the lamp table beside the phone and wrapped her arms around herself. Her apartment was no longer hot but had turned freezing cold. There was, she realized, nothing wrong with the air conditioning. It was her internal thermostat. She was terrified.

Papa was her rock, her world, the only person she'd ever been able to count on one hundred percent. She loved him with all her heart and even though he was pushing seventy—probably from the far side if he'd only admit it—she'd never thought of him as old. Until today.

The possibility of losing him—the knowledge that one day she would lose him—hit her full force.

She lifted the glass of wine again and stared at the pale liquid as it shimmered and shook...shook because her hand was shaking.

"Not yet, Papa, please."

Then when? Next month? Next year? Ten years from now?

Never.

She drained the glass without tasting it.

***

"She's awful worried about me, Emma. I hope we're doing the right thing, letting her know about you and think I'm losing my marbles so she'll come running down here." The Sheriff of Briar Creek County ran a hand through his thinning hair.

"We are, Jerome," his wife said firmly. "I love our Katie every bit as much as you do, and it breaks my heart to have to worry her. But this is like the time when she was just a little thing and you had to restrain her from eating that entire chocolate cake. We have to get her down here immediately, before she can have that surgery, and we have to get her here without that Spencer person. That man is so wrong for her."

"What is our Katie thinking, wanting to marry a man with a yard-stick stuck to his spine?" Jerome Fallon shook his head and leaned back on his comfortable old sofa. "Did you hear the way she talked about the wedding? They're going to be sensible and invest their money instead of going on a honeymoon."

"I heard that and I heard what she said about my dress. The reason she doesn't want to wear my dress is because she knows this is all wrong. Deep in her heart, she doesn't want to marry that Spencer. She'll thank us for this one day."

Emma laid an affectionate hand on his leg. Well, *in his leg* probably described the action more accurately. She was upset about Kate, not paying close enough attention to form, and her hand sank in about an inch. He experienced the familiar tingling sensation. It felt pleasant, just as it had been many years ago when they were young and she was alive. Well, today she was still alive, so that wasn't the right word. *Physical.* That was the best way he could describe it. When she'd still been physical and had laid her hand on his leg.

"Emma, you're sinking."

"Oh, sorry, dear." Emma pulled her hand back to skin level. "I really hope I can make contact with our Katie again. If we can just get her to open her heart, I know I can. At a time like this, a girl really needs her mother."

"No more than I need her." Jerome leaned over and kissed his wife on her translucent cheek. After so many years of practice, he got it just right, barely touching the surface of what Emma insisted on calling her body. Jerome didn't understand a lot about atoms and electricity or any of that sort of stuff, but it seemed to him his wife's *body* now consisted of the sparkling, electrical energy she'd possessed when she'd been physical.

A large white cat with gold markings and blue eyes leaped onto the sofa beside Emma, rubbed alongside her arm and purred.

"Well, Leo, it's about time you got up." Emma stroked his head and back, causing the fur to rise slightly wherever she touched. "Our Katie's coming to see us." As if he understood her words, Leo lifted his head to look at her with his perpetual feline grin, meowed and purred even more loudly.

"Do you think we should tell Luke she's coming?" Jerome asked.

Emma ran her hand along Leo's tail as it lifted and

13

curled in the air. "I think not. I remember when he was little how much he liked surprises."

Chapter Two

Kate pulled up in front of the sheriff's office on Main Street in Briar Creek, Texas, just before noon the following Friday. Her hands clutching the steering wheel were damp though she'd driven from Dallas with the air conditioning blasting all the way.

She turned off the engine and sat in her small, compact car for several minutes as the noon sun beat through the windows, driving out the artificial cool and turning the interior into an oven. For the first time in her life, she was reluctant to see her father. Seeing him today might confirm that something was wrong, and she didn't know how she could stand if it that were true.

The day after her conversation with her father she'd convinced herself that pre-wedding jitters combined with the knowledge that Papa was getting older had caused her imagination to run rampant. She hadn't heard her father correctly. He hadn't really been talking to Mama.

She'd called him again that evening after work. Papa had been his usual cheerful, easy-going self, aware and alert, except for that one tiny little quirk. Though he hadn't offered to put Mama on the phone, he had relayed information from Mama in an upbeat, three-way conversation.

The next day Kate had requested and been given a week of vacation starting that Friday. She had to see her father. If something really was wrong...well, she'd face that when and if she had to.

Possibly it was only the news of her impending marriage that had sent Papa out into temporary *lala* land. Maybe it would help if she could reassure him that this change in her life would be minimal, would in no way affect her close relationship with him.

The heat in the car became unbearable, and she had

15

to get out, go inside, face reality, whatever that reality was.

An icy fist wrapped around her heart as she climbed from the car, crossed the sidewalk and pushed open the door, uncertain what she'd find in the familiar office where her father had presided as sheriff for as long as she could remember.

The reception area was empty. Evelyn had probably already gone to lunch. She strode across the room toward the offices on one side occupied by Papa and his deputy, Pete.

"Papa?"

A quick scan of the first small room told her he wasn't there. In the second, the deputy—someone new, definitely not Pete—glanced up from sifting through a chaotic collection of papers on the old wooden desk while carrying on a phone conversation. When the man's gaze fastened on her, his brown eyes widened and his lips came to a sudden halt in the middle of a word.

Kate ran a self-conscious hand through her hair, checking to see if she'd suddenly sprouted horns, and backed out of the doorway.

The deputy picked up his phone conversation again, but his eyes never left her.

She sank down in a chair in the reception area, out of range of that unnerving scrutiny. Even so, she had to admit she was little flattered at being admired by someone as attractive as the new deputy.

Well, actually, *attractive* didn't have quite the right ring to it. The word was too bland. His tanned face was craggy, all angles, his black hair unruly, his eyes dark with unexplored depths. There was nothing smooth about the man, but there was something familiar and strange and overwhelmingly intriguing.

Sexy.

16

That word fit a lot better.

A pang of guilt niggled at her, but she brushed it away.

So she was engaged. That didn't mean she couldn't look and appreciate. And Papa's new deputy was certainly not anyone she'd do more than look at. Even one glance at him told her he was the opposite of everything she valued in Spencer.

Where the heck was Papa?

She got up and paced impatiently around the reception area. As she passed the deputy's door, her gaze was drawn to him again.

His broad shoulders did amazing things to that crisp, tan uniform. Black hairs escaped from the open neck, and the short sleeves revealed tanned, well-muscled arms.

Again his gaze met hers and something in the depths of his eyes—depths that swirled into spaceless infinity yet reflected back her image—seemed to reach out to her as if to someone familiar. She ought to turn away, sit down, stop acting like a school girl. Instead she stood there staring at him, mesmerized by his eyes.

The long fingers of his big hand curled around the phone in a somehow intimate fashion, and she stopped herself from running one of her own hands up her arm as if his gaze was a physical touch on her skin.

What on earth was the matter with her?

She had never been given to drooling over strange men even before she became engaged. The shock of worrying about Papa's sanity, his sudden relationship with Mama's ghost, must be affecting her equilibrium.

The deputy hung up the phone, and Kate settled her lips into a prim smile. "I'm—" she began.

"Katie?" He slid the chair back, rising to an impressive height.

Kate blinked, clutching at the elusive memory the

17

single word evoked. He could have heard her childhood
name from her father, she told herself, and she'd come in
calling for Papa. That was easy to figure.

But there was something about the voice that teased
at the edges of her memory, taunting her then flitting away
before she could grasp it.

His lips stretched into a lazy, sexy smile as he went
around the desk and came toward her. "Katie Fallon? Is
that really you? You're—" He stopped inches away and
spread his hands as if suddenly seized with awkwardness.
"You're all grown up. It's me, Luke Rodgers."

Kate went cold then hot as a thousand emotions
swept over her at once, emotions that ran the gamut from
joy to anger and fear.

"Luke?" She clapped her hands to her cheeks,
wishing she could cover the blush she knew stained her
whole face.

Of course his voice was familiar. She'd heard him
call her name a thousand times when they were
children...and a thousand more in sad, poignant dreams
after he'd moved away when she was eleven.

*And she'd just been having sexual thoughts about
him!* That was perverted! Luke had been like a brother.
She really was losing her equilibrium. Maybe her sanity.

"Luke?" she repeated. "I don't believe it. What are
you doing here?"

He spread his arms wide, showing off the uniform as
well as the breadth of his chest. "I'm the new deputy
sheriff. I'm surprised Sheriff didn't mention it." She
noticed that he called her father by the nickname the town
had given him over the years, shortened from Sheriff of
Briar Creek. When they were young, more often than not,
he'd called her father *Papa*, just as she had...just as she'd
often called his parents *Mom* and *Dad* in imitation of him.

But that was long ago and far away.

"No. No, he didn't mention it." *How could Papa have failed to tell her something that important?* Was this further evidence of his mental deterioration?

For a moment she thought Luke was going to pull her into his open arms, hold her the way they'd held each other when they were children...a lifetime ago. For a moment she wanted him to, desperately needing the innocent comfort and friendship they'd once shared.

But they'd lost that years ago, lost it irretrievably. Besides, it wasn't innocent friendship she'd been feeling only a few moments ago. It wasn't innocent friendship that made her want to bolt into his arms.

He hesitated as if reading her mind. It was only for a fraction of a second, and someone who knew him less well would have missed it.

He took her hands in his and smiled down at her. "It really is you. Did you just get into town? Did Sheriff know you were coming?"

Of course her father knew she was coming. Why hadn't he told Luke? Had he forgotten? Kate's fingers clenched Luke's, holding on more tightly than she should, an automatic gesture of need she thought she'd left far behind.

"I talked to Papa this morning. Didn't he tell you?" Gently she took her hands from Luke and was dismayed to find that her palms were clammy.

"No, he never said a word. Maybe he wanted to surprise both of us."

Surely that was it. A surprise reunion party, like a surprise birthday party. "That's probably it."

Luke checked the large, utilitarian watch on his left wrist. "It's almost noon. Have you had lunch? I was just getting ready to run over to Dodie's Diner for a burger. Why don't you come with me?"

"I can't do that. Papa asked me to meet him here and

19

go to lunch with him." Luke could be right about Papa wanting to surprise them. It would be just like him to have set up the whole thing so the three of them could go to lunch together.

Luke's forehead creased in a brief frown. "That's funny. Sheriff left half an hour ago to check out a vandalism report. Somebody painted a big, round face with a frown on Homer Grimes' barn. Kind of appropriate from what I remember of Homer Grimes. I offered to go, but Sheriff insisted on doing it himself. Said he'd known Homer for a lot of years and knew how to deal with him. It must have slipped his mind that you were coming. He'll be gone at least another hour."

People forget appointments all the time, Kate told herself, trying to push aside the chill. "Yes, it must have slipped his mind."

She forced a smile and restrained herself from an urge to run out of the office as fast as she could, away from this man she'd once blindly trusted in a way that only a child could trust, to go home and wait for Papa in the safety of the old house.

But that was silly. What happened between Luke and her when they were children was long ago and far away. Of no consequence now. Luke was Papa's deputy, worked with her father every day. He could tell her if Papa was all right, if he ever mentioned Mama, how many things he forgot and, putting aside her selfish concerns for his welfare, whether he should be allowed to run around town carrying a badge and a gun.

If he was talking to Mama, would he soon be talking to Billy the Kid and Jesse James? *Shooting* Billy the Kid and Jesse James?

"Then let's go get one of Dodie's burgers with her special sauce," she said brightly.

Luke caught her arm as she headed out the door. She

turned back and was again sucked into that intense gaze.

"Katie, I'm sorry I never answered any of your letters. I was going through a rough time."

She slid her arm from his grasp. "It doesn't matter. We were just children." His apology, rather than taking away the transgression, recalled the haunting, unbearable pain of loss she'd moved to the dark corners of her mind years ago.

She shook off the unpleasant sensation. She'd been eleven years old. She was, as Luke had said, *all grown up* now, no longer a child. It had been an eternity, more than half her lifetime, since a little boy who no longer existed broke the heart of a little girl who also no longer existed.

"Of course it matters," he said softly. "You sent me those long, wonderful letters full of life and energy and—" He shrugged and grimaced. "I'm sorry. It wasn't because I forgot you or because I didn't miss you—"

"It's okay," she interrupted, wanting him to stop dredging up things that no longer had any relevance in her life, things that were over and done and couldn't be changed. Apparently Luke shared the trendy preoccupation of some people for exhuming and examining, ad infinitum, events whose resurrection served no purpose except to upset them all over again. "I'm starved. Let's go get those burgers." *And forget the past.* She had plenty to worry about in the present.

She'd been a little disconcerted at seeing Luke again after all these years, but it wasn't anything that really bothered her. So they'd been friends and playmates once upon a time. That was long ago. Things were different now. They were both adults. Her only connection to him now was that he was her father's deputy.

***

Luke followed Katie outside, into the blast of summer heat. However, it wasn't one damned bit hotter than he'd felt in that office with Katie. What the hell was the matter with him, letting his hormones go haywire over a woman who was not only Sheriff's daughter but also his own best friend, his virtual sister, from years ago?

When he'd glanced up to see her standing in the doorway, he'd thought for a minute he was hallucinating. He'd just been thinking about her, though her image in his mind had still been that of a skinny, freckle-faced eleven year old girl. The woman in the doorway had looked very much and very little like his old friend, and he'd been so shocked and confused he'd had a hard time making sense out of his phone conversation. He'd finally had to tell the court clerk he'd call her back later.

For seventeen years he'd yearned to be with Katie again. Now he was, and he felt as awkward as if he were still a teenager.

He locked the door of the sheriff's office behind them—as if anyone in Briar Creek would bother anything inside the office—then turned to Katie and smiled. "It's really good to see you."

Oh, yeah, any sophistication and conversational skills he might have acquired over the years had gone right down the drain.

As they started along the sidewalk, he automatically passed his arm around her waist, his hand coming to rest on the curve of her hip.

His Katie wasn't supposed to have curves!

He moved his hand away, aghast at the feelings when he touched her—when he looked at her. This was *Katie*, for crying out loud. Sheriff's daughter. His *friend*. He'd lost her once. He wasn't going to let himself do anything stupid and risk losing her again. He was not a teenage boy at the mercy of raging testosterone. He was a grown man with at least a little control.

He walked beside Katie, careful not to touch her

again.

The sun blazed down as it always did in Texas in the summer, pulling the smells of asphalt and hot concrete into the air. But those odors were overpowered by the delicate scents of honeysuckle and spring rain that drifted to him from Katie.

He cleared his throat and tried to clear his mind, though the latter wasn't so easy to do. From the moment he'd first decided to move back to Briar Creek, he'd looked forward to seeing Katie again, to the possibility of resuming their friendship, but nothing could have prepared him for the reality of her, her rounded breasts barely concealed by the scooped neckline of her sleeveless white dress, her slender legs that stretched for miles before disappearing under the short skirt of that dress, her full lips...

He cleared his throat again. "So you live in Dallas now," he said. It was the most mundane thing he could think of to say. The only mundane thing, actually.

She nodded, the movement sending sunlight dancing in her red-gold hair as it swung about her shoulders—her bare, creamy shoulders that would, he felt sure, feel smooth and satiny beneath his fingers.

He looked straight ahead, avoiding that silky hair, those bare shoulders, the way the sheer fabric of her dress swirled about her legs.

Now if he could just shut off the images in his mind.

"I work for an investment company," she said. "I'm a systems analyst—a computer programmer."

"That sounds...interesting." Actually, it didn't sound the least bit interesting, and it didn't sound like a career the Katie he remembered would enjoy.

"It can be interesting," she said. A little defensively, he thought. "It's very rewarding."

"*Rewarding.* That's good. So, how long are you

23

staying in Briar Creek?"

He wasn't looking at her, but he knew she scowled. He could feel it, a disturbance in the air surrounding them. They'd always had that sixth sense about each other.

"I don't know," she said, her taut tone confirming his thoughts.

She wasn't happy about this visit. Something was wrong.

Whatever it was, he'd figure out a way to make it right. He'd let her down once, but he'd make it up to her. He'd take care of her this time and not screw up.

They reached the faded green building that was Dodie's Diner.

"Papa and I haven't come here in years. We usually go to one of the restaurants up on the highway. But this place is just like it was the last time we were here. Some things never change," Katie said.

Luke scanned the wooden screen door, the plastic geraniums in pots beside the front steps, the neon sign that had read *D ie's Di er* even before he'd left. "Nope, it hasn't changed," he said, then grinned. "I like that in a diner. And a town. Briar Creek is the town where time stood still."

Katie laughed, and even though it had an edge of tension, the silvery sound tinkled through the still summer day like wind chimes, like music from his childhood. "But you've changed," she said.

"Yeah," he said quietly, "I guess I have. But only on the outside." He opened the tall, wooden door, then stood back to allow her to enter. "Katie, do you remember our thorn?"

Her expression softened. "Omigosh! Yes, I remember that. The day before you had to leave, we took a thorn from the big old locust tree down by the creek and each pricked our thumb with it."

24

"Then we buried it in the cave floor and swore we'd always be friends, that the mingled blood on the thorn would always bring us back to each other."

Her eyes—the blue shade of morning glories in the sun's first rays—seemed to mist, but her tone was crisp. "Weren't we silly little kids? It's a wonder we didn't get an infection!"

"We didn't. And it worked. We've found each other again."

She turned away abruptly and moved through the door.

He was right. Something was bothering her.

He followed her inside and sat down across from her in one of the red vinyl booths.

Katie wrinkled her nose. "Grease."

"Be pretty hard to make fries without it. And Dodie's has *the best* fries."

She arched an eyebrow. "*The best*? All this grease has clogged your arteries to the point your taste buds are completely out of kilter."

A waitress with steel gray hair pulled into a tight bun plunked down two menus and two glasses of water.

"How's it going, Nadine?" Luke asked.

"Busy. You want your regular?"

"Sure. If you've got a good thing going, why change?"

"How about you, honey? Same thing?"

"What's your regular, Luke?"

"Bacon cheeseburger, fries and a cherry Coke." It had been her regular, too, seventeen years ago.

She grimaced. "Do you have a chicken sandwich?"

"Sure do."

"I'll have that and iced tea."

Nadine left, taking the unused menus with her.

Luke leaned across the table. "That chicken sandwich

25

is a fried chicken breast."

Katie tried to grimace again, but a smile tilted the corners of her luscious mouth. "Why doesn't that surprise me?"

Luke shifted uncomfortably. He couldn't recall ever noticing Katie's lips before. Had they always been that full? Did women's lips change as they got older, the way their bodies did?

"So tell me what you've been doing the past seventeen years," she invited. "How on earth did you end up back here in Briar Creek?"

Luke shook off the inappropriate thoughts about her lips...and her body. He leaned back against the vinyl of the booth, trying to absorb some of its coolness, and focused on her question. "Well, let's see. Seventeen years in a capsule. After we moved to Houston, I went to school and graduated from school. Got a degree in criminology and joined the Houston Police Department. Got married to my high school sweetheart and got divorced. No kids. Called Sheriff and found out Pete was retiring and he was looking for a new deputy. Kicked the renters out of my old house, bought it from Mom and here I am."

Katie laughed. "Whew! That's the fastest seventeen years I've ever lived through. I think I have jet lag! So you came back here because Papa needed a new deputy?"

Luke shook his head. "No. I was coming back anyway. My heart's always been here. I missed all the trees, the clean air, seeing familiar faces everywhere you turn. I never felt like I belonged in Houston. Sheriff needing a new deputy was a fortunate coincidence." *If you believed in coincidences.* From the first, it had been as if outside forces had facilitated his move here, so much so that sometimes the whole thing felt a little eerie.

"I guess that worked out well for both of you."

"Yes, it did."

26

"How's your mother?"

"Mom's fine. She got married again just a few months ago."

"That's wonderful!" Katie enthused. "I'll have to get her address and send her a card."

"She'd like that." Irritated with himself, he bit back the pang that thoughts of his mother's remarriage always brought, the irrational worry about her and the equally irrational feeling that her marriage to another man had somehow taken away the last remnant of contact with his dead father.

"Do you think she'll remember me? It's been so long."

"Remember you? Hey, you were like her own daughter. When I told her I was moving back, she gave me strict orders to find you."

Katie smiled wistfully. "Remember how your parents and Papa used to embarrass us by telling everybody we'd been friends so long, we'd worn matching diapers?"

Luke nodded and turned his water glass between his hands. "I remember. You were like my sister, except we never argued like most brothers and sisters. We never disagreed about anything." He knew comparing the relationship of children to that of adults wasn't fair, but he couldn't stop himself from comparing the bitter fights and even more bitter silences he'd had with his ex-wife, Cindy, to the halcyon days he'd spent with Katie.

Her eyes seemed hazy with memories, too, and she wrapped slender fingers around her own water glass, unconsciously mimicking his actions just the way she used to do. "No, we never had disagreements in spite of the amount of time we spent together. I stayed at your house a lot what with Papa working such odd hours."

"When you weren't at my house, I was usually at yours."

"Until your dad died and you moved to Houston to live with your Aunt Myrtle," she said briskly, lifting the glass of water to her lips, and he could tell the nostalgic mood was shattered.

He nodded. "I thought surely my world had come to an end when I was forced to leave you and Briar Creek right on the heels of losing my dad. Twelve was the worst year of my life." *Except maybe for this past award-winning year.* "Katie, the reason I never—"

Nadine appeared and set their food on the table.

"I didn't order fries," Katie protested, inspecting her plate.

"Comes with the sandwich. You don't want 'em, don't eat 'em."

Katie grinned. "I'll eat them. That's the problem."

For a few minutes they ate in silence.

Then Katie lifted her morning-glory eyes to his, and he saw the urgency there. Maybe now he was going to find out what was bothering her so he could help her, so he could make it up to her for abandoning her all those years ago. "How long have you been working as Papa's deputy?"

It wasn't a very urgent question.

"Two weeks. I moved back a month ago, but it took me that long to get the old house cleaned up. It's sure a nice change of pace working here after all the big-city crime and drugs in Houston."

She swirled the straw in her tea, watching the activity intently as if were somehow important. "A month and he never mentioned it to me."

"Maybe he thought you wouldn't want to see me, that you were still angry at me for not writing or calling."

She looked up at him. "Of course he didn't think that." She bit her lower lip while the straw continued making its rounds in her glass of tea. "Has

28

Papa...umm...has he changed much?"

"Sure, some. He's older, his hair's almost completely gray and there's less of it. He's gained a few pounds. About what you'd expect in seventeen years. But you know that already."

"What about mentally? Do you think he's losing any of his mental acuity? He's at least seventy, you know."

"Really? I had no idea he was that old. No, mentally, he hasn't changed at all. He's as sharp as I am." He grinned. "Probably sharper."

She continued to play with that straw. She was definitely nervous, and it had something to do with Sheriff.

"I don't think he's ever really accepted Mama's death. Has he said anything to you about her?"

"Your father's always talked about your mother. Of course he hasn't accepted her death. How can anyone ever accept the loss of someone they love?"

"People can. They do. They have to." Her voice was brittle like the leaves in winter.

"Katie, are you worried that your father's senile? Is that what's bugging you?"

She didn't answer.

"Well, he isn't. He always talked about your mother like she was waiting on the other side of the door. You know that. You certainly never thought he was senile when you were a little kid and he made her live for you. He gave you a mother. He did it because he's a good person. There's nothing wrong with him. Because your mother died, you're being overly-protective of your dad."

She looked up and gave a weak smile. "You're right, of course. I shouldn't worry so much. It's just that—" She spread her hands in a helpless gesture. "No matter who else came and went in my life, Papa's always been here. I can't bear to think that one day he might not be."

29

She picked up her sandwich and took a huge bite, changing the subject by her action, veering away from the thought of losing her father.

"Sheriff's got a lot of years left," he said, as much for his benefit as hers. He didn't want to think about losing Sheriff, either. It would be like losing his own father all over again.

What he wanted to do was take Katie's slim hand in his and explain why he'd never contacted her after he moved, beg her forgiveness, reassure her that he was back for good, that he'd always be there for her now, that their relationship would be an unchanging reality they could both hang onto for the rest of their lives.

Thomas Wolfe was wrong. You could go home. He'd done it.

He was back in Briar Creek, living in his old home, doing the job his father had done, and Katie, his surrogate sister, his best friend, was sitting across from him.

Katie, wearing a thin summer dress that clung to her rounded breasts so he could see them swell with every breath she took. Katie, who somehow made sensual the act of closing her lips around the straw in her tea.

He chomped viciously into his burger, biting down on those thoughts he shouldn't be having about Katie.

He was home, back where he'd been happiest, and this time he wasn't going to screw it up or let any of it slip away.

Chapter Three

When Kate and Luke returned to the office, Evelyn was still gone, but Papa was waiting.

A huge smile spread over his face as he rose from behind the same big old wooden desk he'd had for as long as Kate could remember. "There's my favorite daughter and my best deputy!" He came around and wrapped her in a bear hug. "Ah, Katie-girl! It's so good to see you!"

For the first time, Kate noticed that he was only a couple of inches taller than she was. He'd always seemed like a giant, larger than life.

When he stepped back, still with one arm about her, Kate was dismayed to see that his twinkling blue eyes seemed a little faded and his hair was, as Luke had said, gray and thin.

When had he gotten old? She'd seen him every couple of weeks since she'd moved to Dallas, but she supposed it had happened so gradually, she hadn't noticed...or maybe she just hadn't wanted to notice.

"We're your *only* daughter and deputy, Sheriff," Luke said with a grin.

Papa waved his free hand. "Insignificant details. Did you two have a good lunch?"

Luke crossed his arms over his chest and gave Papa a mock-glare. "Sheriff, you wouldn't, by any chance, have planned to be out of the office when Katie got here, now would you?"

Papa winked and wrapped his other arm around Luke. "I knew you'd make a good law enforcement officer. See how easily you solved that one?" He looked from Luke to Kate then back again, his face glowing with happiness. "You have no idea how good it is to see you two back together. Luke, you were barely a year old when we brought Katie home from the hospital. You toddled right over to where she sat in her mama's lap and gave her a big kiss! From that day until your dad died and you had to move, you two were inseparable. You even wore matching diapers."

Luke looked at Kate, and they both burst into laughter.

"Papa," Kate protested, "all diapers were white in those days."

"Which means yours and Luke's matched."

She laughed again. "Okay, you win! Well, I'd better let you two defenders of justice get back to work. Luke, it was good to see you again." She was surprised at how true her polite comment was, how good it had felt to be with him, and a part of her pulled up short at that realization. She and Luke had their time of friendship, they'd parted, that was over and done, and they couldn't go back.

"I hope I get to see you again before you leave," he said.

"I'm sure you will," she replied, but this time she really was only being polite. There was no point in seeing Luke again. He belonged to the past, and nothing beneficial ever came from trying to resurrect the past...especially when parts of it hadn't been very pleasant the first time around.

"Course you'll see him again," Papa said. "Luke, why don't you drop by tonight for a little porch sitting. Or maybe you and Katie could chase lightning bugs like you used to."

Kate froze. Was Papa teasing or was he as confused about Luke and her as he had been about Mama two days ago? Did he think they were still children who chased fireflies in the evenings?

"Sounds good, Sheriff. See you then, Katie."

Kate fled the Sheriff's office, got into her BMW and drove down the familiar streets with unfamiliar thoughts

32

tumbling round and round in her head.

She didn't want to see Luke again tonight.

She did want to see Luke again tonight.

There was no reason to see Luke again, ever. Not only did he represent a part of her life she didn't choose to revisit, there was still her engagement to Spencer to think about. She wasn't free to spend time with another man, not even Luke.

Not that she saw Luke in that kind of a light, of course. Well, maybe when she first saw him, but that was before she knew who he was. Okay, maybe even then she still hadn't been able to get her head or her hormones completely straightened out about his identity. But she would, soon. He was just Luke, her former childhood friend, emphasis on the word *former.*

Spencer had been completely understanding when she'd suddenly decided to take a week of her vacation early and come to Briar Creek without him. To help her father set up an income tax system, she'd said, which was an out and out lie, and for a final visit with him and old friends before getting married. The last part was the truth.

She'd just had no idea those *old friends* would include Luke.

Not that it would have made a difference if she had known.

Except she could never have anticipated those inappropriate feelings when she saw her childhood friend.

To add to her anxiety about Papa, she now had to deal with her bizarre reaction to Luke.

He hadn't really changed that much, she supposed. His dark hair had always been thick and tousled even right after he'd combed it. His eyes had always been the deep brown of polished mahogany. And even as a child, he'd been tall.

So what if he'd added a few muscles and some hair

33

on his chest.

But that didn't account for all the differences. That didn't explain why he exuded an earthy masculinity, why he made her feel yearnings she shouldn't be feeling for someone who was just an old friend, yearnings she didn't want to feel for anyone.

She was going to marry Spencer. He made her feel safe and comfortable. That was what she wanted.

She and Luke had once had a very special friendship that had made her feel safe and comfortable.

For a while, when they were very young.

Then he'd moved away, and her foolish attempts to hang onto the past had fizzled—as did all such attempts eventually. A person couldn't live in two time continuums at once. People who tried only succeeded in losing the present. She'd had to turn loose of first her mother then her best friend. She'd learned not to look backward. She wouldn't do it now.

She slowed as she drove past Luke's house. He'd really cleaned it up. The renters over the years had let it run down, but now it looked just the way it had when they were kids—immaculately white and tidy with a new roof, the trellis of roses a happy splash down one side. Well-trimmed hedges served only as a boundary of the yard, too low to constitute a fence. He'd done a lot of work on it.

She pulled up in front of Papa's house two blocks away and sighed fondly as she got out of the car. It was pretty much the opposite of Luke's house in every respect. Though she'd made repeated efforts to help Papa keep it up, he'd successfully resisted almost every one of them. She had managed to hire a team of painters to paint the exterior of the big old house while he was at work one day, but that was pretty much the extent of what she'd been able to do.

Weeds—wild flowers, Papa called them—covered

most of the yard. Honeysuckle leaned heavily on the picket fence along one side.

Of course, she had to admit as she went down the cracked sidewalk, their house had never been as well kept as the Rodgers'. It hadn't been a priority with Papa. Raising a motherless girl must have been a full time job, and she couldn't complain about his priorities in that area.

And if it was her turn now, if Papa was losing it, she'd give back the same love and care he'd given her. Though she wasn't sure she could ever take care of Papa as wonderfully, as lovingly, as he had cared for her. Worse—she wasn't sure she could ever accept the fact that Papa, the rock of her life, might need to be cared for.

Papa's big cat, Leo, eased himself out of the porch swing, arched his back in an elegant stretch then strolled over to greet her as if she'd only been gone a couple of hours.

She leaned down to scratch his ears and rub under his chin. "Hi, big fellow. You been controlling the mouse population?"

Leo yawned.

"Come on in. I'll bet Papa's got some kitty treats in here just for you."

She drew in a deep breath and straightened her shoulders as she opened the front door. Whatever happened, she'd be there for Papa as he'd always been there for her. He'd been the one person in her life who'd never deserted her, never left her, and she wouldn't desert him.

***

Before Papa got home that afternoon, Kate made a pitcher of sweet tea and shoved a chicken with a couple of potatoes into the oven. The house with no air conditioning was hot even though she had turned on the attic fan. No wonder they'd eaten so many sandwiches in the summers

35

of her youth rather than heat the house by using the kitchen stove. Of course, they'd eaten sandwiches in the winter, too...both during her youth and more recently.

Over the years when she'd come to visit, she'd either picked up something in Tyler on her way in or they'd made sandwiches or gone to the pizza place or the Chinese place on the highway. Sundays after church everyone went to the Grand Street Café for fried chicken. Neither she nor Papa had ever done much cooking.

But for some unknown reason, Papa now had a kitchen full of food, some of it unusual, like two bottles of white wine, fresh mushrooms, frozen asparagus. Papa had always been a meat and potatoes person. The odd items of food gave her one more thing to worry about.

She'd chosen to bake a chicken and a couple of potatoes for dinner. That pretty well strained her culinary expertise. She was a computer geek, not a cook.

She stood at the big old sink tearing up lettuce for a salad when the slam of the front screen door announced her father's arrival.

"Smells wonderful," he greeted, his heavy footsteps creaking across the wooden floor as he came into the kitchen to give her a hug.

"I had plenty of food to choose from," she observed. "I've never seen your pantry so well-stocked. You have just about as big a selection as Clifford's Grocery Store, all unopened except for the bread, bologna and cheese. You've never kept this much food in the house, not even when I was growing up. Are we expecting company?"

She waited tensely for his answer, unable to stop herself from wondering if he thought Mama was going to bring along other family members for a ghostly reunion. She could do all her genealogical research first hand.

He took off his hat, more cowboy style than standard issue for the sheriff, and set it on the table, then pulled out a wooden chair and plopped his stocky frame onto it. Leo strolled in and wound himself around Papa's leg.

"How'd your day go, Leo?" He scratched the cat's ears and ignored Kate's question.

When Leo had received his requisite petting and strolled regally out of the room, Papa lifted one foot. "Don't know why I wear these damn boots. They're harder'n hell to get off."

Kate turned from chopping tomatoes and wiped her hands on a dish towel. "Let me help you," she said, straddling his leg backward and tugging on the recalcitrant boot.

He had a boot jack upstairs in his bedroom closet, but when she was ten years old she'd seen a little girl in a movie take off her father's cowboy boots. From that day on, she'd insisted on performing the service for Papa. Soon it had become a ritual—a ritual she thought pleased her father as much now as it had pleased her years ago.

With both boots off, he leaned back and wriggled his toes, one of which protruded through a hole in his sock. He sighed happily. "What more can a man ask for?"

Socks without holes in them? Kate thought. When she came to visit him or he came to Dallas, they spent their time talking, laughing, eating, going places. She'd never stopped to really assess his lifestyle, to wonder how he got along when she wasn't around. He'd taken care of her; of course he could take care of himself.

But not forever.

"Maybe a glass of iced tea?" she suggested, washing her hands.

"You always could read my mind, Katie-girl."

She poured the amber liquid into a glass.

He took a sip and smiled. "Delicious. Just the way your mother used to make it."

"Papa," Kate began, settling into the chair next to

him, "let's talk about mother."

"Did you have a good visit with Luke today?"

With a sigh, she stood and moved back to the sink, continuing her dinner preparations, accepting the change of subject. If he wasn't ready to talk, dynamite couldn't force him.

"Yes," she replied. "We had a very nice visit. But I wish you hadn't asked him to come by later. I thought you and I could spend some time together."

"We've got plenty of time, sweetheart. I'd've asked him to dinner if I'd known what a great spread you were putting on. We could call him. He probably hasn't eaten yet. We owe the boy a few meals considering how often you ate with his family."

"That was a long time ago. Anyway, I'm here to spend time with you, not him."

"If you weren't at his house, he'd be over here," Papa went on as if he hadn't heard her. "I don't think there were too many meals the two of you didn't share."

"That's when we were children, Papa." She searched futilely through the cabinets trying to find two matching bowls and plates. "Maybe another time," she hedged.

"Okay." Papa was silent for a moment. "How about tomorrow?"

"Tomorrow?" She turned to him in frustration, taking in his inexplicably pleased expression. She couldn't refuse, but she couldn't agree either. "Look at this," she pleaded instead, opening the cabinet door wide. "We don't even have any dishes that match."

"We have service for sixteen. Your mother's china is in the hutch in the dining room."

Mother's china. It gave her the perfect opening to bring up the subject that had brought her flying down to Briar Creek.

She hesitated, not really wanting to know, but then

forced herself to plunge in. "Do you think mother would mind if we used her china for our dinner with Luke?" She studied him closely as she dropped the loaded question.

"Of course she won't mind. She's the one who suggested it."

Chapter Four

For just a moment the years seemed to slide backward as Luke stood on Sheriff's rickety front porch in the warm summer evening and knocked on the wooden frame of the screen door.

For just a moment he was twelve years old again, coming to see Katie, his best friend in the whole world.

For just a moment he could almost believe that tomorrow night, instead of standing at the sink and eating corned beef hash from a can in his kitchen, he'd go home, probably taking Katie with him, and find the big wooden dining room table covered with food, Mom and Dad sitting at either end.

He heard Katie's familiar, "Come on in" accompanied by a pattern of creaks as her quick, light steps crossed the floor of the old house. Time swirled around him, circled and folded back on itself, and he half-expected an eleven-year-old Katie with short, golden-red curls and shining eyes to appear in front of him.

But then the sensuous, unknown woman in the fashionable white summer dress opened the door and smiled up at him with Katie's smile.

Time jerked itself straight, becoming linear again. The warm, secure feeling from the past vanished, leaving his mind filled with the memory of how this woman had felt when he'd so briefly slipped his arm around her waist.

The whole thing was very disorienting.

"Evening, Luke," Sheriff called, the sounds of his heavier, slower tread approaching from the dim interior.

Wordlessly, Katie stepped back, holding the door open for Luke to enter. Was it his imagination, or had she hesitated just a second too long, gazed up at him just a little too intently? Could she read his thoughts?

He felt a flush creeping to his face.

The Katie he used to know had been able to sense his thoughts before he spoke them.

He strode past her into the living room. She might look like a glamorous stranger, but deep inside, beneath those breasts that would just fit into his hands, those curves he yearned to caress, and that hair that looked like somebody had been running his fingers through it, she was still his Katie.

As the screen door thunked closed behind him, Luke looked around the familiar room and was again possessed by the instability of time. The place was tidier now than it had been when they were children. Books, shoes and various paraphernalia were no longer scattered randomly about, but the furniture could have been the same he and Kate had romped on twenty years ago—except he felt sure they'd totally destroyed that furniture.

While Sheriff had laid down the law in no uncertain terms about many things, the man had never been particularly concerned with the house, and neither had they. The sofa and chair must be replacements, he decided, though worn to the same faded, nonintrusive condition as their predecessors.

Leo leaped onto the sofa arm—with no rebuke from Sheriff—and stretched toward Luke, offering his head to be stroked. He wasn't the same cat Katie used to have, of course, but he was big and white and gentle, just like Jingles had been.

The big man—Luke still thought of Sheriff that way even though he himself now stood a good two or three inches taller—clapped him on the shoulder. "It's cooling off real nice out there. Going to be a great evening for porch sitting. Katie made a fresh pitcher of the best iced tea you ever tasted."

"You all go on out. I'll bring the tea," Katie said. "Luke, how do you like yours? Do you still want an extra three spoons of sugar?"

"Nah, I've cut back to two and a half."

His teasing was rewarded by a smile from Katie—a surprised smile, he thought, as if she hadn't expected to be amused, as if she hadn't been amused in some time.

Being a systems analyst for an investment company—how had his laughing Katie ever become one of those?—probably didn't provide for a lot of amusing situations.

"Tonight I think I'll take it straight," he told her.

She disappeared in the direction of the kitchen, and he followed Sheriff back out to the porch.

Sheriff eased himself onto the top step. The care with which he executed that movement was one of the changes Luke had noticed but hadn't mentioned to Katie.

Or maybe it wasn't a change. Maybe, as a child, he'd just never noticed that Sheriff had always sat down deliberately and carefully. He was, after all, a big man.

Not as big as you, and you don't sit so carefully, some annoying little voice whispered in his head. He shoved the voice aside. Katie's fretting about her father was getting to him, making him look for problems. Sure, Sheriff was a little older, but he was the same as he'd always been.

Luke couldn't stand to consider any other scenario.

"You ever able to make any sense out of those records?" Sheriff asked.

"Records? Oh, you mean all that paperwork in the office? It's a pretty big mess. Not to speak ill of Pete, but I think it kind of got away from him. Evelyn said she helps both of you as much as she can, but she doesn't know what to put in the blanks if you don't tell her, and she has a terrible time trying to read your handwriting."

Sheriff's deep laughter rumbled into the soft, gathering dusk. "When your dad and I were young, there

42

wasn't so damn much paperwork. A man got drunk, shot off his mouth or his gun, we threw him in jail then let him out the next day when he sobered up. Once in a while we had to hold somebody over for the judge, but even that didn't take a pile of paperwork higher'n my hat brim."

"I'll admit paperwork is not my favorite part of law enforcement."

Sheriff grunted agreement. "Grimes is making such a fuss about that harmless paint on his barn, I guess I'll have to write all that up, too."

"In triplicate."

"Lot of work for nothing. Crazy old man thinks somebody's out to get him. I told him he wasn't that important to anybody."

Luke chuckled. "You have a way with words, Sheriff."

A firefly—lightning bug—blinked over near the honeysuckle. Soon the yard would be full, but he and Katie wouldn't be chasing them now. They'd be sitting on the porch where their parents had once sat to watch them.

"You know," Sheriff drawled, "I've been thinking maybe we ought to get us a computer."

"A computer?" In the Sheriff's office in Briar Creek?

"Yeah, they've been after me for some time to get a computer system. Then we can be connected to all the other law enforcement agencies around the country. We could get on a computer right here in Briar Creek and compare Homer Grimes' DNA to somebody's DNA in New York City. Imagine that." He shook his head as if in disbelief. "You used one in Houston, didn't you?"

"Yes, but it doesn't eliminate all the paperwork."

"Good. Then you could train Evelyn."

"I don't think—"

"Sure make it a lot easier to run driver's license checks and get all that stuff from National Crime

43

Information Center. It's in the budget. Been there for a while. I was just waiting for Pete to retire. He didn't like new-fangled gadgets. Too old to learn, I guess."

Luke smiled since Sheriff was at least six or seven years older than Pete...maybe more.

A burst of harsh light interrupted their conversation. He turned to see Katie coming through the door with a tray of glasses. Leo brushed past her, gliding onto the porch like a ghost.

Kate felt an unexpected rush of warmth at the sight of Papa and Luke sitting on the steps just the way she'd seen them so many times when she was a child...except now Luke was taller than Papa.

"Katie-girl," Papa said, shielding his eyes, "why don't we turn out the porch light? You can't see the lightning bugs."

"Oh, sorry." She leaned back inside to flick it off, and a gentle, shadowy world changed Papa and Luke from real people to dark silhouettes.

A shiver darted down her spine. So easily they seemed to leave, though she knew it was only a trick of the darkness. Luke and Papa still sat on the porch.

However, the reality was that Luke had left years ago.

Were Papa's mental lapses the first sign that he was leaving her?

No. She couldn't accept that.

She handed out the glasses of tea and took a seat in the ancient porch swing beside Leo who'd already made himself comfortable. The swing creaked alarmingly, but it always had even when she and Luke were children.

"It's nice out here," Luke said.

"Mmm," Papa agreed. "June's a good month in Briar Creek."

Kate laughed, loving him so much it was almost

painful. "You say that about every month, even August."

"No." Her eyes had finally adjusted to the darkness, and she could see the grin on his face. "Surely not August."

"Even August," Luke confirmed, giving her a conspiratorial grin.

She responded without thinking, a smile on the inside as well as on her lips. Just a reflex, a habit left over from the past. With one foot, she pushed back and forth in the groaning swing, the action providing some release of the tension inside.

Papa seemed perfectly normal now. Since their discussion of Mama's dishes, the only thing he'd done that concerned her was to slip away upstairs to his bedroom and close the door right after dinner. When he'd been up there for almost half an hour, she'd considered going up to check on him, but then Luke arrived and he came down full of energy and seemingly fine.

Now, as they sat outside in the summer evening, he talked only of inanities, of friends and neighbors and weddings, deaths and births. So far as she could tell, Papa's mind was sound except for brief excursions into that one area.

"The Gardners had a big barbecue last month to celebrate their fiftieth wedding anniversary," he said. "It was quite a shindig. All the kids and grandkids came back. Must have been a hundred people there. Well, at least fifty. Too bad your mother had to miss it. She grew up with Helen Gardner, and she sure was partial to Helen's chocolate cake. Me and your mama went to a lot of barbecues together."

"How long were you and Mama married?" Kate asked. She knew the answer, but it was a game they played. Papa wanted to reminisce about Mama, and she always indulged him, asking questions so he wouldn't feel badly about repeating information over and over.

"Let's see," Papa said, counting on his fingers.

Maybe she shouldn't have asked, shouldn't have encouraged his reminiscences in view of recent developments. She could only hope he wouldn't say something that would reveal his problem to Luke. This was private, between Papa and her. She didn't want outsiders to ridicule him. And Luke was an outsider. The closeness they'd once shared was gone. A part of the past.

She tensed, waiting for Papa's answer to her question.

"Nineteen years."

She breathed a sigh of relief. At least he hadn't said forty-five, hadn't included the twenty-six years since she'd died.

The affection in his voice, even in those few words, was unmistakable. He still loved his wife even though she'd left him so long ago.

Kate's heart ached for his loss.

"Seventeen before Katie was born," Luke said softly, and she was surprised that he remembered.

"Seventeen before Katie was born," Papa repeated. "We'd given up on having children. What a surprise you were! All those red curls and those big eyes—you were the spitting image of your mother." He chuckled. "She always said you were stubborn like me, but I'm not so sure you got that trait from me."

"She said I was stubborn? But she died when I was two years old." *Was his mind wandering again?* "How stubborn could I have been at that age?"

As soon as she asked the question, she wanted to retract it. She didn't want Luke to hear the answer. She didn't want to hear the answer herself. She held her breath, desperately wanting him to come up with a logical reason for his comment.

"Oh, Katie-girl. You were the queen of the house

from the day you moved in," he said cheerfully, and Kate let out a small sigh of relief. Still she wasn't sure if he'd slid through the sticky situation accidentally or if he was simply sharp enough not to let Luke know that he didn't believe death had parted him from his wife.

"Luke," he continued easily, "do you remember when you two decided you absolutely had to have a horse or your lives wouldn't be worth living?"

Luke laughed softly, his gaze warm on Kate's face. It was tempting...so tempting...to fall into that gaze, to lean against that broad chest just the way she used to when it was thin and skinny instead of broad and sexy.

She lowered her head, turning her attention to stroking Leo and to studying the cracks between the boards of the porch.

Even if she weren't engaged to Spencer, she couldn't lean on Luke. She didn't need to lean on anybody, for that matter. People who could stand on their own made it just fine; those who leaned on somebody were sure to fall when that person went away.

"Yeah," Luke said in answer to Papa's question. "I remember. My mom and dad said *no* the first hundred times I asked them, then they just ignored me. You found somebody outside town who'd let us come out and ride every weekend. We thought we were real cowboys."

Sheriff stood, drained his glass and tossed the leftover ice into the yard. "Well, I think I'll go upstairs to watch reruns of *Golden Girls*. Moved the little TV to my bedroom when Katie gave me that big one for Christmas two years ago."

Kate rose from the swing. "Are you all right, Papa?"

"I'm fine, sweetheart. Since you're not usually here on weeknights, I guess you don't realize how set I am in my little routines like going to bed early and getting up early for work. Why don't you kids go on down to the root beer stand? You used to beg me to take you there almost every night. Now you're all grown up and you can drive yourselves. And you can stay out as late as you want."

He brushed past her, opened the door for Leo to enter, then turned back to them. "Katie, don't forget to invite Luke for the dinner you're cooking tomorrow night."

Nothing wrong with his short-term memory.

"Dinner? Does this mean you've learned to cook?" Luke teased. "You won't burn the marshmallows this time?"

"Katie's a great cook. Takes after her mother. See you tomorrow night." Papa entered the house, letting the screen slam behind him.

"Sounds great, Sheriff," Luke called after him.

"Uh, Luke, about this dinner..." She shrugged and grinned. "I probably would burn the marshmallows as well as the salad. I'm afraid Papa's a little confused." That was putting it mildly.

Luke stood, walked over and took her hand, smiling down at her. "Your father's proud of you, Katie. He thinks you can do anything."

His fingers stroked her palm, an innocent, friendly gesture, but his touch created sparks so intense she looked down, expecting to see them flaming brightly in the darkness.

As though he could sense her response, Luke dropped her hand abruptly, strode to the edge of the porch and gazed out into the night. Kate stared after him, heart pounding, thoughts whirling chaotically, an equal mixture of embarrassment and desire sending the hot blood rushing to her face.

"Don't worry," he said. "I'd have been disappointed if you'd turned into a gourmet cook. You wouldn't be the same Katie. We'll eat whatever you burn."

48

"I'm not the same Katie," she said weakly. There was another understatement if she'd ever heard one. The Katie he'd known had held his hand hundreds of times without ever feeling that burst of heat lightning.

"Can I bring anything for dinner? A bottle of wine?"

"A bottle of antacid would be more like it. I'm not sure what kind of wine goes with peanut butter sandwiches."

Luke laughed. "I'll have to think about that. How do you feel about heading on over to the root beer stand like Sheriff said? I had a float there just the other night, and it was like a trip back in time."

"Thanks, but I don't think so. I'm pretty tired after my drive down here." *Liar, liar, pants on fire.* The childhood chant rang through her head, taunting her. She wasn't tired at all. In fact, she felt exhilarated as well as terrified. Those two emotions should keep the adrenaline pumping until close to dawn.

"I understand. I'd better be getting on home myself. Walk out to the street with me. There's something I want you to see." He reached toward her hand, hesitated then continued the movement upward and ran his fingers through his hair instead, turned and started down the walk.

Was he afraid to touch her? Had he sensed the way she felt?

Did he feel the same thing?

This was crazy.

She moved down the walk beside him, careful to keep just the right distance...near enough to show that she wasn't worried about being close to him and far enough away that their bodies wouldn't accidentally touch.

The only thing she could see in the street was a big old convertible.

He opened the door and gestured her inside. "Remember this?"

"No. Should I?"

"Dad's old Chrysler. We went to the root beer stand plenty of times in this."

"So we did." Kate brushed her fingers across the flawless paint that glowed a deep cranberry red even in the faint light that filtered down from Papa's upstairs window.

"I just couldn't bear to part with the old girl," Luke continued. "So I fixed her up instead."

"You did a terrific job." She knew he wanted her to sit on the leather interior, to admire his obviously prized possession from every angle.

But the idea filled her with the same ambivalent feelings Luke did—a desire to recapture long faded sunshine and a fear of the storm that came after. The irrational feeling that she might suddenly, inexplicably, be whisked into the past kept her feet planted firmly on the ground.

Ridiculous.

She forced herself to slide onto the seat.

"I replaced the entire dash," he said, leaning inside to point out the immaculate area, now missing the crack in the vinyl that had been there when Luke's father purchased the car used.

"It's beautiful. You've put in a lot of work."

"It was worth it."

"You'll have to take me for a ride tomorrow after dinner," she heard herself saying, much to her astonishment. Damn! The blasted car *had* jerked her back into the past!

"I'd love to."

He seemed to lean closer, or maybe it was only a trick of the shadows or her imagination. She could smell his familiar scent of soap and peppermint chewing gum and something new, something male and tantalizing, something that tugged at her inner recesses. The darkness of the new moon hid his expression, but she could feel the energy, the strength, the masculinity, emanating from him.

The same as when they were children but different.

They weren't children anymore.

They were adults. A man and a woman.

Hidden from the rest of the world in the night.

Of their own volition, her lips parted, anticipating—

The soft strains of a hauntingly familiar tune drifted to Kate's ears on the summer air, tugging her back to reality.

She swallowed. "Where is that music coming from?"

Luke pushed away from the car, from her, and stood rigidly straight. "I don't know."

She scrambled out of the Chrysler, onto the sidewalk, into the present. "It's coming from Papa's bedroom." She pointed to the window on the second floor of their house where the open curtains fluttered in the breeze, a perfect frame for the scene inside.

As she watched, Papa moved slowly, rhythmically, back and forth across his room, arms extended at odd angles.

"What's he doing?" Luke asked.

Kate shook her head. "I don't know. That song...do you remember? He used to play it a lot when we were kids. It was one of Mama's favorites. *The Anniversary Waltz.*"

Kate continued to stare in hypnotic fascination at Papa's window. He almost looked as if he were dancing. He certainly wasn't watching television.

Then it hit her. He was playing old phonograph records and dancing with Mama.

For just a moment she got caught up in his fantasy and could have sworn she saw the faintly glowing outline of a woman in Papa's arms.

She blinked to clear her head.

"Now that you mention it, I do remember that song," Luke said. "But what's going on with your father? Is he dancing by himself?"

"Of course not. He's...he's doing aerobics," she blurted.

"Aerobics?"

"Very low impact. For senior citizens. Well, it's been great seeing you, Luke. Let's get together and do it again soon." She started up the walk.

Luke chuckled, a low, sensual sound, halting her in mid-step. She'd never before noticed he had a sensual chuckle. "How about tomorrow?" he asked. "You're cooking dinner for me. Remember?"

"Of course I remember."

The phone rang, and Papa stopped dancing, moved across the room and out of her field of vision.

"Omigosh! That's probably Spencer! I forgot to call him." And she'd left her cell phone in her room. Had he tried to reach her and then called Papa's number?

"Spencer?" Luke asked.

Kate looked at Luke, horror washing over her. She'd been with him twice today. They'd reminisced about old times and talked about their new lives. She'd found herself attracted to him in an inexplicable way she shouldn't be.

And she'd totally forgotten her fiancé.

"Spencer Osborne. We're..." Why was it always so hard to say? "We're engaged."

"Oh."

"Yes, he's a very nice guy. I know you'll like him. He works for the same company I do. He's stable and reliable and helps me keep my feet on the ground and he played golf with the CEO of our company today." Oh, Lord! Had she really said that? Why was she babbling?

"Well, congratulations."

Luke turned away, walked around his car from the

past and slid into the driver's seat.

"I think she went to the root beer stand with an old friend." Papa's voice, unaccustomedly irritated, floated down from his bedroom window. "I don't know when to expect her. I'll have her call you when she gets home."

She raced to the house and darted inside, closing the door behind her and leaning against it.

Great. This was just what she needed.

She'd forgotten to call Spencer, who expected strict punctuality. Papa was upset with Spencer who was undoubtedly upset with her.

But somehow that worry paled beside her other concerns. Papa had been dancing with Mama's ghost, and she had the hots for her former best friend, a friend who'd left her and broken her heart seventeen years ago. And tomorrow night they would all four have dinner together, a meal she was supposed to cook when she had trouble making toaster waffles.

Served on Mama's best china because that was what Mama wanted.

Chapter Five

Kate tiptoed upstairs though she wasn't sure why she was taking such pains to be quiet. Papa was obviously awake, and Mama, she thought wryly, wasn't likely to be frightened into hiding after all these years.

She tapped lightly on her father's door. "Papa, was that Spencer on the phone?"

For a long moment there was silence broken only by soft sighs—or whispers? Was Papa talking to himself? Was he answering himself?

"Yes," he finally said, "but he wants you to call him tomorrow. He's going to bed now." Papa sounded resigned, as if giving her the information against his will.

Distressed, Kate leaned her forehead against her father's door. Her pending marriage had obviously upset Papa, and that surprised her. He had always been on such an even keel. He'd even taken her rebellious teenage years in stride.

Was this another aspect of the aging process, another sign that Papa was getting older and changing?

She didn't like that possibility.

A yearning flowed over her to confide in Luke, to share the burden and figure out some way to make everything turn out right, the way they'd shared their burdens for the first eleven years of her life.

She liked that thought even less than the one about Papa getting older.

She was an adult. She could stand on her own. She had to stand on her own.

Too bad she hadn't talked to Spencer. He was reason personified. He'd get her back on a rational track and away from these insane mood swings.

But it was probably for the best. She couldn't tell him the truth about what was going on. She would not expose

Papa's problems to a stranger, not even his future son-in-law. Anyway, she couldn't call him back. Spencer's schedule was inviolate. By now he'd already brushed his teeth, put on his pajamas, turned down the bed and fluffed his pillow.

Too tired and too emotionally stressed to try to comprehend the feeling of relief that came with that conclusion, she went on down the hall to her own bedroom.

When she checked her cell phone, she noticed that Spencer had called three times, left three messages. She'd listen to them later, when she was in a better mood.

As she lay in bed, thoughts of Spencer, Papa, Mama and Luke chased each other through her head in sleep-destroying chaos.

Spencer would be irritated that she hadn't called earlier, hadn't answered her cell and then had been out when he'd called.

But he could just get over it. She had more important things to worry about.

Like Papa's sanity.

Like Luke's reappearance in her life and the strange attraction she couldn't explain or control. She'd adored Luke at one time, but she'd gotten over that ages ago. She was an adult now and past that sort of all-consuming need, that need that could destroy one's soul and rip out one's guts.

And, of course, she was engaged to be married which meant she didn't have the right to that blatant and unaccustomed sexual attraction. She'd always refused to let herself be controlled by any outside forces, not by emotions or by physical urges. But she'd never experienced anything quite this strong before. She was going to have to keep a tighter rein on her emotions and urges.

For a long time she lay awake beside her open window, trying to clear her mind, to focus on the night sounds instead of all the problems that had suddenly arisen in her formerly well-ordered life.

The dark silence was broken by the occasional barking of a dog, the eerie hoot of an owl, the chirrup of a cricket and sounds of the leaves on the cottonwood tree as they danced in the breeze, rustling like satin gowns, becoming still then dancing again.

She'd been coming to visit Papa regularly ever since she left home, but this was the first time she'd really listened to the night in years.

Finally the scent of lilacs from Mama's lilac bush drifted in, caressing her senses, soothing the turbulence and bringing elusive sleep.

Just the way that scent had soothed her to sleep when she was a child and worried about something.

But...didn't lilacs bloom in the early spring? The question was too much trouble to think about as sleep blurred the sharp edges of her problems. She'd ask Luke about the lilacs tomorrow. He'd know. He always knew everything. He was her best friend in the whole world.

***

Feeling unbelievably peaceful and loved, Kate sat under the big oak tree, her head pillowed on her mother's lap while a mockingbird trilled happily overhead.

"Katie, my precious daughter," Mama said, "it's been too long since we talked. Papa and I are so proud of the woman you've become, of all your accomplishments. But you still have some very important things to learn."

"They're sending me to a seminar in California in October. I'll learn about everything new that's coming out. I'm up for a promotion." Kate kept talking because she sensed she hadn't yet said what her mother wanted to hear.

Mama smiled. "That's wonderful. You always were bright. But that's not really what I mean. You need to realize that you never lose someone once you love them, no matter how far away they may go."

More birds of different varieties joined the first, their songs becoming louder.

"I lost you. I lost Luke. I'm losing Papa," Kate protested, though how could she believe what she was saying when her mother was right there with her?

Mama smiled and stroked Kate's hair, just the way she'd done when Kate was a little girl. Her lips moved as though she were speaking, but the bird songs had become so loud, Kate couldn't hear the words.

Kate awakened with a start and the realization that the trills of an entire choir of birds originated outside her window and not in her dream.

She sat up, pushing aside the compelling wisps of the dream. She'd dreamed about Mama a lot when she was a child, but this was the first time it had happened in years. Undoubtedly brought on by Papa's delusions about Mama.

Slipping into her robe, she padded down the hall. As she passed her father's room the scent of lilacs drifted out...the same scent that had lulled her to sleep last night. It had been Mama's favorite scent, and Papa had planted the bush for her when they'd moved into the house. It was now quite large.

She must be wrong about it being past time for lilacs to bloom. Or maybe the odor had permeated the walls of the old house over the years.

She started to move on when she heard the sound of Papa's voice. He was speaking quietly, presumably to himself, and she couldn't hear the words. Briefly, she considered putting her ear to the door or even looking through the big, old-fashioned keyhole. In light of his recent actions, spying would be justified.

But she couldn't make herself do it, couldn't treat her father with so little respect.

She started to move on down the hall, but halted with one foot in mid-air. Her father's voice had stopped, and for an instant she could have sworn she heard a soft, airy female voice replying.

She hurried away, making haste to get downstairs and start the coffee. A little caffeine should clear her head, and apparently it needed clearing.

As she shoveled the dark grounds into the filter, her mind raced. Either her father had a woman in his room or she was having auditory hallucinations or—she sighed and leaned against the cabinet with relief as the answer occurred to her—he had risen early and turned on the television set he'd moved up to his room.

Of course. It was all quite mundane.

This whole business was making her edgy, imaginative, ready to ascribe paranormal meanings to perfectly normal events.

She jumped as the coffee maker began to gurgle then laughed at herself. It just proved her own assessment of her mental state.

However, even in the best case scenario, this still meant Papa was carrying on a conversation with the television set.

"Good morning, sweetheart. Coffee sure smells good."

She turned to see her father amble through the doorway, lay his gun belt and hat on the cabinet, pull out a chair and sit down at the table. He was dressed neatly in his uniform, wide awake and beaming. He was happy in his delusions, she had to give him that.

"Guess you don't get to come down to the smell of coffee brewing very often," she said, holding her breath as she waited for his answer.

"Not since the last time you were here."

Well, at least Mama didn't make his morning coffee. That was, she supposed, a positive sign.

"How about a little breakfast, Papa?"

He nodded. "That would be real nice. I bought some bacon and eggs and some of those instant grits."

It was the meal he always ordered when they went out for breakfast.

She got the bacon from the refrigerator and laid it in the big iron skillet but then stood staring at it.

Bacon and eggs.

Cholesterol.

Papa didn't really need anything clogging his arteries, restricting the flow of blood to his brain.

"How about some..." She hesitated. She couldn't remember seeing anything even vaguely resembling a bran muffin, bagel or whole grain cereal in the well-stocked pantry.

"Some what?" Papa asked.

"Some coffee while you wait for the bacon," she improvised. What the heck, one more shot of cholesterol shouldn't make much difference. She'd go buy some bagels or cereal and skim milk today. "I think the coffee's just about ready." She took from the cabinet his oversized mug that read *World's Best Father.*

As they ate breakfast, Kate found herself relaxing. Everything was comfortably ordinary and familiar...the sun coming through the faded yellow curtains on the kitchen window as the morning breeze puffed then dropped them, the scarred wood of the round table top, her father's drawling comments. This was the way it had always been. It simply wasn't possible that Papa really had a problem, that he'd changed so drastically.

Papa finished everything on his plate—there was nothing wrong with his appetite—then poured himself another cup of coffee, added cream, and sat back down.

"What did you plan to fix for Luke for dinner tonight?" he asked.

Kate cringed. She'd hoped he might forget the dinner. "I hadn't really thought about it. What would you like, keeping in mind that my cooking repertoire is very limited."

"Oh, I was thinking maybe we could start with stuffed mushrooms for an appetizer, follow that with a spinach salad, then that chicken in wine stuff with the little potatoes and onions in it, asparagus on the side, nice bottle of white wine, and top it all off with chocolate brownie pie."

White wine, stuffed mushrooms—the strange items of food she'd seen in his pantry began to make sense. In a senseless sort of way.

"You already bought all the ingredients. You planned this before I got here."

Across the table, he met her gaze unflinchingly, innocently. "I had to go to Tyler to get the wine, but Clifford's had everything else. No fresh asparagus. It's out of season. But Mama said the frozen would be all right. They freeze that stuff in seconds, you know. Purely amazing. I can still remember when we used to keep stuff cool in an ice box with just a chunk of ice in the top."

Kate lifted her hand to her forehead as if she could somehow grip the irrational situation and force it into something rational. "*Mama said*—Papa, Mama's dead! She died twenty-six years ago."

"Some might say that."

Some might say that? What kind of a reply was that? Not a good one.

She dropped the subject and switched to something he couldn't equivocate about. "I don't know how to cook any of that stuff."

"Don't worry. We found recipes for everything, and I'll be home around noon to help you." He sipped his coffee as casually as if he hadn't been dropping bombs all over the place.

"Help me?" she croaked. "Look, this is just you, me and Luke. Why don't I do another baked chicken? Or maybe even a steak. I can grill steaks and make baked potatoes. Luke isn't expecting a fancy meal."

Papa looked out the window. "I guess that would be all right. It's just that it's been such a long time since I had stuffed mushrooms and that chicken and wine stuff with the French name. What do you call it?"

"Are you talking about *coq au vin*?"

"That's it. *Coq au vin*. I surely do miss all those things."

This was very strange. How could he miss something she'd never known him to eat? Even on their visits to the nicer restaurants in Tyler and Dallas, Papa had never ordered anything other than the basics...fried chicken, steak, chicken fried steak. She'd never heard of a sudden yen for gourmet foods being part of senility, but what did she know?

"If that's what you want," she said. "If it'll make you happy, I'll do my best."

What the heck. It was, as she'd pointed out, only Luke and her father. If it turned out totally inedible, they could always have sandwiches or order a pizza. Luke would understand.

A knock sounded from the front door, and Kate jumped. For a split second, she'd thought it was Mama come to help her cook this crazy meal for Papa.

"That must be Luke," Papa said.

"Luke? What would Luke be doing here this early in the morning?"

"I called him before I came down for breakfast and

asked him to pick me up. One of the tires on my car is a little low. I thought since I'd be home this afternoon anyway, I'd just wait and get it fixed then." He stood and took down another cup from the cabinet. "Would you let him in while I pour him some coffee?"

Let him in? Reluctantly, Kate rose, appalled that she'd gone abruptly from worrying about Papa's sanity to worrying about Luke seeing her in her faded robe with her hair an unruly mess, her face pale, lipstickless, blushless and mascaraless—the last of which translated to eyelashless.

Not that what she looked like mattered. Luke had never been more than a friend, and now he wasn't even that. He was an acquaintance, someone out of her past, someone who'd disappear back into her past as soon as she did whatever she had to do for Papa and left town.

She marched to the door and yanked it open.

Luke stood on the porch, again wearing his tan uniform, gun belt strapped around his waist, hat held politely in one hand. "Good morning," he said, and his voice and eyes were distant, giving verification to her mental assertions about their relationship...or lack of one.

"Good morning. Come on in and have a cup of coffee."

He shoved his free hand into his back pocket. His boots were planted firmly on the porch, a shoulder's width apart. She could tell from his stance and his expression that he was going to refuse.

That was good. She didn't want him to come in for a cup of coffee or anything else.

"Papa's pouring it now," she added.

Papa wasn't the only one with sanity problems. She *did* want him to come in. What was up with that?

He hesitated, and a thousand emotions fought for ascendancy in Kate's fickle brain. Or maybe they were originating in her heart. Surely nothing from her brain could be that illogical.

"You're probably in a hurry. I'll fix you a to-go cup," she forced herself to say.

Did a shadow of disappointment cross his face, or was it just a shadow from the oak tree?

"Thanks." He sounded relieved. His expression she'd thought she'd seen had been only a shadow from the leaves overhead.

She went back to the kitchen, took down a disposable cup and poured in the last of the coffee.

"What are you doing?" Papa asked.

"Luke's in a hurry. He's in too big a hurry to come in and have coffee."

Papa stood, taking his time about fastening on his gun belt. He took the cup from Kate then leaned over to kiss her cheek. "See you around noon, Katie-girl."

As Kate watched Luke and Papa drive away, she felt more concerned and confused than ever. In fact, some of her concern was for herself. She had to keep a level, unemotional head in order to deal with this whole situation, and she didn't seem to be doing that.

It was hard enough to view Papa's problem objectively, but her incomprehensible feelings about Luke were complicating matters.

Maybe she was reacting too strongly to her childhood loss. Maybe she could be Luke's friend now. As an adult, she'd learned that caring about someone didn't mean diving in head over heels and drowning in emotions. She certainly didn't have that sort of insane relationship with Spencer. They were compatible, shared the same interests, had the same goals and were almost always in agreement. That was a sensible kind of relationship.

She dropped the curtains and headed upstairs to get dressed.

Too bad she hadn't brought the mint green silk dress for tonight. She always got compliments when she wore that.

She stopped with her hand on her closet door, horror washing over her as she realized what she'd just thought.

Who did she think she would be dressing up for?

Not Luke.

Certainly not Luke.

She'd wear her cutoffs. The kitchen would be hot from all that cooking, and cutoffs would be practical.

Maybe she couldn't be his friend after all.

Papa's possible mental lapses in talking to Mama began to seem less significant in view of her own mental lapses since she arrived here yesterday.

Maybe there was something in the town air that made people crazy. She certainly hadn't been herself since she arrived yesterday.

Chapter Six

"So, Sheriff, what's your future son-in-law like?" Luke asked casually as he steered his car away from Sheriff's house...from Katie who, without makeup and wearing an old robe, looked heart-breakingly like the Katie he'd known all those years ago. He'd wanted to grab her, pull her into his arms and hold her so tightly he'd never lose her again.

Except, of course, he didn't have her to lose again.

When Sheriff didn't answer immediately, Luke stole a quick glance away from the road to study the older man's face. Sheriff was frowning slightly and looking very contemplative. Neither expression was usual for him.

"You do know about Katie's engagement, don't you?" Luke asked as the thought occurred to him that perhaps Katie hadn't told her father just as she hadn't told him until late last night.

Sheriff nodded slowly even as he contradicted that nod with his words. "I wouldn't go so far as to call it an engagement. She doesn't even have a ring."

Luke knew he shouldn't feel so relieved over that small detail. "People don't have to have a ring to be engaged," he pointed out.

What difference did it make to him if Katie was engaged? He'd wrestled with that question most of the night and had concluded somewhere around two o'clock that morning that he was being possessive of something he didn't own. Anyway, all he wanted from Katie was her friendship. It didn't matter if she was married. He would probably like any guy Katie picked out. They could all be friends.

If that conclusion didn't seem to be exactly on-target, it was only because he'd drunk too much tea at Sheriff's house last night, been unable to sleep, and felt lousy today. Things got all skewed when he was tired. Maybe he ought to try to work in a short nap before going to Sheriff's house for dinner.

Sheriff grunted. "Katie wouldn't really get married without her mama's wedding dress, and that's still stored in the attic. She's here because she needs to think through some things. What's that expression you young people use? Get her head on straight. Did you see that red car run that stop sign up there?"

"Sure did. Think we ought to go after him and give him a ticket?"

"Nah. There wasn't anybody else around. He didn't hurt anything. Probably running late. You got time to help me with those forms this morning? I might as well tell you, Pete used to do the paper work for both of us."

Luke laughed. "You mean, Pete *was supposed* to do the paperwork for both of you."

Sheriff grinned. "Something like that. Once we get this new computer system, we'll get things in order."

Sheriff seemed determined about the computer thing. He probably should have done it years ago. The new equipment was going to look odd on the top of that fifty-year old solid wood desk in Sheriff's office. Luke wasn't even sure they had the necessary wiring to support a computer system. The building itself was at least fifty years old, maybe older.

He pulled into the parking lot behind the jail.

As he and Sheriff got out of the car, it dawned on Luke that Sheriff had successfully diverted the conversation away from Katie's engagement.

Deliberately?

He suspected so. Sheriff hadn't seemed too thrilled with the prospect of his new son-in-law. Maybe Sheriff was having as much trouble dealing with Katie's being grown up as Luke was.

He leaned on his open car door and looked down the alley on both sides at the backs of the stone, brick and frame buildings. It was Saturday and a couple of places were closed, but most had cars parked behind.

Luke took a deep breath of the clean air, scented with that early morning fragrance that belonged only to Briar Creek. He was home. Life was good.

Katie's engagement was good. That news would surely put an end to all those wild thoughts and desires he'd been having about her.

Katie would marry that Spencer person and he, Luke, would find someone to focus his desires on. Maybe he'd even get remarried one day. He and his wife could play cards with Katie and her husband on Saturday nights. Dallas wasn't that far away. They'd all be the best of friends. Their kids would go to each others' birthday parties.

He slammed the car door behind him and wished with all his might that he could believe that crock, that he could be happy for his friend's impending marriage, convince her to forgive him for his childhood lapse and resume their friendship. Most of all he wished he could stop thinking of her as a woman, stop lusting after her. That seemed almost sacrilegious. She was Katie, his friend and Sheriff's daughter.

Well, if he couldn't stop doing it, he could at least learn to ignore those thoughts.

***

Kate spent the morning cleaning house. A couple of years ago she had tried to get Papa to let her pay a bonded service in Tyler to drive over and do weekly cleaning, but Papa insisted he'd managed just fine for twenty-six years, including her messy childhood. Now that he only had himself to pick up after, he sure didn't need help.

His concession was to hire a local woman to come in

on a monthly basis and clean. But it had obviously been at least three and a half weeks since her last visit, judging from the amount of dust.

With the main floor finished, she marched upstairs. She had about an hour before Papa was due home and they were scheduled to start cooking his bizarre meal.

She finished her room and the two guest rooms then paused at the open door to Papa's room. She hadn't been in there more than a dozen times in her life. He'd never forbidden her to enter, never kept the door closed except at night, but she'd always valued his privacy as much as he'd valued hers. Now she hesitated to go in even to clean. From the doorway she could see that the bed was made and the room was tidy. Whatever chaos had reigned in the rest of the house when she was growing up, Papa's room had always been tidy.

It hadn't changed much. He still had the same blue recliner, faded and getting a little threadbare. The walnut dresser and chest of drawers he and Mama had found at a used furniture store and refinished still had the doilies Mama had crocheted to protect their surfaces.

When she was a child, the spread on the four-poster bed had been pale blue with a lace overlay and curtains to match. It had only been about five years ago that she'd talked Papa into getting rid of the tattered lace curtains and spread. She'd expected him to choose something masculine or at least in a solid color. Instead, he'd selected a print of lilacs and leaves with the comment that Mama would have liked it.

Or had he said, *Mama likes it?* When had his delusion begun?

She'd never noticed before, but he'd always talked so much about Mama, she hadn't paid close attention. There hadn't been any reason to pay close attention. She'd always considered Papa invulnerable, the unchanging center of her life.

Leo rubbed against her leg then strolled into the room and leaped gracefully onto the lilac-print bed spread.

"Leo!" she chastised. "Come here!"

Papa never complained about Leo getting on the furniture, so it was probably all right. Nevertheless, she went in to retrieve the cat.

Leo tilted his head up and back then down again, arched his back slightly, raised and lowered his tail...as if he were being stroked by an invisible hand. It was one of his favorite tricks. Kate assumed it meant he wanted to be petted.

She sat down on the bed and began to stroke him. Leo often seemed to have more than his fair share of static electricity, and her hand tingled for an instant as it passed over his fur. "You're a good cat, Leo. I miss you when I'm in Dallas. Did you know that? How would you and Papa like to come to Dallas to live?"

As she spoke the words, she realized she'd been considering that option in the back of her mind for some time. Papa's delusions, the holes in his socks and the realization of the enormity of keeping up this big old house had brought it to the front. Surely Papa was close to being ready to retire especially now that he had someone competent to pass the sheriff's job to.

Maybe she could convince him to move into her condo after she and Spencer found a larger one. Hers was on the third floor of the building, but there was an elevator. If he didn't like it, they could sell it and find him another one on the ground floor, maybe in the same complex as Spencer's. That would be better. She could be close in case he needed her.

A breeze billowed the curtains that matched the spread.

A mockingbird whistled a liquid trill of notes.

A locust whirred its raspy song.

Peace wrapped invisible arms around Kate.

Sitting in Papa's room made her feel the way Leo must feel as she stroked his soft fur, like purring.

On the nightstand beside the bed sat the familiar picture of Mama and Papa at their wedding. She picked it up to dust off the glass, but it wasn't dusty. Papa must look at it regularly.

His hair was dark and thick in the picture, his face unlined, his smile wide.

Mama was beautiful. Even in the black and white print, her hair seemed to have a red cast to it. It had been, Papa said, darker than Kate's, and curly rather than wavy. Her dress was beautiful, too. Mama's mother and Aunt Viola had spent weeks making the dress so it was perfect. It was a simple design with a scoop neckline and long sleeves, the ivory satin nipped in at the waist then falling sleekly to the floor.

Papa wanted her to get married in that dress, but it wouldn't fit with Spencer's and her plans. It was too formal.

And somehow it just didn't feel right.

She set the picture back down and studied it. That dress was for a fairytale wedding, like Mama and Papa had, two people with stars in their eyes. But she was having a practical, down-to-earth wedding. Those stars had a way of exploding in your face, and fairytales happened only in story books she was too old to read. Even Mama and Papa's fairytale had ended unhappily with Mama's death.

Would things have been different if Mama had lived? Would Mama and Papa still have stars in their eyes?

Would she have grown up believing in fairy tales and happy-ever-after?

Probably not. Such notions were outmoded, a thing

of the past. The divorce rate verified that romantic love was a temporary state of mind. Even Mama and Papa's stars might have turned to dust with the pressures of everyday living.

Mutual respect, mutual interests, mutual goals, those were the things that made for a successful partnership in today's society.

She checked her watch, surprised to find she'd been sitting there for half an hour. She ought to go down and peel onions or do something productive.

The curtain billowed in the breeze again, and the cool scent of lilacs drifted to Kate's nostrils, wrapping around her. The fragrance made her feel as if she could almost touch her mother. Probably because Papa had so often mentioned how much Mama liked that scent, how he'd planted the lilac tree for her.

Or maybe she actually remembered something of her mother. Maybe on a subconscious level she could recall the smell of lilacs while being cradled in soft arms, her crying comforted, her pain soothed, surrounded by love, secure in the knowledge it would always be that way.

Just so the breeze seemed to caress her now, brushing along her cheek with a pleasant tingle, inviting her to relax, to remember being a trusting child, to remember...

Her fifth birthday party when she'd been shocked to see that she'd blown out all but one candle which meant her wish couldn't come true, but Luke had clapped so hard so close to the candle that it went out, and then he'd sworn she blew them all out and her wish would come true.

Her first day of school when Bart Greene, two years older, had pushed her off the merry-go-round and taken her spot and Luke had descended on the older boy in a fury, snatched him off the ride and bloodied his nose.

Playing dolls with Luke. He'd never complained, though he had insisted that half a day spent playing house

71

should end with half a day spent playing cowboys and arresting and hanging the dolls.

The phone rang, jolting Kate out of the nostalgic trance she'd somehow fallen into.

She snatched up the receiver. "Hello?"

"Katie, could you come get me? Luke had to go out on a call. I know it's nearly one, and I should have phoned you sooner, but I kept thinking Luke would get back here any time."

"Sure, Papa. I'll be right there."

"Are you okay, Katie-girl? You sound kind of out of breath?"

Kate rubbed a hand across her eyes in an effort to clear away the wispy remnants of fog that still clung. "I'm fine. I just dozed off. I'll see you in a few minutes."

She hung up the phone and stood, tentatively drawing in a deep breath. The scent of lilacs was gone. Had that fragrance, so familiar from her childhood, caused her to relax so completely she'd fallen asleep and dreamed? It had seemed to have that effect last night, but today had been more like a hypnotic trance.

She snatched up her dusting cloth and started to leave, then remembered the reason she'd come in.

Leo was doing his stroked-by-the-invisible-hand routine again. She picked him up under one arm and strode from the room, closing the door behind her. Visits to the past were futile and a waste of time. There was only one way to move and that was forward, into the future.

Papa and maybe even Luke were trying to recapture a part of that past with the dinner tonight. Both were doomed to disappointment as well as some really awful food.

When she went to her car, she noticed that the tires on Papa's blue Oldsmobile looked fine. He'd apparently imagined a low tire, too.

She sighed. She should have checked herself. Then she wouldn't have had to see Luke this morning.

***

"Get the chicken started first," Papa advised. "It takes longest to cook. I marked the recipe page with a rubber band."

Tea towel tied around her waist, Kate approached the vintage cookbook as if it might attack her. A rubber band, a paper clip, a letter opener, a twist tie from a plastic bag, and a used envelope protruded from its pages. Tentatively she flipped it open to the rubber band. "*Coq au vin*," she read. "Six slices of bacon, diced." So far, so good. Dicing bacon couldn't be all that hard.

"Don't dice them until they're cooked," Papa advised. "Mama says it works better that way."

"Right." She ignored the present tense verb. She could only deal with one crisis at a time. "*Two-thirds cup chopped scallions.*"

"Clifford's didn't have scallions. Mama says green onions will work."

"Right." Mama's ghost was obviously an experienced cook. But then, she supposed ghosts had lots of time to perfect things like that. They didn't have to go to an office or shop for groceries. And they could just whip up any old recipe since they didn't have to worry about gaining weight or having a heart attack from high cholesterol.

A high-pitched giggle escaped Katie's lips, and she realized she was on the edge of hysteria. Or maybe she'd fallen over the edge.

"You okay, Katie-girl?" Papa asked solicitously.

"I'm fine." One crisis at a time, she reminded herself. Get this food ruined and move on to Papa's mental condition.

Kate scanned the rest of the list, her gaze stopping at the specification for two cups of burgundy wine. She

opened the refrigerator door and took out the bottles she'd
set in that morning to chill. "Papa, you have two white
wines. Burgundy is red. Do you have another one
somewhere?"

"Mama always uses white."

Of course she does. *Hence the expression, white as a
ghost.* She smothered a giggle at her silly joke.

"So which one do I use? These are different kinds."

Papa studied the bottles then shook his head. "I don't
remember. I'll go ask her."

"Okay."

Okay?! Kate stiffened. For just a second there she'd
almost bought into Papa's delusion. Maybe that lilac scent
was some kind of hallucinogen, olfactory LSD.

She stood frozen in place, one hand on the cookbook,
the other clutching a bottle of wine, and watched Papa
leave the room. His footsteps crossed the dining room,
mounted the stairs, went down the hall to his bedroom,
and then she heard the sound of his door closing.

Should she go after him? Was he going to hold some
kind of séance and try to contact Mama? Was he going to
have a conversation with himself?

Before she could decide on a course of action, she
heard the door open and his heavy tread coming back
down the hall, down the stairs, returning to the kitchen.

He walked over and selected one of the wines. "Cook
with this one, drink the other."

Kate licked her dry lips. Papa looked as normal as he
always did, totally composed and happy. Not like a man
who'd just been to visit a ghost.

Maybe he had some of Mama's notes in his bedroom,
and he'd gone up and consulted her wine list.

Maybe. But that would mean he was lying, and she'd
never known Papa to do that. Certainly he wouldn't lie in
order to convince her he *was* seeing ghosts. Any sane

person would do the opposite.

She took out the big iron skillet and turned on a burner on the gas range.

"I'll chop the green onions," Papa volunteered.

"Thank you," she said numbly and had to resist an urge to wrap her arms around him and hold him tightly so he couldn't slip away.

Instead she took out the bacon and laid six slices in the skillet.

When she had the bacon and green onions cooked and draining on a paper towel with the chicken breasts browning in the skillet, Papa instructed her to begin the pie crust, the recipe marked by a paper clip.

Kate could feel the panic creeping up her spine even as the perspiration crept down it. She studied the page Papa indicated.

Pie crust. Four ingredients. How tough could that be?

"*Sift flour and salt into a bowl*," she read. "*Add half of the shortening and cut it in with a pastry blender or two knives until mixture looks like coarse meal. Cut in remaining shortening until it looks like large peas?*" Her voice rose another octave with every word past the pastry blender.

Papa smiled at her panic. "Use the next recipe, the one where you pour in the oil and milk at the same time. Mama says it's just as good and a whole lot less trouble."

"Oh."

The pie crust proceeded reasonably well until time to get it in the pan. Between trips to the stove to turn the chicken, she followed the directions explicitly, pressing the dough into an uneven, lopsided circle with a rolling pin while squeezing the torn parts back together. The result wasn't great, but she supposed it could have been worse. Anyway, it was going to go underneath the pie, not on top. Nobody would see it.

She consulted the recipe again, folded that circle twice, laid it in the greased pie pan and unfolded. Or tried to.

For the first time in too many years to remember, Kate thought she might burst into tears as she surveyed the shreds of pie dough. Even Papa looked dismayed.

"I'd better go talk to Mama," he mumbled.

Kate sank into one of the kitchen table chairs and laid her head in her hands. She'd known before she came to Briar Creek that things could be bad, but somehow she hadn't quite believed it, hadn't wanted to believe it. This was bad and getting worse. The whole situation was totally out of control.

Papa was losing his mind, talking to Mama, getting cooking directions from her, directions his daughter couldn't follow, and in a few hours her childhood friend, Luke, who'd grown into a sexy man she barely recognized, would come over expecting dinner and would find total chaos and inedible food and what did she care if he did? He'd left her all alone, hadn't written or called once in all those years, and now she was supposed to cook dinner for him?

She bit her lip, focusing on the physical pain to control the hysteria that threatened to bubble up and overtake her.

"It's okay, Katie-girl." Papa wrapped one big arm around her and stroked her hair.

He was still taking care of her when she should be taking care of him.

She lifted her head and forced herself to smile. "I know. I'm just a little tense. I'm not accustomed to this cooking business."

"It's going to be fine. Mama says to throw out that batch of dough, mix it up again and put it between two sheets of waxed paper to roll it. Then peel off one, plop it in the pan and peel off the other."

The method worked perfectly.

Every time she had a question or a problem, Papa went upstairs to consult Mama and returned with the right answer.

Papa couldn't cook. What the heck was going on?

When he went up to ask a question about the stuffed mushrooms, Kate tiptoed into the hallway to where the telephone sat in a built-in niche. She waited tensely for a few seconds after she heard his door close then quietly lifted the receiver. Papa had a phone in his room. He could be calling someone in town to ask the questions, though, again, she'd never known him to be deceitful.

All she heard was a dial tone.

Papa's door opened, and he started down the hallway.

Kate hastily hung up the phone and raced back to the kitchen, her heart pounding. Had he somehow known she was going to listen on the extension and not made a call this time?

But again he had the correct answer to her question.

Did Papa have a split personality who was a gourmet chef?

She tore spinach for the salad and resolved not to think about it until this dinner was over. Even if it was edible...which was highly unlikely...she was going to have to decide if she was thrilled at the thought of seeing Luke again or if she was dismayed or if she was dismayed at being thrilled.

And she still hadn't decided what to wear.

Oh, yes, she had. Her cut-offs.

Or maybe the long turquoise halter dress. Not because it looked great with her hair or because it was slenderizing, but only because it was cool and the house was hot.

77

She ripped a spinach leaf in two with a vicious tear. That argument would be all well and good for someone outside her head, but she couldn't hide her motivation from herself. She wanted to look good for Luke.

Okay, so she was on an ego trip...wanted to impress an old friend who hadn't seen her in years.

Nice try, but if that was all it was, her knuckles wouldn't be turning white.

This was nuts. She never obsessed about her appearance. Maybe she was over-compensating since Luke had been the first—and only—man to break her heart. There had to be a logical reason for her strange attraction to him. If she'd paid more attention in psych class, she'd surely be able to figure it out.

But she hadn't. She'd been far more interested in her business and computer classes, something tangible rather than the vagaries of the mind.

So the best she could do was ignore the whole thing for the short time period she'd be in contact with him. She had plenty of other problems to occupy her mind what with Papa bringing Mama in as a cooking consultant. At least he hadn't asked her to set a place at the table for Mama.

Yet.

***

Jerome sat on the edge of the bed to pull on his best boots, getting dressed for Katie's dinner.

Emma *tsked*. "Jerome, you really need to buy some more socks. You've got a toe sticking out of this pair, too. People will think I don't take good care of you."

"Now, Emma, who's gonna see my socks except you?"

Emma fisted her hands on her hips. "Jerome!"

"Okay, okay, I'll buy some more socks. Katie'll probably give me some for Christmas if we wait."

Emma rolled her eyes.

He stood and tucked the tails of his green, western-cut shirt into his blue jeans.

"Jerome, you're still the best-looking man I've ever known," Emma said.

He smiled at the image of the faint aura just behind him. He could barely see his wife in the mottled glass of the ancient dresser mirror. "Emma, I think you're blinded by love, and I'm awful glad you are."

Emma laughed softly and planted a tingling kiss on his cheek. "You're the one whose eyesight's failing. But you're right about the love part. I do love you and our little girl. She and I had a nice visit today. I haven't had a chance to tell you what with all the dinner preparations."

Jerome lifted one eyebrow. "You had a nice visit? I wish I'd been here to see that. What happened?"

"She was standing at your door, looking in, and I was sitting on the bed. Leo came in for me to pet him, and she came after him, though I like to think part of the reason she came in was because she sensed I was here and wanted to talk to me. A girl needs her mother when she's thinking about getting married, especially if she's thinking about marrying the wrong man. Anyway, she sat on the bed and I held her in my arms, just the way I used to when she was a baby, and we reminisced."

"About Luke?"

"Mostly." Emma sighed and walked over to the window. "I don't think she's ever completely recovered from his leaving her when they were children."

Jerome drew a comb through his remaining hair. "I know she hasn't. That was hard on her. She was so brave about it, not wanting to worry me, but I knew."

Emma sighed. "I felt so helpless. She cried herself to sleep every night and was so distraught, I couldn't get through to her. Then she built that barrier around her, and we were never close again."

Jerome turned and planted a quick kiss on his wife's cheek. "Somewhere inside, she's always known you were still there. Don't go thinking you've failed her. You've done a great job."

Emma smiled. "Things are getting better. I'm pretty sure I made contact last night when she was asleep and again this afternoon. Not like it used to be when she was little, but being with Luke is having a good effect on her. Those two have been given another chance. It's up to you and me to keep them together long enough for them to realize that. You and I just need to give them an extra little nudge."

Jerome chuckled then wrapped his arms around her. "*A little nudge?* Emma, sweetheart, do you think you might be confusing *a little nudge* with *a giant shove*?"

"Whatever it takes, Jerome. We'll do whatever it takes to get those two stubborn people back together so they can be as happy as we've been."

"Yes, we will, Emma. Whatever it takes." Jerome held his wife as tightly as he could without his arms passing through her. Only one thing marred the moment. When their daughter's happiness was assured, would Emma's *special dispensation* be up?

All those years ago when Katie was just a baby, Emma's return until Katie was raised, until she found her true love, had seemed a long time. But the years had flown and he was no more ready for her to leave him than he had been the day of her car wreck.

Nevertheless, she was right. They'd do whatever it took to be sure their Katie was happy.

Chapter Seven

Luke sat on the faded, comfortable sofa sipping iced tea and talking to Sheriff while Katie made final dinner preparations in the kitchen.

"Whatever she's doing in there smells wonderful," Luke said. "The way she talked yesterday, I expected bologna sandwiches."

"Katie can do anything she sets her mind to. She just needs a little encouragement sometimes to kind of jumpstart her on something new." The older man leaned back in his recliner. "How'd it go at Homer Grimes' place today? You were sure out there a long time. What's his problem now?"

"Somebody ran a tractor down four rows of soy beans and totally destroyed that part of the crop. He wanted me to rush right over and arrest Seth Flanders, but there wasn't any evidence that Seth did it."

Sheriff frowned. "I know those two old codgers have hated each other for years, and I don't doubt for one minute that Seth painted that frown face on Homer's barn. Heck, Homer's barn needed painting anyway. Seth just gave him a head start. But I can't see Seth destroying something that Homer depends on for his livelihood."

Luke shrugged. "I went over and questioned him. Of course he denied knowing anything about it. Why do those two hate each other? They've lived on adjacent farms since they were kids, haven't they?"

"Yep. Sure have. Used to be best friends, then one day they weren't. Nobody knows what started the feud. Seth claims he doesn't know, either, and that he tried to end it a lot of times. One thing's for sure, Homer's not ready to shake hands and make up."

"That's a shame. Two old men, all alone...does either one of them have any family?"

"Nope. Seth was married once a long time ago, but she

ran off to California with some traveling salesman passing through the town before they had a chance to have any kids. You're right. It's a crying shame they can't get along."

Katie appeared in the doorway wielding a wooden spoon like a baseball bat, her expression slightly frantic, her skin shiny and translucent from the heat, her hair a little wilder than usual as if to coordinate with her expression.

She was beautiful.

"It's ready, guys," she said. "As soon as you sign a waiver, we can eat it."

Sheriff chuckled as he slid from his chair. "It's not like you to be so modest, Katie-girl." He clapped Luke on the back. "I tell you, Luke, this is going to be one of the finest meals you've ever eaten."

Katie grimaced, casting an appealing glance at Luke. "We've got peanut butter sandwiches for backup."

Sheriff motioned Luke ahead of him, so he followed directly behind Katie into the dining room. She was wearing a dress that tied around her neck and left most of her back bare. He'd seen Katie's back a thousand times when they were growing up, but for some reason tonight he couldn't pull his gaze away from the slight movement of her shoulder blades as she walked, the porcelain shade of her skin, the way her back tapered down to her slim waist.

She was close enough he could smell the spicy scents of the food she'd been cooking as well as that honeysuckle fragrance that was the essence of Katie.

She was close enough he could touch that bare skin if he just lifted his hand.

She stopped abruptly and turned to him with an apprehensive look on her face, and he thought for a minute he'd been caught admiring her erotic back.

Then he realized she was waiting for his reaction to the room where they'd never eaten in all the years he'd known her, the room where dust usually lay thick on the formal table.

Tonight the rich wood of that table gleamed in the light from the overhead chandelier which had also been dusted. The table was set with the china he'd only seen in the past decorating the interior of the hutch, and three cloth napkins rested in three polished silver napkin rings.

Katie had set a gorgeous table, but that wasn't what caught his attention.

In amazement he noted the stuffed mushrooms and spinach salad already on their plates, the food in the serving dishes, the wine and the pie on the sideboard.

Katie had prepared all his favorite dishes, even bought his favorite wine.

Had he mentioned his preferences to Sheriff? He didn't think so. It wasn't something that came up in casual conversation.

Sure, he used to think he and Katie could read each other's minds, but not in that much detail. And in those days his favorite foods had been hot dogs and Cokes.

But somehow she knew and had gone to a lot of trouble to please him. He felt a little embarrassed. While he'd been mentally yowling around her door like a tomcat in heat, she'd been planning this special meal for him.

He made a firm resolution to keep his mind off her bare back and her...well, all those other parts of her that sent his blood rushing straight to his lower extremities.

Extremity.

"What's the matter?" Katie asked. "Why are you frowning? You haven't even tasted it yet."

"Nothing's the matter. It looks wonderful. I'm not frowning. I'm just a little surprised."

Hurt followed by anger flashed in Katie's blue eyes as she plopped down at the table and jerked out her napkin.

"Not at your cooking skills," he hastily added, taking his seat across from her. "Just the food choices. How did you decide on the menu?"

"Katie, would you pass the salt, please?" Sheriff asked, cutting off his question. It surprised Luke a little. Sheriff was always unfailingly polite.

Katie frowned. "Are you sure you need extra salt? Doesn't it raise your blood pressure?"

"My blood pressure's just fine, so I'd be much obliged if you'd pass the salt, Katie-girl."

It was a small thing, but Luke felt again that Katie was patronizing her father. He wanted to tell her—and would at the first opportunity—that there was nothing wrong with Sheriff. He was the same man he'd always been. Briar Creek was the same town it had always been.

Only Katie had changed.

Well, so had he, whether he wanted to admit it or not. He was having a very hard time remembering that Katie was his friend and that he wasn't going to do anything to ruin their relationship this time.

They ate in silence for a few minutes.

"Katie, these stuffed mushrooms are wonderful," he told her.

"They sure are," Sheriff seconded. "Can't say as I've ever had anything quite like this before, but I sure wouldn't mind having it again." Almost before the last word left his mouth, Sheriff clamped his lips shut and looked guilty, as if he'd said something wrong.

Katie's eyes widened, and she seemed to pale. "But Papa, you said—" She glanced at Luke then down to her plate. "I'm glad you both like them," she said softly.

Luke had no idea what that interplay was all about. "They're great, Katie," he said. "The best I've ever eaten. And you said you couldn't cook. I'm impressed."

"Thank you," she mumbled without looking up.

When they finished, Sheriff leaned back, rubbed his stomach and groaned. "I'm as stuffed as a Thanksgiving

84

turkey. I haven't eaten so much or so well since your mama was doing the cooking. She'd have been real proud of you, Katie-girl." He scooted his chair back and stood, picking up his plate and silverware.

"Put that down, Papa. Let's all take our coffee and go in the living room. We can have our pie in there, and I'll clean up later."

"I'm so full, I couldn't possibly eat pie right now. Your mama always washed the dishes before they got dry and all that food stuck on there. She said it was a heck of a lot easier that way. You did all the cooking, Katie. I'll do the cleaning. You kids go on."

Katie took the dishes from him. "I didn't do all the cooking. You helped. You and Luke take your coffee to the living room, and I'll do the dishes before the food dries on them. Then I'll join you for pie."

"Well, I don't know. That's an awful lot of work for one person. Maybe I could help you." Sheriff's voice seemed a little uncertain, and Luke wondered if he was tired. Not surprising if he'd had a part in cooking all that food.

"I'll help her," Luke volunteered.

"Okay," Sheriff agreed...amazingly easily, Luke thought. With a smile of gratitude, the older man took a fresh cup of coffee and headed for the living room.

That wasn't like Sheriff to be eager to sit down and rest. Was it possible Katie had reason to worry about him?

"You don't need to do this," Katie protested as he began to gather up the dirty dishes.

"I don't mind. It's kind of like when we were kids and we each had to wash our own milk glass and sandwich plate." Except when they were kids, her fingers hadn't been long and slender and graceful as they wrapped around a glass, and she'd certainly never worn a dress like the one she had on tonight.

And he hadn't wanted to touch those fingers and the

Gh

smooth bareness of her back the way he did now.

What the hell had happened to those good resolutions he'd made just before dinner? He mentally cursed his libido and wondered if Sheriff would welcome him into his home, would treat him like a son, if he had any idea of the kind of thoughts Luke was having about the man's daughter.

For sure Sheriff wouldn't be sending them off to the kitchen alone.

He carried his load of dishes to the kitchen sink and returned for another while Katie began scraping the plates. When he brought in the last bowls, she was squirting soap into the sink under the flow of water from the growling faucet.

She looked up at him and smiled distantly...or was it nervously?

No, he was the one feeling nervous...among other things.

"Thanks for your help," she said. "I'll finish up."

He opened the drawer that had always contained clean dishtowels, took out the last one and closed the drawer. "You wash, I'll dry."

She shrugged and plunged her hands into the soapy water, her attention focused on her task. In the dark glass of the window over the sink Luke stared at their reflections. How many times had he seen those same images in that glass? A few inches shorter, maybe, but not so different.

Katie handed him a soapy plate, and he rinsed and dried it.

Not quite the same, he supposed. They'd never eaten off the good dishes before.

"Your dad's quite a guy," he said after a few minutes of working in silence...an uncomfortable silence, not like the ones they used to share.

Katie nodded. "I know."

"He hasn't changed a bit in all these years."

Her hands stilled in their underwater movements, and she looked at him for just a moment with the same trusting, hopeful expression he recognized from years gone by.

But immediately she looked away and resumed washing dishes. "We've all changed."

He wouldn't have called her tone hard exactly, but definitely *solidified*.

"Katie, you said last night you were worried about your father. Why? He seems fine. Maybe a little tired, but we all get tired sometimes. He's not as young as he used to be, and he works hard every day."

She washed the last dish and handed it to him, then pulled the plug so the water could gurgle down the drain while she dried her hands on the kitchen towel. All done with her gaze averted from his.

He laid down the dish towel and took her hand in his. It was warm and moist from the soapy water and still as soft as it had been years ago, but the fingers were longer now, the skin sleeker. He needed to take an hour or so and trace out the small differences, sample and memorize each one.

What was he thinking about? He was supposed to be comforting her, not seducing her. He curled one finger of his other hand under her chin and gently tilted her face up so she had to look at him. "What's the matter, Katie?"

"Nothing," she denied then seemed to relent. "I guess I'm just having a hard time accepting the fact that Papa's getting older, that I could lose him. He's the only one I have left."

That pinched a little. He and Katie had sworn their allegiance to each other many times. Maybe he had left her, but it hadn't been his fault. Okay, abandoning her had been. But now he was back. She needed him, and he wouldn't let her down this time.

He reached up to stroke her cheek bone with his index finger, feeling the silky heat of her skin, then trailed along the slight roundness of her cheek, entranced by the sudden slide into softness. Her eyes, twilight blue in the dim lighting, dominated her face, seemed, like her cheek bones, to be larger, more prominent in this face that was and wasn't Katie's.

His finger stopped as it reached the curve of her lips. She'd eaten off her lipstick, but her lips were still pink and full and slightly parted as though waiting to be kissed.

Everything but her lips became blurred and out of focus. He was pretty sure he'd made some sort of good resolution earlier, but he couldn't remember what. He tried to concentrate on the fact that this was only his old friend, but his body didn't believe him.

Somehow, without his quite realizing how it had happened, his hand had dropped hers and snaked around her waist, pulling her against him. Her hands rested on either side of his neck, and he could feel his pulse throbbing wildly against her fingertips.

His friend, Katie, had never felt like this, so alive and supple against him. Katie had never made his blood boil with desire.

He knew he ought to release her, stop this insanity, but his body wasn't taking orders from his brain any longer. Instead of releasing her, he stroked her bare back, his fingers touching skin above the line of her dress—sensuous skin.

He knew he was breathing too fast. She was bound to notice. He didn't see how she could fail to notice his growing hardness as he held her body against his.

He tried to focus on her face, her eyes, to see what she was thinking, if she was appalled at the way he was acting, if she wanted to push him away.

All he could see was her lips, those strange-familiar lips he couldn't wait to kiss.

He moved his hand from her waist to her head, sliding his fingers through her hair. Her eyes closed and her face tilted upward, making those lips more accessible.

From another world, far away, he heard chimes. The sound was pleasant, blending with the world created by Katie's nearness.

But then the sound came again, and Katie pulled away. "My phone," she said, "in my purse." She whirled around and strode toward the sound.

Luke stood alone in the kitchen feeling deserted and embarrassed. What had he nearly done? Kissing Katie sure wouldn't help get their friendship back on an even keel.

And unless he was greatly mistaken, she had been about to kiss him back.

In the muggy summer night, a wave of cold enveloped him.

What the hell did he think he was doing? Deliberately trying to lose her again? Trying to mess up his relationship with Sheriff?

From the living room he heard Katie's voice pitched a couple of octaves too high and just a shade on the shrill side. "Spencer! It's so good to hear from you!"

The words were like ice water tossed into his face.

Katie was talking to her fiancé. That should be enough to get him back on track and make him stop acting like a teenager who'd just discovered sex.

***

Kate clutched her cell phone tightly as if she could thereby stop the spinning, whirling turmoil going on inside her head. How was she supposed to talk to Spencer with anything resembling coherency when she was pretty sure Luke had almost kissed her?

"I've been waiting for you to return my calls," Spencer's voice accused.

"What? Okay, yes, that's right."

She needed some time to figure out what had just happened...or almost happened...or what she'd just imagined almost happened. She needed to recall the circumstances, Luke's expressions, the feel of his arms about her...recall it and examine it in minute detail. Surely it wasn't possible that Luke had almost kissed her...or that she had desperately wanted him to kiss her. How could that have happened?

Had it really happened?

Did hallucinations run in the family? Papa saw ghosts and she thought her old friend wanted to kiss her?

From her position in the hall, she could see through the dining room to the kitchen door. She watched that door intently, waiting for Luke to emerge, waiting to see how he looked, to see if she could read anything from his appearance.

"Kate, I asked what you meant when you said *that's right*?" Spencer's even tone held a trace of annoyance. "What's right? That I've been waiting for you to return my call?"

Why was he asking her all those questions? Why couldn't he be quiet for a minute?

Oh, jeez! She couldn't have that kind of thought about Spencer. She was going to marry him. She couldn't want him to be quiet so she could think about Luke, figure out if he wanted to kiss her. This was not a good sign. She'd only been around Luke for two days, and already he was causing problems.

"I forgot to call. I'm sorry. Things have been hectic here. I was going to call you on Saturday."

"Today is Saturday," Spencer persisted.

"So it is. And here I am."

"Kate, is something wrong?"

"No, everything's fine." It was the second time she'd lied to Spencer.

Luke strolled through the kitchen door and into the living with three plates of chocolate brownie pie topped with whipped cream. He didn't as much as glance in her direction.

"Are you sure? You don't sound all right. Do you need me to come down there? I can be there tomorrow morning. I don't have anything on my schedule until Monday morning."

That's all she needed, for Spencer to come down and find his fiancée lusting after her childhood friend and that same fiancée's mother's ghost performing the other-worldly version of Julia Child's cooking show.

"No! Really, everything's fine. We, uh, we have company. A neighbor. An old friend. We were just having dinner."

"My apologies. I didn't mean to interrupt."

"You didn't." She pressed a hand to her forehead as if she could somehow press the chaos in her mind into some sort of order. "Of course you didn't interrupt. Things have been a little crazy. As soon as I get it all straightened out, I'd like you to come down and meet Papa but there's no point in your coming tomorrow."

"I understand. We'll schedule it for another time. I'm looking forward to meeting your father."

Papa's touch on her arm startled her. "Where's your mother's pie?" he whispered. "She just wants a tiny piece. Always worried about her waistline."

"*What*?"

"I said I'm looking forward to meeting your father," Spencer replied.

"Not you."

"You don't want me to meet your father?"

Papa smiled beatifically and held up his dessert plate. "She can have part of mine if there's not enough."

"There's enough. There's plenty of pie for her, too."

Good grief! What was she saying?

"Obviously I've caught you at a bad time," Spencer said. "I just wanted to let you know that I'm leaving town Monday morning, and I'll be back on Thursday. I've got to meet with the Larimer people in Connecticut. If you need me, you can check with my secretary and she'll give you the number of the hotel, and you have my cell number. Call me back tomorrow if you get a chance. If not, I'll phone you in a day or two."

"She doesn't want whipped cream on hers," Papa whispered, then patted his own expanding waistline. "Calories."

"A day or two. Fine. Great. No whipped cream. Good-bye, Spencer." On the third try, she managed, with a shaking hand, to disconnect the call and return her phone to her purse.

Papa was already back in the living room by that time.

Kate hurried after him, hoping to catch him before he could tell Luke about Mama's request for a piece of pie, hoping to spare him the embarrassment of an outsider knowing his mental condition.

If she wasn't already too late. If he hadn't already told Luke.

The two of them were deep in conversation, Papa relaxing in his recliner and Luke on the sofa.

Luke was nodding. "I can take care of that," he said.

Take care of what? Getting Mama a piece of pie with no whipped cream?

"There you are, Katie-girl!

"Yes, here I am!"

"The pie's great," Luke said.

"Thank you."

Both men looked at her expectantly, and she realized she was still standing...hovering, actually, waiting.

She perched on the sofa beside Luke.

Then moved one cushion away.

"Katie, Luke's going to go to Dallas Monday and pick up some copies of legal documents at the Dallas County

Courthouse for me. Would you mind going with him to show him where the courthouse is?"

"She doesn't need to do that. I can find my way around." Luke's protest was adamant, and she felt again the sharp, cold stab of rejection as clearly if it had happened yesterday rather than seventeen years ago.

Or today.

Maybe it wasn't quite the same thing, but he'd just made it clear, after almost kissing her, that he didn't want her with him on his trip to Dallas.

And she didn't want to be with him, either.

Determinedly she brushed aside that stab of rejection. When she was eleven years old and lonely, Luke had been able to hurt her. She'd needed him. She'd written him countless letters, begged him not to desert her.

But she was no longer a child, no longer lonely and no longer desperate for his or anyone else's friendship. That was all in the past, dead and gone.

"Papa, I came to visit you, not run back and forth between here and Dallas."

Papa smiled at her. "I understand. Of course you don't want to make that long drive on your vacation. I'll do it." He concentrated on cutting off his next bite of pie with his fork.

"Sheriff, I can get those papers for you!" Luke cast Kate a frustrated glance.

They were, at least, united in their efforts to take care of Papa.

Papa chewed and swallowed his bite then waved his fork in a dismissive gesture. "I've done it before. I know exactly where the courthouse is. If you don't know, you could get lost in all those one-way streets in downtown Dallas. Back when I first started going down there fifty years ago while I was still a deputy, it wasn't like that. Dallas is big now. Huge."

"So was Houston. I didn't have any trouble finding my way in Houston," Luke protested. "I have a good sense of direction."

"But I'd get lost in Houston, just like you'd get lost in Dallas. Nope. I'm going on Monday. And while I'm there I'm going to get us a computer system."

"A computer system?" Kate echoed in shock. "You want a computer? I gave you a laptop for Christmas, and you made me take it back! You said you'd lived this long without one and didn't need it now!"

"I changed my mind. You've got to stay in step with the times, you know. Anyway, this is for the office. Luke used one when he was in Houston, and he's convinced me they can save a lot of time and paperwork."

A quick glance at Luke's face told her he was a little confused by this information about his part in this situation.

"Pete used to do all the paperwork," Papa went on. "I never was too good at it."

Kate had no trouble accepting that last. Papa had always been an action-oriented person, not a desk-work person. "Okay," she said, "you and I will go to Dallas on Monday. I'll help you get your computer system, and you can pick up your papers at the courthouse."

Papa ate his final bite of pie, chewing thoughtfully. Finally he nodded. "That'd be fine, Katie. We can do that."

Kate was relieved the matter had been settled so easily. Thank goodness she wasn't going to have to drive all the way to and from Dallas with Luke beside her.

Knowing how stubborn Papa could be, she'd half expected him to protest, to insist that she and Luke go together.

She'd half wanted him to protest.

Her insanity was worse than Papa's. His at least made him happy. Continued contact with Luke Rodgers wouldn't make her happy and could make her very unhappy if she didn't get all those rampant hormones and emotions under control.

Yes, it was a good thing that she wasn't going to Dallas with him on Monday. A very good thing.

Chapter Eight

The choir had already started to sing Sunday morning when Kate and her father hurried into the big stone Methodist church on Grand Avenue. Papa had forgotten his Bible, and they'd had to return to the house, so they were running a few minutes late.

Not being on time for any event made Kate nervous. This occasion she'd looked forward to as a soothing time of quiet and solace, a respite from the increasing tensions of her life, had already become stressful even before they got there.

The church was filled almost to capacity but Papa guided her unerringly toward a pew halfway down. As they approached, the dark haired man on the end turned to look at them, and Kate's heart lurched.

The stress was intensifying.

Papa had chosen the pew where Luke sat, where there was room for only one more person, someone about the size of a six year old child.

She tugged on his arm, trying to steer him toward the other side where she'd spotted a larger space, but he ignored her.

Luke, just as delectable in a suit and tie as he had been in his uniform, smiled up at them and obligingly scooted over as far as he could, practically into Mrs. Lawther's lap.

Mrs. Lawther looked up and Papa smiled charmingly at her. She smiled back and moved closer to Mrs. Moncrief who also smiled at Papa, gave him a finger-waggling wave with one gloved hand, and moved closer to Mr. Moncrief...which was probably, Kate reflected, the closest those two had been in at least twenty years.

There was barely enough room for Papa and her to squeeze in if she sat really close to Luke. And that was something she didn't want to do...because it felt so darn good.

For a moment her gaze met his...as luck would have it, just as the choir burst into the Hallelujah chorus.

She turned her eyes determinedly toward the front.

Luke's shoulder and thigh pressed against hers. In his lap his hands were folded on top of a black Bible that was identical to if not the same one she remembered his mother having in their childhood.

An eerie sensation of past and present merging swirled around her, tugging her in different directions.

The way his body against hers made her feel was very definitely the present, something entirely new.

But as children, she and Luke had spent many Sunday mornings in this church, and a part of her seemed to be back in that time. The hymns sounded the same. The stained glass with the sunlight making the Madonna's halo glow was the same. Even the scents were the same...perfume and powder mingled with the light fragrance of the fresh flowers on the altar and the slightly musty paper odor of all those hymnals and Bibles. Like a wispy thread woven through all of it was Luke's essence...earthy and clean and masculine with a trace of peppermint gum.

He was at once a young boy and a grown man, her friend and a sexy stranger.

Kate swallowed hard and tried to focus on the music, on spiritual matters, on anything except Luke, past or present.

From the corner of her vision, she could see his knuckles turning white.

He was as tense as she.

That observation only increased her own tension.

She felt wedged between the past and the present.

Pulling her in one direction were the wonderful years

she'd shared with Luke when they were children. But the pain that had come with depending on him for so many years then losing him battered her from another direction. She didn't want to be reminded of all that. She'd dealt with that childish dependence and pain and put it behind her years ago. There was no reason to resurrect it now.

Yet neither was she prepared to deal with her responses to Luke the adult. As an engaged woman, as a reasonably intelligent woman, she shouldn't become breathless in his presence, her heart shouldn't speed up, she shouldn't want to reach over and touch the dark hairs that sprang from his white-knuckled hands.

The church service crept by with an agonizing slowness. Several times Kate surreptitiously checked her watch, certain it must be long past noon.

Actually, the service ended five minutes early.

Kate shot to her feet, released at last from the delicious torture of sitting beside Luke.

To her chagrin and her body's delight, the crowd pushing to get out kept her pressed to Luke's chest, her bottom to his groin, his warm breath on her neck.

Her head whirled with the confusion of desire and suppressing that desire.

Finally they burst into the open air, and the sultry summer temperatures were much cooler than the air-conditioned proximity to Luke had been. She had to get away from him, get home by herself where she could think clearly and rein in her confused emotions, get them untangled and back into their proper slots.

The crowd milled around in the church yard, friends and neighbors visiting, discussing the sermon, smiling, nodding, shaking hands, hugging. In the parking lot only a hundred feet away she could see her car, her vehicle of escape. She was almost safe.

"Well, Luke," Papa said, squinting into the sun, "how

about some lunch at the Grand Street Café?"

Her heart fluttered and sank and fluttered again. It was as confused as the rest of her.

Luke hesitated, and she saw that his forehead glistened with a sheen of perspiration as if he, too, had been fighting his own personal demons. "Well, I—"

"Then we'll see you there," Papa said, clapping him on the back. "Won't be as good as Katie's meal last night, but Helen fries up some mighty tasty chicken. We'll save you a chair at our table."

Kate's only consolation was that half the congregation went to the Grand Street Café for Sunday lunch. With that many people around to dilute Luke's presence, surely she could maintain an impersonal attitude.

After lunch she'd have the rest of the day to get everything straightened out in her mind. That was all she needed, a few hours away from him. Since she'd arrived in Briar Creek two days ago she'd been thrown together with him almost constantly. Between his disturbing presence and Papa's relationship with Mama's ghost, it was no wonder she was in a state of total confusion.

She'd have the rest of the day and night alone at home with Papa, then tomorrow a trip with him to Dallas, and by the time she got back, she'd be prepared to face Luke with all her jumbled emotions sorted out and under control. She'd have Luke properly catalogued and contained in one of the compartments that held her past.

But then after lunch Papa invited Luke over for an evening of porch sitting.

Luke demurred.

Papa insisted.

And Luke could no more deny Papa anything he wanted than she could.

***

99

As soon as they got home after lunch and changed clothes, Katie took two glasses of iced tea and went to join Papa in the porch swing. Even in the sweltering midday heat, the shade of all those trees kept it cool enough to sit outside...provided you drank plenty of iced tea.

Leo jumped into Papa's lap, and Papa stroked him.

"Good sermon," Papa said.

"Umm," Katie replied noncommittally. She wasn't real sure what the sermon was about. "Papa, have you ever thought about retiring?" she asked.

"Oh, sure," he said, and she looked at him in surprise. "Thought about it and decided not to."

"I see. Well, maybe you should give it some thought now that you have Luke to take care of things. I can understand why you didn't want to leave Pete in charge—"

"Pete was too old."

"Pete was younger than you!"

"Only in age."

She couldn't argue that. "Anyway, this might be a good time to think about retiring. When Spencer and I get married, we're going to move into his condo because it's larger, and you could have mine."

He cut his eyes around at her.

"Or we could sell mine and get you a different one," she hastily amended.

Papa turned to her and smiled. "That's real nice of you to offer, Katie-girl, but I'm not planning to retire just yet and I sure don't want to move to Dallas. Not that you don't have a nice place, but this is home and I'm going to stay right here." He lifted his glass and took a big drink of his tea as if the subject was closed.

Katie sighed. "Papa, did you ever think there might be a reason why people retire when they get older?"

"Well, sure. Lots of reasons. They're tired and don't want to work anymore. They don't like their jobs. They

100

have something else they want to do. None of that applies to me. As long as the people keep electing me, I'll keep doing my best to take care of them."

"But what if you can't? What if there's a big shoot-out and maybe your reflexes aren't quite as fast as they used to be and what if you get killed?"

Papa chuckled and patted her leg. "Katie-girl, you've been watching too many movies. Nothing ever happens here in Briar Creek. Bob Fenton may get drunk and pick a fight with his wife and she'll lay him out cold and call me to come drag him to jail for the night. Homer Grimes and Seth Flanders may carry on their little feud. Clarissa Jordan runs that red traffic light on Main Street just about every day, but nobody's ever coming from the other direction. Don't you worry about me getting into a shoot-out. Only things get shot around here are a few deer and wild turkey."

Leo slid out of Papa's lap and went to the door, then looked back and meowed.

"Leo must be hungry," Papa said, rising from the swing. "I'll feed him and then I think I may take a little nap. Sunday afternoons are made for taking naps."

Kate sat on the porch for a long time after Papa went in. She was pretty sure he'd used the excuse of a nap to avoid talking any more about his potential retirement.

That suspicion was verified when the sound of voices drifted down from his bedroom window on the still summer air. He was watching television.

She leaned back in the porch swing and rocked gently. The rhythmic creaking blended with the songs of the birds and insects.

She couldn't really blame Papa for not wanting to leave here. Now that she thought about it, she didn't really want him to leave. As much as she enjoyed the fast-paced excitement of living in Dallas, coming back here was like...well, it was like a Sunday afternoon nap. If he moved to Dallas, sold this house, she wouldn't have a home to visit.

Papa's laugh floated down to her, as it had so many times over the years when she and Luke played on the porch.

But Papa had only had the television set in his room since she'd given him the big flat screen for Christmas two years ago.

Which meant...what? That Papa used to sit in his room alone and laugh?

Or had he been talking to Mama even in those days?

***

That evening Kate pleaded a headache and went to her room before Luke arrived. Fortunately, her room faced the rear of the house and she couldn't hear the conversation from the front porch no matter how hard her ears strained. She probably ought to get up and close her bedroom door so she wouldn't even be trying to listen, but she wanted to hear when Papa came up to bed, to know that he was all right.

She sat in bed reading for an hour. Then Leo came in, jumped up beside her and, shoving his head under her hand, insisted that she pet him. In a few minutes, however, he moved away from her to the edge of the bed and went through his invisible-hand routine.

And then somehow Kate felt as if that invisible hand was stroking her, draining the tension and soothing her. The breezes coming through her open window became softer and cooler and brought the scent of those lilacs she'd forgotten to ask Papa about. She hadn't noticed any blooms on the tree.

She closed her book, turned out the light and fell into a sleep so deep she didn't hear Papa when he came up to bed.

***

Jerome knew Emma wasn't in their bedroom even before he looked in. Katie's door was open, and he could tell from all the way down the hall that she was in there with their daughter. He was never quite sure if he could feel or sense or see the glow of her energy, but he recognized it in the open doorway.

He walked down the hall as quietly as he could, trying to avoid the boards he knew creaked. As he approached, her familiar scent of lilacs drifted to him. He knew she couldn't have put on any perfume over the last twenty-six years, but she always seemed to trail the scent. It was as much a part of her as the glow.

Sure enough, Emma stood beside the bed where Katie and Leo lay sleeping.

His wife looked up and smiled as he walked in. "Isn't she beautiful?"

Jerome wrapped an arm around his wife's waist, looked at their daughter and nodded. Katie couldn't hear her mother, but if he spoke, his voice might wake her.

"I'm so glad I could come back and be here for all these wonderful years with her, especially now that she really needs guidance."

"I'm glad, too," he whispered softly against her ear.

"She's awfully stubborn, isn't she?"

Jerome smiled. "She's your daughter."

"And yours," she replied archly. "But our plans for tomorrow should be enough."

"I hope so. Now come to bed. You worry too much."

"I'm a mother. That's what we do." She leaned down and kissed Katie's cheek.

Katie stirred in her sleep. "Mama?" she murmured softly.

"Yes, dear, I'm here."

Katie sighed and went on sleeping.

"See? She's starting to hear me again. It's connecting with Luke that's causing her to open up."

Jerome nodded. "Being in love opens your eyes to all sorts of miracles you might miss otherwise."

Soon Katie would have her true love, and then Emma would be free to go on. It was the way of life. He'd follow her soon. He knew that. Still, he was going to miss her.

He extended his arm to his true love. Emma linked her arm with his and they went down the hall to their bedroom.

Chapter Nine

Luke woke Monday morning with a vague sense of unease, as if things weren't quite right.

Oh, yeah. Sheriff and Katie were going to Dallas for the day.

Holding down the Sheriff's department by himself for the first time shouldn't bother him. After Houston, he could handle the inconsequential problems of Briar Creek in his sleep.

But Sheriff had been in that office for as long as he could remember. It would be a little strange to be without him today.

And even though things weren't working out so hot with Katie, he'd been with her so much the last few days, even this one day without her would also be strange. Last night, sitting on the porch with Sheriff and knowing Katie was upstairs but wouldn't join them had been strange, kind of empty. He hadn't stayed long. He'd been unable to focus on the conversation, his mind wandering continually to the subject of Katie, wondering if she wouldn't come down because of the scene in the kitchen the night before when he'd almost kissed her.

It was kind of like being a teenager all over again. He'd dated several women since his divorce and had found the experience quite different from the days of high school with his sweaty palms and clumsy kisses. As an adult, he'd found it much easier to relate to women, to relax and enjoy their company.

But Katie had just set him back about fifteen years.

He showered, shaved, dressed and went downstairs to put on some coffee. While it brewed, he rummaged around in the kitchen until he found a can of sardines in mustard sauce and some crackers. That would do for breakfast.

He stood at the counter, eating, swigging bad coffee and surveying his home.

He'd put in a lot of work restoring the place, but there was still a lot to be done. Structural work, plumbing and electrical, paint inside and out, sanding floors...all those things were priority and he'd completed them first.

However, the only furniture he'd acquired was a bed, nightstand and chest of drawers for his room upstairs. The necessities. He could get along for the time being without a table or a sofa or paintings on the walls.

Though the place did look kind of bare. Not much like it had when he and his mom and dad had lived there, when he and Katie had raced up and down the stairs and played stick ball in the back yard.

Katie wasn't the same as she'd been in those days, either.

And it wasn't just that she was a woman now, and a darned sexy one. She'd lost her spontaneity. She had a reserve that she hadn't had when she was young.

He supposed some of that was a natural result of becoming an adult.

But not all of it.

When he'd left Briar Creek, she'd written him almost every day, lengthy letters penned in her precise, rounded handwriting, pouring out her heart.

He'd treasured every word.

But he'd never been able to answer a single one.

He'd hurt her badly, and now she didn't consider him her friend anymore.

And he didn't blame her.

It had taken him a lot of years to come to terms with his dad's death and the changes in his life. His divorce from Cindy and his mother's remarriage had forced him to take stock and evaluate, to return to his roots, to try to reclaim all those things he'd shut away when his dad died,

106

those things that were so sweet he hadn't even been able to think about them without feeling again the gut-wrenching pain of their loss.

Katie was one of those things. He'd never meant to hurt her. He'd cared for her so much he'd had to relegate her to the shadowy corners of his mind along with all of Briar Creek—Sheriff, his home, his friends and his dad's memory. Now he wanted to retrieve the things he'd lost, the things he'd closed his heart to for all those years.

Katie was at the top of that list, but being attracted to her, desiring her the way a man desires a woman, wasn't on that list at all, not even on the very bottom. He'd already done that with Cindy. She'd been his Katie-replacement, or so he'd thought at the time. She had red hair and a big smile. She was outgoing and vivacious. Over the years they'd made the gradual transition from friends to dating to going steady to marriage to complete indifference.

Friends were forever, but lovers were temporary.

During all those years, he'd never stopped loving and missing Katie.

He had to make up to her for all the pain he'd caused her by his abandonment.

And if he had any chance of doing that, he was going to have to ignore his raging hormones. Every time she got close to him...hell, every time he thought about her...he wanted to touch her soft skin, hold her body against his, feel the weight and roundness of her breasts in his hands, taste her lips.

Damn!

He opened the pantry and tossed the empty sardine can in the trash.

While Sheriff and Katie were gone to Dallas today, he would figure out some way to deal with all that.

He drained the last of the pot of coffee into his cup,

turned off the switch and was locking the front door behind himself when the phone rang.

He considered not answering it. He'd be at the office in ten minutes. If it was an emergency, he could take the call then.

But it might be his mother.

He twisted the key to unlock the door, turned the knob, pushed on the door which still stuck in spite of his efforts to repair it, and spilled coffee on his right pants leg when the door finally gave and opened. With a heartfelt curse, he strode across the living room to where the phone sat on the polished floor.

"Hello?"

"Luke, this is Sheriff. How you doing this morning?"

"Fine, Sheriff, just fine. How about yourself?"

"Fair to middling. But I don't feel like making that long trip to Dallas. You wouldn't mind going with Katie, would you?"

A two hour drive to Dallas and two hours back, trapped in the relatively small confines of his car with Katie. Heaven and hell along I-20.

"Of course I don't mind, Sheriff. I'll be right over to get her." He looked down at the stain on his pants leg. "I'll be over in fifteen minutes."

"I'll call the court house, and they'll have the documents waiting for you. I sure do appreciate it, Luke."

"No problem." Yet. But he had a feeling there'd be a lot of those before the day was over. "Sheriff, you never did say what these documents are...Sheriff? Hello?"

***

"I hope Sheriff's all right," Luke said as he pulled onto the highway with Katie beside him and her elusive scent of honeysuckle flowing around and through him. The interior of the big old car seemed small and intimate.

"Papa'll be fine," she said.

108

"Did he tell you what was wrong? All he said to me when he called was that he didn't feel like making the trip."

"I know. That's all he told me. I think he just didn't want to go to Dallas. He felt fine at breakfast. I made him a toasted bagel with cream cheese, and he got out the skillet and made bacon and eggs to go with that bagel."

Luke laughed. "That sounds like Sheriff. He didn't seem sick when I talked to him on the phone, then at your house when he came out on the porch to say good-bye, he didn't look sick. Still, it's not like him to ask anybody to do anything for him. Usually it's the other way around. He wants to do everything himself."

"He likes to take charge."

She'd been distant from the time he'd picked her up. Now she hugged the passenger door as if she didn't dare get too close to him.

For several minutes they sped along the concrete ribbon in silence. The highway was six lanes wide, but even so the trees and hills on each side, the confines of the car, his own thoughts, made him feel suddenly claustrophobic.

"Katie, will you stop sitting on the door handle? You act like you're afraid of me."

"Don't call me that," she said.

"Don't call you what?" he asked in exasperation.

"Katie. My name is Kathleen. My friends call me Kate. Only my father calls me Katie."

"Damn it, I've always called you Katie! Why should I stop now?"

"Because it sounds like a little girl's name, and I'm not a little girl anymore."

He knew that only too well. Maybe that was why he refused to stop calling her by the diminutive. Maybe he thought somehow he could convince himself she was still that little girl he'd loved with the uncomplicated love of children.

"You're acting pretty childish right now," he said.

With his gaze fixed on the highway, Luke could only see Katie peripherally, so he felt as much as saw her glare at him.

But then the atmosphere inside the car seemed to lighten. Katie smiled. Again it was something he sensed more than saw.

"Yeah," she said, "I guess I am. Sorry. I've had a lot on my mind lately."

She'd finally admitted what he'd known all along, something was bothering her. "I hope you know you can always talk to me. You used to tell me everything."

She shook her head slowly, sadly. "That was a little boy and a little girl who don't exist anymore."

He couldn't argue that point with her. If they were still those same children, his libido wouldn't go into overdrive every time he got close to her. "I'd still like to be your friend."

She didn't say anything, and he could feel the tension building again.

"Katie, I'm more sorry than you can ever know that I didn't answer your letters."

"Luke, I told you, that was a long time ago and it doesn't matter anymore." Her voice was dignified and smooth on the surface, but he could hear the soft underbelly of her words. He knew her too well for her to be able to fool him. It *did* matter.

He licked his suddenly dry lips. "I guess we need to talk about it."

She looked out the window, away from him. He thought he heard her whisper the single word *Don't,* and something shifted inside him.

He felt callous for daring to expect her to forgive and

110

forget. He'd hurt her. A lot. More than he'd realized. However difficult it might be for him to talk about it, he had to do it.

"I've never been good at this sort of thing, expressing my feelings, I mean. So I probably won't do this too well."

"Then don't say anything. We don't need to do this. I don't want to do this."

Her words were tough, verging on harsh, and that told him how much it still bothered her. He was going to have to open himself up as he hadn't done since he and Katie were kids, expose himself in a way he'd never done for anybody.

But this wasn't just anybody. This was his Katie. For her, he'd been in fights with boys bigger than he was. He'd tried to take all the blame when the two of them broke his mother's favorite lamp, though Katie hadn't let him. He'd visited her when she had chicken pox and she'd done the same for him when he caught it from her.

Then ultimately he'd let her down.

He leaned forward in the seat. "When I first made up my mind to come back to Briar Creek, I wanted to see you and make things right, ask you to forgive me. I guess I thought you could absolve me of guilt for what I did to you and make me feel okay again. Well, today, right now, that's not as important as making *you* feel better. I was a jerk. You were wonderful and giving and caring, and I was a jerk."

She didn't contradict him.

He had no choice but to continue.

"When my dad died and we left Briar Creek, I wanted to die, too. I'd never heard the term *depressed* in those days, but that's what I was. So depressed I didn't want to get out of bed in the mornings or eat or talk to people. I was twelve years old. I didn't know what to do. My mother was doing all she could just to hang on. She had to get a job which meant she left early in the morning and came home late at night. Aunt Myrtle kept telling me if I loved my mother, I'd be strong, be a man, and stop worrying her by being sad all the time. She said I was the man of the family, and I had to take care of my mother and grow up."

"Let it go, Luke. It was a long time ago. We were kids. It's no big deal." She kept her head turned away from him, and her tone was as impersonal as if she were talking to the scenery rushing past them.

"Yes," he insisted, "it is a big deal. You may never be able to forgive me, but I need you to understand. I managed to send all the pain to a dark corner of my mind so I could be strong and not worry Mom. But the only way I could do that was to put everything related to that part of my life into that corner, too. If I thought about you or Sheriff or Briar Creek, I'd think about my father and everything I'd lost, and I'd get depressed again. I suppose in today's psycho-babble terms, you'd say I blocked everything."

"Blocked," Katie repeated softly. "I've never understood why a process that saves your sanity should be considered harmful. I've always thought it's a good thing if you can get away from something that hurts. If we have a headache, we don't focus on it and concentrate on the pain. We take an aspirin and try to divert our attention so we won't notice the pain so much until it's gone."

"You're right. Unless that headache turns out to be a stroke and you've ignored it until it's too late. I did such a good job of ignoring my pain that I lost the best part of my life. My best friend."

He thought her shoulders quivered a little, and his heart sank. Had he made her cry?

It was hard to tell. He couldn't look away from the road for longer than a quick glance. She was holding herself so tautly upright, it could have been a quiver from the tension of her muscles.

He wanted to stop the car, get out, go around, haul her into his arms, hug her and make all the pain he'd caused her go away.

Instead he continued to drive down the highway at seventy miles an hour, his hopes sinking with every mile, with every heartbeat. Katie was not going to forgive him. Could not forgive him. Should not forgive him.

Finally she turned in her seat and faced forward again. "Luke, I understand." Her voice was quiet with none of the distance he'd heard in it earlier. "If you need my forgiveness, you have it. If you want to resume our friendship, that's not so easy. We've both changed a lot. Our lives only move in one direction. Forward. We can never go back. I lost my mother, you lost your father, we lost each other, and we moved on. We found other people. You married Cindy, I'm going to marry Spencer. We're both very different than we were seventeen years ago."

He couldn't argue with that. Seventeen years ago she'd been a skinny little thing with eyes too big for her face and freckles across the bridge of her nose. Today she was a beautiful woman with curves in all the right places.

Seventeen years ago she could have been another guy for all the difference her sex made in their relationship. Today he was only too aware that she was a woman. She made it difficult for him to remember she was engaged to another man, that his only interest in her was friendship. At least, friendship *should* be his only interest.

"I know all that, Katie. But in spite of those early efforts to put everything behind me, I don't think there's been a day I haven't thought about you. I'd really like to start over and see if these new people we are can become friends."

She was silent for several minutes. The only sound in

113

the car was the hum of the engine and the muffled thumps as the tires traveled over the highway. Luke had plenty of time to think of how important this was to him, how desperately he wanted Katie back in his life, how much he'd missed her.

He also had plenty of time to wonder how he would keep his desire for her tamped down and how he would deal with her impending marriage.

"Of course we can start over," she finally said. But she hadn't mentioned resuming their friendship, and her voice had a distant echo, as though she spoke to mollify him, to end the discussion.

Still, it was a beginning. That's all he'd asked for.

For the rest of the trip, they made small talk. Finally they arrived in Dallas, and she directed him through the downtown mix-master of highways to the exit that led to the Dallas County Courthouse.

Their trip was half over, and he wasn't sure how much he'd accomplished with his time alone with her.

When they entered the courthouse, they found that the clerk knew nothing about any legal documents for the sheriff of Briar Creek County.

Chapter Ten

"Obviously there's been some sort of a mix-up," Kate said smoothly, though she felt anything but smooth inside. Was this one more piece of evidence of her father's confused mental state? "I'll just call the sheriff and find out what's going on."

Luke's words, his offer of a renewal of their friendship, had been uncomfortably seductive. She certainly needed a friend right now. But something inside refused to break down, to let her get close to him again.

She moved to a corner of the room, took out her phone and called Papa's office.

Evelyn answered. "Sheriff's not here right now, Katie. I heard you were in town for a few days. How's everything going?"

"Pretty good." *Compared to a national disaster, anyway.* "Did Papa say when he'd return?"

"Oh, honey, you know how these things go. No telling when he'll come dragging back in here. Now you be sure and come by to say *hi* before you leave town. I'll show you pictures of all my grandkids. I've got five now."

"I'll do that. Did Papa leave a message? He asked Luke and me to pick up some documents from the Dallas County Courthouse, but we're there, and they don't know anything about it. He didn't tell us what those documents are. Did he tell you anything?"

Evelyn laughed. "No, he never said a word to me. That's just like Sheriff. I swear, he'd forget his head if it wasn't attached to the end of his neck."

A shiver ran down Kate's spine. That really wasn't what she wanted to hear. She looked at Luke standing a couple of feet away, politely pretending he wasn't listening to her conversation. She desperately wanted to confide in him and just as desperately wanted to keep her problems and her heart to herself.

"We've got some more errands to run while we're here. Have him call me on my cell when you talk to him."

"Will do! So you're spending the day in Dallas with that big, handsome deputy, huh? Well, you two have a real good time!"

Kate wanted to protest that she and Luke were there strictly on business, but there was no point in it. She'd be trying to convince herself as much as Evelyn. "We'll do that," she said instead.

She disconnected the call, moved over beside Luke and repeated what Evelyn had told her except for the part about the *big, handsome deputy*.

Luke shrugged. "Okay. So we get the computer stuff then come back by here on the way out of town. I'll drive you wherever you want to go, and I'll help carry the boxes, but that will be my sole contribution to that portion of our trip. The only thing I know about computers is that they have some little green man inside to make them run, and if you spill coffee on him, he gets mad and goes on strike."

Kate laughed in spite of their problems. "That's a good start. That little green man doesn't like to have soft drinks or tea spilled on him, either. I speak from experience."

They spent the rest of the morning and much of the afternoon looking for computers and all the necessary accessories and peripherals and the appropriate software. In between, they made a stop at her office to get a copy of a technical manual she wanted, ate lunch and tried to call Papa two more times with no success.

They left the last store with the last item, and were barely able to cram it all into Luke's trunk and back seat.

"I'm going to try Papa one more time," Kate said. "If he's still not in his office, we might as well head back home. The courthouse closes in an hour and a half."

Luke shook his head. "I don't understand. That's not like Sheriff."

No, Kate thought. It wasn't like him at all. Something was definitely wrong, and the thought gave her heart a painful twist.

Luke pulled over into a convenience store parking lot. "I'll get us something cold to drink while you call Sheriff," he said.

Kate nodded, got out of the car and stood in the shade close to the store front. The day had become unbearably hot, the heat intensified by all the concrete and asphalt in the shopping centers they'd visited. Knowing what they would face, Kate had worn a light cotton blouse, long skirt and sandals, but even so, the heat assaulted her with a vengeance every time they stepped out into it.

Evelyn answered on the first ring. "He's right here," she declared happily. "Sheriff, it's Katie again."

"Papa, we went by the courthouse this morning and your papers aren't ready." She kept her voice calm and refrained from asking where he'd been all day. On a picnic with Mama? Shopping for a *mother of the bride* dress for her wedding? "Is there a problem?"

"Oh, I didn't know you were going to the courthouse first. I thought you'd go computer shopping and then swing by to pick up those papers last."

Kate sagged with relief that Papa had a reasonable explanation. "Well, we've got the computers and we're ready to swing by the courthouse again. Have you talked to them yet? Are the papers ready now?"

"To tell you the truth, I haven't called yet. I just got in. Had to go out and talk to Homer Grimes and Seth Flanders again. I sure don't know what to make of that situation. Somebody took wire cutters to a section of Homer's fence, and some of his cattle got out. I just can't imagine Seth doing something like that. On the other

117

hand, I can see how Homer could drive you to desperate measures, always complaining and carrying on. I think he might need some of that Prozac stuff I'm always hearing about. Seth says he didn't have anything to do with it, and I believe him, but Homer's ready to take the law into his own hands. Took me a long to get him calmed down."

The temperature rose at least ten degrees as Kate bit her lip and waited impatiently for Papa to finish his story. "Can you call the courthouse now?" she asked when he finally concluded.

"Of course I can, Katie-girl. You kids get a cold soda pop and call me back when you're through so I can tell you what I find out."

"Why don't we just go on down to the courthouse? If you call right now, the papers should be ready when we get there, shouldn't they?"

"Maybe. Maybe not. Getting everything copied is kind of complicated. Depends on how busy they are down there, and you know they're always busy in Dallas."

Kate lifted her hair off the back of her neck in a futile attempt to find relief from the heat. "If getting it copied is that complicated, shouldn't you have called earlier?" As soon as she spoke the words, she wished she could take them back. She hadn't meant to criticize Papa. That wouldn't help, and she didn't want to make him feel badly about his lapses.

But he didn't seem upset. "I probably should have called earlier," he admitted blithely, "but I didn't. You go on back to the courthouse right now if you want to, but it could turn out to be a wasted trip."

"We'll get a cold drink," she mumbled. "Call me on my cell after you talk to the court house."

"Why don't you just call me back in a little while? You know I hate those cell phones and all those modern gadgets."

118

"But—" She started to protest that calling her on her cell would be no different on his end than if he called her on a land line. Instead she said, "Fine. I'll call you back in a little while."

Kate disconnected the call and saw Luke standing beside her, holding two cold Cokes. She accepted one gratefully and took a long gulp, then reported the conversation with her father.

"Are you sure that's what he said, that he just didn't do it?" Luke asked in amazement. "This whole situation isn't like Sheriff at all. He's always so conscientious about everything. Well, maybe not paperwork, but anything to do with getting the job done."

No, Kate thought dismally, it isn't like him. At least, not like he used to be. "I'm sure that's what he said. Let's go inside where it's cool and finish our sodas."

They went inside and stood to one side sipping their drinks, waiting for *a little while* to elapse.

"What do you think?" Luke said. "Does this remind you of when we were kids and used to stop off in Clifton's Grocery to get a cold soda after playing in the heat all day?"

Kate lifted her red can, turned it and studied it from all angles, then shook her head determinedly. "No," she said, pulling herself back from the brink of nostalgia that Luke was so good at taking her to. "Clifton's store was older. It had wooden shelves and a wooden counter. It smelled like bananas and apples and, in the summer, peaches and cantaloupes. This store is all steel and glass, and it smells like plastic."

Luke grinned and shrugged and looked so darn good in that uniform, Kate could feel the temperature rising again even in the air-conditioned store.

"Okay," he teased, "other than those few little things, I mean."

She smiled in spite of herself. "I'm going to try Papa again."

"Why don't you let me talk to him this time?"
Why?

Because Luke might find himself talking to a ghost, for one thing.

However, so far Papa seemed to have been able to hide Mama's existence from everyone but her. When Luke was around, he never spoke of Mama in the present tense.

What the heck, Luke was with Papa all day, every day. If Papa hadn't revealed his peculiarity by now, she supposed one phone call couldn't make much difference. She handed her phone to him, and he punched in the number, walking outside as he did so. That brought a smile to her face. Good cell phone manners. Better to sweat in the heat than have a phone conversation in a restaurant or even a convenience store.

She gulped down the rest of her soda and tossed the can in the trash then went out to join him.

Luke frowned. "Then we'll come home and drive back up here tomorrow."

It sounded as though the papers wouldn't be ready in time and they'd have to make the trip again. Well, Luke knew the way now. He could come by himself tomorrow.

"They *what*?" Luke's face flushed darkly and he ran a hand over the back of his neck. "No, I don't think that's a good idea....Well, sure, I understand, but...yes, but...I think you'd better talk to Katie."

With a panic-stricken look that seemed out of place on his rugged face, he handed her the phone.

"Papa? What's the problem?"

"You were absolutely right. I should have called those folks earlier. They're real busy and they can't get those papers ready before the courthouse closes."

"Then we'll pick them up tomorrow morning. Luke

can come back to Dallas."

"No, I wouldn't want him to go to all that trouble. I'm trying to work something out with a friend of mine there who says he might be able to stay a few minutes late and have what I need messengered over to your little apartment."

"Condo," she corrected automatically.

"Okay, your condo."

"But we're not at my condo."

"It would be a much nicer place for you to wait than where you are now. You must be outside. I can hear a lot of noise, cars honking. I can just see you standing there in that heat and those exhaust fumes, your backs hurting from all the walking you've done today. Your little apartment will be quiet and cool, and you'll have a comfortable place to sit."

The idea of Luke and her alone in her condo was far too tantalizing. "Papa, I don't think—"

"Why don't you and Luke pick up a couple of steaks and some potatoes on the way home so you won't have to leave in case the messenger doesn't get there for a couple of hours and you get hungry? We've made some mighty tasty steaks on that little grill of yours when I came to visit."

She could feel her hand clutching the phone so tightly it hurt. This must have been the point at which Luke handed the phone to her, but she had nobody to pass it on to.

"I don't think that's a good idea," she said.

"Why not?"

What could she say to that? There was certainly no reason Luke shouldn't go to her condo with her, grill steaks and wait for Papa's messenger. No reason except the way she felt every time she got close to him. No reason except the way he'd almost kissed her in the kitchen the other night. No reason except the dust devil of confusion swirling around in her own head.

A car pulled up to the store.

Someone got out and brushed past Luke and her to go inside.

Someone else came out, got in a car and left.

Papa waited patiently for her answer.

"No reason," she finally said, pushing aside her absurd thoughts. She was an adult, and adults didn't have to act on every impulse they had. "I was just anxious to get home. To your home, I mean. But we'll go to my condo and wait for your messenger."

"Thanks, Katie-girl. I really appreciate it. And don't forget those steaks. Charge them to the sheriff's office since you're on official business."

Kate hung up the phone and turned to Luke, bracing herself as if she expected him to protest. Well, he was tired and ready to get back to Briar Creek, too. He probably would protest. "We're to go to my place to wait for someone to bring us the papers. And on the way, we're to pick up steaks and potatoes for dinner in case the messenger's late."

Luke stared down at her for a long moment, his eyes narrowing and darkening until she could barely distinguish the pupil from the iris. Finally he nodded and looked away. "If that's what Sheriff wants us to do, as long as you've got air conditioning and something cold to drink, I guess we can do it."

Of course they could. She was being silly to fret about it.

Chapter Eleven

They arrived at her place half an hour later.

Luke managed to cram a couple more of the smaller boxes they'd purchased into his trunk, then lifted out the remaining two large boxes from the back seat.

"I don't think we should leave them in a convertible even for an hour or so," he explained. "We could in Briar Creek, but not in Dallas."

Katie picked up the bag of groceries and didn't argue with him. He was right.

He locked the door, and they headed for the elevators in the middle of the small complex.

"Nice place," he said as they reached the central courtyard with a swimming pool and landscaping. "I like the trees."

"My unit's on the back side, overlooking a creek."

They got on the elevator and Kate punched the third floor.

See? she congratulated herself. The elevator was a tiny space, putting her only inches away from Luke, so close she could feel the heat of his body, smell the starch of his uniform, the dark scent of masculine power. All that and they weren't groping each other.

Of course, on the practical side, any sort of groping would be pretty difficult while Luke held those two big boxes and she had a bag of groceries.

He looked at her, his eyes dark and fathomless in the dim interior, and it seemed the heat radiating from his body intensified.

The elevator dinged and came to a lurching halt.

Kate bolted through the doors before they were completely open.

"My unit's down this way," she called.

Balancing the groceries on her hip, she unlocked the

123

door and preceded Luke inside, turning on lights as she went. For a moment, she thought she detected a faint, lingering fragrance of lilacs, but that wasn't possible. Her room deodorizer was cinnamon scented.

"Nice place," Luke repeated, setting the groceries on the breakfast bar and looking around.

"That's what you said about the exterior."

She could almost see her home through Luke's eyes and suspected he didn't really care for the contemporary furnishings, the off white carpet, the glass coffee table, the stark white sofa and chair with turquoise and purple patterned throw pillows, the matching swaths of fabric draped above the white mini-blinds.

"And I meant it both times," he said.

"It's very different from Papa's house and from yours."

Luke laughed and drew a bottle of chilled white wine out of the bag. "Do you have a corkscrew?"

Katie opened a kitchen drawer and handed the tool to him then took down two glasses while he worked on the cork.

"Yeah, this is different from my house all right. You'll have to come over and see it some time. Just be sure and bring your own chair."

"What?"

"I don't have any furniture except a bed."

For a second their eyes met as she wondered if he knew how suggestive that sounded.

He looked away and poured the wine.

Of course it didn't sound suggestive. Her hormones or guilty desire or something was working overtime.

She picked up her glass of wine and started across the room. "The grill's on the balcony. I'll get the fire going."

Luke followed her out and took the bag of charcoal from her. "I'll do it. I still remember when our Sunday school class went on a wiener roast and you caught the woods on fire."

She laughed and relinquished the bag to him. "You're welcome to do the work, but you're not being completely fair. It was that flaming marshmallow that fell off my coat hanger into a pile of dead leaves that caused the problem. Could have happened to anybody."

"It could have, but it didn't. According to Mrs. Oliver, you still have the dubious distinction of being the only person in Briar Creek to commit arson on a Sunday school picnic."

Luke dumped charcoal onto the grill, and Kate walked to the edge of the balcony where the branches of a big elm tree had grown past the rail. She rubbed a leaf between her fingers, feeling the rough texture, then stood looking down at the creek below. The muffled noise of nearby traffic barely filtered through.

"It's amazing what a few trees can do to clean up the air and noise that we humans produce," she said.

The acrid smell of lighter fluid was followed by a soft *whoosh* and the smell of burning charcoal.

Luke came over to stand beside her. "When you said you had a condo fifteen minutes from downtown Dallas, I imagined something in a high rise, surrounded by parking lots and office buildings."

"You're not far wrong. We're just a few blocks from some luxury high rise condos and office buildings on Turtle Creek. The Oak Lawn area—that's where we are— is an old section of Dallas that started out as wall to wall apartments for swinging singles and hippies during the sixties. It went downhill in the seventies then got converted to condos, quaint little shops and offices in the eighties. It's cozy here. You get to know your neighbors, just like in a small town."

"Almost like," Luke said. "You can't leave your new

computer equipment in the back seat of your car here like you can in a small town. Why settle for *almost* when you can have the real thing?"

"I guess it's a trade-off. Dallas has a lot of things Briar Creek doesn't—jobs, theaters, department stores, restaurants, just to name a few. I happen to think this area combines the best of both worlds. We're walking distance to my favorite park, Reverchon. It has some wonderful structures built out of native stone—winding steps up the hills, benches—one shaped like a throne—and so many trees, you feel like you're in a forest, completely hidden from the rest of the world."

"Can you walk in that park alone at night?"

Kate lifted her chin. "I could if I wanted to."

"Sure, if you wanted to get killed or raped."

"How often do you go for a midnight stroll in Briar Creek?"

"Occasionally." He looked down toward the trickle of water below, then lifted his glass and took a sip of wine. He swallowed and turned to her. "This reminds me of the creek at home where you and I used to play, where we found that cave and buried our friendship thorn. What did we put it in? An old aspirin box?"

Kate frowned. "I don't remember, and I don't see the resemblance. Of course there's some similarity. I mean, a creek's a creek and a tree's a tree."

He gave her a look which told her he didn't believe she was being completely honest then leaned on his elbows on the rail. "You like it here."

"I do, yes."

"I was all prepared not to like your condo in Dallas, but this is—" He stopped, looked up at her and smiled. "A nice place."

She rolled her eyes and laughed. "You really need to increase your vocabulary, learn some synonyms for *nice*."

"Okay, how's this? It's like being in a tree house only you don't scratch your legs climbing up and you have air conditioning and a grill for steaks and you can drink wine."

"That's nice, Luke, real nice."

The sound of Luke's laughter blended with the summer air, warm and mellow, a caress to her ears.

"I've missed you, Katie."

"I missed you for a long time." Kate spoke without thinking, from her heart not her head. If she had taken time to think, she wouldn't have admitted that she'd ever missed him.

Nevertheless the words couldn't be recalled, and she found that she was actually glad she'd spoken them. Relieved. A weight lifted from her chest, a barrier between Luke and her came down, and she realized how tired she was from holding that barrier in place.

He half-turned, hoisting one foot onto the rail, draping an arm over his knee, and smiled...and the years fell away. It was Luke's smile, her best friend's smile.

Of course he was no longer her best friend. But the rational part of her mind where that knowledge existed had somehow disengaged. She smiled back.

"The outside's changed," he said, studying her, "but you're still the same Katie."

She wanted to tell him that wasn't true, that she'd changed all the way to the core of her being.

But she was no longer sure if it was true, or if it even mattered.

She turned and leaned back against the rail, her arms folded across her chest. "Your outside's changed quite a bit, too."

Luke shrugged, his gaze warm on her, comforting and compelling like the approaching shadows of evening. "When you walked through the door of Sheriff's office on

Friday, I thought at first I was hallucinating, that I wanted to see you so much, I'd pulled you straight out of my own thoughts."

Was that what Papa had done, missed Mama so much, wanted to see her so much, that he pulled her out of his own thoughts and into his version of reality?

"I still think it's odd that Papa didn't tell you I was coming down," she said.

"Katie, in your father's eyes, you and I will always be two little kids, following him around and getting into mischief. Surely you remember how he used to love to surprise us."

She nodded, her heart swelling with love for her father. "Like the horse rides."

"Every year he had surprise birthday parties for us."

"And we let him think we were surprised, even when we knew, after so many times, he was going to do it."

"Sheriff knew I wanted to see you. I told him so. I'm sure he planned the whole thing, getting you down to Briar Creek and then getting himself out of the office when you came in."

That theory put a different light on things. If it were true, that would make Papa's mind as sharp as ever rather than foggy with the early stages of senility.

"He did make a determined effort to get me down here, now that I think about it."

He'd even put Mama on the phone when all else failed.

Okay, maybe Papa's mind was as sharp as ever—though some of his efforts misguided—except for one small hallucination.

Or was it possible that Mama, too, had been part of his effort to get her to Briar Creek? Had he pretended to be seeing a ghost so she'd rush down to check on him?

No. Papa never lied. If he said he was putting Mama

128

on the phone, he believed it.

"You haven't seen any real changes in Papa?" she asked.

He studied her intently for several seconds before answering. Well, it was about the fifth time she'd asked him. Luke was probably beginning to worry about her sanity by now.

"Nothing out of the ordinary. Like I said, he's a few years older, a few pounds heavier. Katie, you've asked me that before. Obviously you're worried about something. What is it?"

A faint breeze rustled the leaves and caressed Kate's cheek.

A dog barked and another answered.

A robin burst into song then went silent.

The words Kate wanted to speak stayed in her throat, refusing to come to her lips.

"Remember that Maypole thing we did in grade school," Luke said, "where they tied colored streamers to a pole and we each took one and went around and around in some pattern I never could figure out?"

Kate laughed in relief at the reprieve from answering Luke's question. "I remember. You got tangled up every time."

"Well, your dad is like that Maypole. He's stability. He stays in one place while everything else revolves around him and gets all tangled and confused and eventually unwinds and finds him there, waiting, the same as when we started."

Kate lifted her glass to her lips and sipped, letting the cool wine roll over her tongue. "Yes," she agreed. "He's the center of my life. I'd be lost without him."

"When I talked to him on the phone about coming to work for him, it was like all the intervening years had never happened. Even so, I was amazed to actually get back to Briar Creek and find how little things had changed, especially Sheriff."

Kate twirled the stem of her glass between two fingers. "Why did you return to Briar Creek, Luke? You've admitted that when you left, you cut all ties, no looking backward."

He stared into the distance for a few moments, his brow creasing. "That's one of the reasons, I guess. I never had a chance to tie up loose ends, take care of unfinished business. The carousel stopped in the middle of the ride, and I came back to finish that ride. I never wanted to leave Briar Creek so it seemed right to return. But also..."

"What?" she asked when he stopped and shook his head.

He shifted, lifting his other foot to the rail, and again stared into the distance. "When my mom remarried, it was like losing my dad all over again, like the last link I had with him had been severed and this time I was an adult and couldn't hide from it. By returning to Briar Creek, moving into our old house, taking Dad's old job, I guess I thought I could find some part of him again, of that life I lost so many years ago."

"Did you?"

"No, not really. But I found Sheriff and you and the whole town of Briar Creek. I found myself again."

For a flickering instant, Kate felt a surge of wistfulness, but that was ridiculous. She had never lost herself as Luke had, so why should she feel wistful over the thought of finding herself?

"You can't turn back the clock, Luke."

"I know. And it's a damned shame we can't. Everything was so much simpler then."

Turn back the clock, once again suffer through the agony of losing one of the two people she'd counted on after she'd already lost her mother? But she couldn't say that.

"Give up my computer?" She shook her head and grinned. "No way."

"Not even for those chocolate chip cookies my mom used to bake?" he teased.

"Oh," she groaned, "no fair! That's a tough one. Would I trade my computer for your mom's chocolate chip cookies? I'm going to have to think about that one."

He moved closer, and the world around them shimmered and became hazy.

"Katie."

He brushed her hair over her ear, and the sensation of his touch reverberated along every nerve in her body. "Tell me what's wrong. I know something is, and I'm pretty sure it has to do with your father. I've talked to you. I've spilled my guts. Now you talk to me. Give me a chance to prove I'll be there for you, never let you down again."

The double assault on her senses, physical and emotional, was too much.

Her body turned toward him like a weather vane turning into the wind. She wanted to lay her head on that broad chest the way she'd once laid her head on it when it was skinny, tell him all about Papa and her worries, feel his arms about her as they soothed away her troubles, feel his warm breath in her hair and on her neck, let all her problems dissolve as her soul and her body merged with Luke's.

One hand curved around the back of her neck while the other slipped down to her waist, and she felt as if she'd come home at last. Luke's eyelids drooped languorously. His lips parted slightly.

"Kate! Spencer! What are you two doing back here? Oh, that's not Spencer, is it?"

Kate jumped back guiltily, away from Luke and from

131

her own insane cravings. What was the matter with her? A sudden bout of masochism, a desire to jump back into the fire after she'd crawled out, scorched and scarred, seventeen years ago?

On the next balcony, Whitney Upchurch, long blond hair streaming down like Rapunzel's, leaned over the balcony and flashed her toothpaste smile.

So much for the idea that knowing your neighbors was a positive attribute of this area.

"Hello, Whitney. This is Luke Rodgers, my father's deputy from Briar Creek. We came to pick up some legal documents for Papa. He forgot to call and they're being messengered over here any minute now." She was explaining way too much, sounding guilty.

Well, she felt guilty.

This had not been a good idea to come here after all.

"Nice to meet you, Whitney," Luke said. "If you'll excuse me, I need to put the steaks on the grill."

"And I'd better get the baked potatoes in the microwave. We have to eat here instead of going out because if we left, we might miss the messenger." She was doing it again! Explaining everything in detail as though she had something to hide. Which she didn't. Not really.

Still, it felt like she did.

***

Luke cooked the steaks while Kate made baked potatoes and a salad, then they sat down at her glass and wood dining table to eat. The atmosphere between them had returned to strained.

"This is very good," Luke said. "I don't know why you keep saying you can't cook."

Kate took another bite of steak, chewed and swallowed. "It doesn't take much ability to make baked potatoes and a salad."

"That meal you cooked Saturday night took a lot of

ability."

Kate slathered more sour cream on her potato. She didn't want to think about that night or that meal.

"I guess Sheriff must have told you those were my favorite foods."

Kate froze with a bite of potato halfway to her mouth. "*Your* favorite foods?"

"Well, not my only favorites, but those are sure on the top of the list."

"But—"

Luke looked up from cutting a bite of steak and frowned. "What? You didn't know those were my favorite foods? It was all a coincidence?" He shrugged and gave a wry grin. "Well, so much for my ego. I thought you were trying to impress me."

"No," she said slowly, her mouth suddenly so dry she could hardly speak, "I don't think it was a coincidence." Luke must have mentioned something to Papa who had then become confused and said they were *his* favorite foods. Then at dinner he had mentioned how he'd never tasted the mushrooms before but hoped he would again. He'd forgotten his own confused story.

She lifted her glass of wine with a shaky hand and tossed down the last swallow.

Luke leaned over the table. "I'm only teasing you. It doesn't matter if you didn't cook my favorite foods on purpose." He studied her intently, his gaze so probing she dropped hers to watch her fingers twisting the napkin in her lap.

"Katie, I know something's wrong. I also know you don't want to talk to me about it, but if you change your mind, I'm here. I'll always be here."

"I don't know about you, but I'm ready to tie into that chocolate cheesecake we brought at the grocery store. I hope it's thawed. If it isn't, we could just eat it frozen.

Probably use more calories chewing that way. Maybe break a few teeth, of course, but—"

He reached across the table and lifted her chin, forcing her to face him. "Stop chattering. If you don't want to tell me your problems, that's okay. You don't have to."

And you don't have to be so seductive—physically and emotionally.

She slid back her chair and went to the kitchen to get the cheesecake. Surely a little chocolate would help to put things back in their proper perspective. Heck, it had as much chance as anything else!

They were just finishing the cheesecake when her cell phone rang.

Kate left the table and went to sit on her sofa. "Hello?"

"Hi, Katie-girl! Did the messenger come yet?"

She'd become so involved in Luke and all the chaos of her own mind, Kate had almost forgotten why they were there. "No, he hasn't come yet, and it's getting late."

"Sure is. I'd better check on things. I'll tell you what, if the messenger doesn't come and you don't hear from me in the next hour, why don't you and Luke just spend the night there, get those papers tomorrow and drive back here in the morning?"

"What?"

Papa couldn't be suggesting what she thought he was.

"I'd sure feel a lot better if you didn't have to make that trip back late tonight. You've had a couple of glasses of wine, not too much, I know you wouldn't do that, but enough to make you sleepy on that long, dark drive back. I tell you, I'd worry myself sick the whole time you were on the road. Luke could have that bedroom where you always put me. That's a real comfortable bed in there."

Kate gave a fleeting thought to wondering how Papa knew they'd been drinking wine and exactly how much, but she had bigger things to worry about.

"Papa, we can't do that!"

"Why not?"

"Because we can't. It wouldn't look right."

Papa chuckled softly. "Katie-girl, this isn't the fifties. I'm your father and I trust you. Who else matters?"

"Spencer! It wouldn't look right to Spencer."

"Spencer doesn't trust you?"

"Of course he trusts me!"

"Then I don't see a problem. You give it another hour then you both go to bed. If the guy doesn't come tonight, you can scoot back to the courthouse tomorrow then head home in the morning."

"Papa! If those papers aren't here in an hour, we're starting home!"

"Oh, Katie, I wish you wouldn't do that. My heart went to bouncing around in my chest like the dickens just at the thought of you and Luke out there on that long, dark drive, and me being the one to get the call and have to investigate." He paused. "It brings back memories of when your mama had that wreck."

Dark, consuming guilt washed over Kate. "I'd never deliberately worry you, Papa. We'll spend the night here. You have a good evening and we'll see you in the morning."

Surely for the sake of not worrying her father she could stay under the same roof with Luke for one night without losing control of her hormones or her emotions. It was, she supposed, a small enough thing for Papa to ask.

She hung up the phone and turned to face Luke who was watching her with a puzzled expression. "Papa doesn't want us to drive home tonight. He wants us to stay here. You can have the guest room."

Luke rose from the table. "Why doesn't he want us to come home tonight?"

"He's afraid we'll have a wreck and he'll be the one to investigate, the way it happened with Mama."

Luke sucked in a quick breath. "Damn. I forgot about that. That had to be a nightmare for him. We'll stay here. No way would I worry him like that."

"We'll clean up the dishes then watch television for a while," she said briskly. That should keep her mind occupied and off him. "If the messenger doesn't get here before ten, we'll go to bed, then we'll get up in the morning, go to the courthouse for those papers and head home."

"No problem. I didn't have anything planned for the evening anyway." He smiled.

She smiled.

***

Emma smiled and squeezed Jerome's hand. Actually, she surrounded it with a flow of energy, but the sensation was close.

Jerome returned her smile but shook his head. "Emma, I'd never have believed you had such a devious mind."

"Neither would I, but I guess it's true that a mother can do anything when her daughter's happiness is threatened."

"I hated to bring up your accident."

"If our daughter wasn't so stubborn, it wouldn't have been necessary. They'll thank us for this on their wedding day."

"You're still so sure it'll come to that?"

"I'm positive. And do you know what they're going to be watching on television tonight? *Harvey*. That old James Stewart movie about a man who could see a six-foot rabbit no one else could, the one they watched a hundred times when they were kids. They loved that movie."

"Kind of fitting," Jerome said. "Sort of like the man

who could see his wife but nobody else could." He patted her hand. "Come on, wife, let's go upstairs to bed."

Together they climbed the stairs. Emma didn't need to go through the motions of walking, but she always did, always stayed beside him.

"How'd you arrange for that movie to come on tonight?" he asked her.

She laughed softly, and the sound flowed around him, like the morning mist scented with lilacs. "If I told you that, you'd be wanting me to make a John Wayne movie come on every night."

"I'm pretty sure one already does, Emma."

His wife was every bit as amazing in death as she'd been in life.

He reached behind and slapped her playfully on the rear.

She giggled and blushed. "Oh, Jerome!"

He was sure going to miss her when they got Katie squared away.

Chapter Twelve

Luke carried the bowl of microwave popcorn into the living room where Katie sat on one end of the sofa, her feet curled under her and hidden by her long skirt. She held the remote control to the TV and was channel surfing from one scrambled picture to another. This whole situation would be one hell of a lot easier if she didn't manage to look so damned sexy even waving that remote control around and swearing at the television.

"Blasted cable. It's on the fritz again. For some reason the only station I can get is one showing that old black and white movie, *Harvey.*"

Luke sank onto the opposite end of the sofa and set the popcorn on the glass coffee table. "That really is an oldie. It was old when we watched it as kids."

But he silently blessed the cable company for their problems. This was good. A trip down memory lane, a blast from the past. Keep his mind in an era when his body didn't get hard just from being around Katie. Much better than one of the new movies. Most of them had nudity and sex scenes. Surely a story about an invisible rabbit, a story he and Katie had shared when they were children, would keep him from having thoughts he shouldn't be having and from doing something dumb.

Something like what he'd almost done in Sheriff's kitchen and again on Katie's balcony.

"Yes, we've seen it a hundred times, but it'll have to do for tonight." She gave up switching channels and sat back. "Popcorn smells good. After that meal, I didn't think I could eat another bite, but I might be able to force down a few kernels."

"Can't have a movie without popcorn, even if it is made in the microwave."

She reached over and took a handful as the movie

began to unfold on the screen.

They watched in silence for a while.

"This is my favorite part," Katie said when the sister of Stewart's character reluctantly admitted that she sometimes saw *that big rabbit* herself. Katie turned to look at him, her face inches from his.

Luke wasn't sure how it had happened, but somehow he and Katie had moved from opposite ends of the sofa to the middle, right next to each other.

Probably it was the bowl of popcorn sitting in the middle, both of them sliding closer to reach for a handful, then not going all the way back to their original spots.

Or maybe his body had just taken charge and moved him over closer to her.

In the flickering glow from the television—when had they switched off the lights?—her eyes were luminescent. For a moment they held his then abruptly she sat back and again tucked her feet under her, distancing herself from him.

This wasn't exactly working out the way he'd hoped. He was still very much aware of Katie the woman sitting next to him. No way could he mistake her for the little girl who used to watch this movie with him. Beneath that thin cotton blouse, her breasts rose and fell with the rhythm of her breathing, in time with the pounding of his heart. She might have her legs tucked under her, but he was only too aware that those legs were long and sleek, the legs of a woman, not a young girl.

"Do you think he's really crazy?" she asked quietly.

It took Luke a moment to pull his thoughts away from her legs and realize she was asking about the movie. "You mean because he sees a six-foot rabbit nobody else can see or because he's always so nice to everybody?"

She laughed softly, but it was a half-hearted laugh. "Just because somebody hallucinates doesn't mean he's

139

crazy, right?"

"No, of course it doesn't. There are all sorts of hallucinations. A lot of people on drugs hallucinate, even prescription drugs. A thirsty man in the desert will hallucinate seeing water."

"Of course," she said thoughtfully. "That makes sense. A person with a desperate need can imagine that need being filled without there being something wrong with that person. In fact, our whole definition of *crazy* just isn't valid any longer. It's all chemical imbalances, and a few drugs can straighten everything out, right?"

"Yeah, but that's what this movie is all about. In the end, Elwood P. Dowd doesn't have the drug treatment because it would be a shame if he no longer saw Harvey."

She chewed her lower lip. "I never thought of it that way."

"You didn't? But we've seen this movie lots of times."

She looked at him, and even in the dim lighting, he could see the agony in her gaze.

"Damn it, Katie, what is it? Are you having hallucinations? Is that what's wrong?"

She shook her head slowly. "No." Her pain was so obvious in her wide morning-glory eyes, so blatant, he couldn't stand it any longer. He pulled her into his arms and held her against his chest, trying to tell himself he was only comforting her.

"It's okay, Katie. Whatever it is, it's going to be okay. I promise."

She wrapped her arms around him and held on tight, just the way she used to, drawing comfort even though neither of them said a word.

But it wasn't quite the way it used to be. Her breasts pressed against him, soft and full. Her scent of rain-kissed honeysuckle wrapped around him, teasing and promising

140

sweet delights. And his body was reacting in a way it sure hadn't in those long-ago days.

He tried to pull away.

No, he didn't. That was a lie. He thought about it, but his body wasn't responding to any such thoughts. His body was only responding to Katie's body.

She was going to hate him. With her head against his chest, she was bound to hear his heart pounding out of control. Her leg was pressed against his thigh and she could surely feel the growing hardness there.

She lifted her head and gazed at him, but it wasn't hatred he saw in her eyes. They were smoky blue with desire. Her lips seemed even more full than usual, as if swollen with the anticipation of his kiss.

But if he kissed her—

He couldn't think about that *if*. His mind wouldn't go there. All he could think about was how desperately he needed to claim her lips.

Lowering his face to hers, he dropped tiny butterfly kisses on her eyelids, the tip of her nose, moved slowly to stake his claim on all of her face, tantalizing himself and her with the nearness of her mouth. He'd waited so long for this, he wanted to savor every delicious second.

Finally, unable to restrain himself any longer, he allowed himself the prize, brushed her soft, full lips with his, felt them reach toward his as she surrendered with a low moan.

She filled his arms and his senses, her body and lips fitting against his in complete alignment as if the two of them had been torn apart leaving ragged edges and now those edges were once again joined seamlessly, forming a whole. His heart raced, beating wildly in perfect rhythm with hers, taking them to a place where only the two of them existed, not the past when both of them were children or the present where so many problems existed to keep them apart. This world was only the feel of her soft, warm body in his arms, her breasts against his chest, her lips moving sensuously on his, the scents of popcorn and honeysuckle blending and becoming a part of the whole, his blood roaring past his ears, roaring and ringing.

Katie stiffened.

The ringing wasn't inside his head, at least not all of it.

Katie's phone shrilled again.

Kate pushed away from Luke, her head swirling with confusion and desire and the ringing of that telephone. Before she could get back to her end of the sofa, turn on the lamp she didn't remember turning off, and gather her senses enough to lift the phone, the recorder broke in, the voice sounding strange even though Kate knew it was her own. "You've reached 555-9627. Please leave a message and I'll call you back."

"Kate, this is Spencer." Kate's hand froze on the receiver. The male voice penetrated the room, out of place, an intrusion, and it took her a couple of heartbeats to remember who Spencer was. "When I checked in with the office today, they told me you'd been there to pick up a technical manual. Now you're not answering your cell, and your father tells me you're not with him and he's trying to give me some idiotic story about your being with a sick friend. I get the feeling he doesn't like me. If you get this message—"

She snatched up the receiver. "Hello, Spencer. I'm here."

"Kate, what's going on?"

"Nothing." Kate flinched as if she half expected to be struck by lightning for telling such an outrageous lie.

Nothing? Everything! She'd just been kissing Luke, her emotions and hormones careening wildly. She'd just lost her mind, that was what was going on.

"Papa wanted me to pick up some legal papers and a computer system for him and that's what I've been doing. I was watching TV, so I guess I didn't hear my cell phone. It's in my purse. Muffles the ring tone." Did she sound as breathless to him as she sounded to herself? As she was? "I'm spending the night here then going back to Briar Creek in the morning."

"Good idea. That's a long drive to be making this late at night. Well, I'm glad I got hold of you. The Larrimer people brought up an interesting request that you can probably help me with."

Kate barely heard the words as Spencer told her what the company wanted. She answered him automatically, but her mind was on other things.

She had to tell Spencer that Luke was here for the night. Beyond the need to be as honest as possible with him...though she didn't think she ought to mention that kiss...Whitney had seen them, and Whitney would be sure to bring it up the next time she saw Spencer. Whitney could never stop talking until she'd had a complete brain dump.

"That should work," he said when they had concluded the discussion about business. "Thanks. You have a good night and I'll talk to you on Thursday."

"Spencer, wait, I need to tell you that I'm not alone here tonight. Papa's deputy came up with me to get those papers, and since the papers weren't ready on time, Papa thought we both ought to stay here and get them first thing in the morning. He worries about me driving at night because of Mama's car wreck." She held her breath, expecting some sort of protest.

"Is that deputy the *Pete* you're always talking about? Well, I hope you get things wrapped up soon so you can get back to Briar Creek and enjoy the rest of your time with your father."

143

"No, it's not Pete. Papa has a new deputy, Luke Rodgers, a, uh, an old friend of mine. A childhood friend."

Silence.

"Okay." Spencer sounded as if he wasn't quite sure why she was telling him that.

"Luke is spending the night in my condo, too. In the guest room, of course."

Another space of silence.

"Kate, you're not worried I'd be jealous, are you?"

"No, of course not." Yes, she had been.

"You know I'm not the jealous type, and I know you're much too rational to get swept up in some tawdry moment of passion. I am not the least bit concerned about your father's deputy spending the night in your guest room."

Kate gave a short, nervous laugh. "Good. Well, I'll talk to you on Thursday then."

She was glad Spencer wasn't concerned about Luke spending the night in her guest room. She was glad Spencer knew she was *too rational to get caught up in some tawdry moment of passion.*

Now she'd feel a lot better if she could be half as certain as he was.

She hung up the phone.

She and Luke rose from the sofa at the same time.

"Well," he said, "if you'll point me in the right direction, I think I'll hit the sack. Long day. Long drive tomorrow."

"Down the hall, first door on the left. Bathroom's on the right."

But Kate didn't go to bed immediately. She sat on the sofa, legs curled under her, and tried to get control of her cartwheeling emotions. It wasn't easy when one part of her wanted to relive, over and over, the incredible sky-rocketing sensation of that kiss.

144

Even more frightening than that was the connection she'd felt with Luke during that kiss and earlier when they'd stood on the balcony talking. For a while she'd fallen back into the past, into trusting him, depending on him, into that old attachment to him that had caused her so much trouble when it was broken.

Luke had made it clear with his aloof attitude when she got off the phone that he regretted what happened. He said he wanted her friendship, but he didn't want to get too close, and that was fine with her. Neither did she. In fact, even friendship was probably too strong a word for what she wanted.

She had to get back to that safe, secure place inside herself where everything was stable and calm. Maybe that place didn't have the balloon-ride highs of kissing Luke, but neither did it have the airplane-crash lows.

Spencer was a part of that place, her rational, logical choice for a husband. Their commitment was based on mutual respect and common interests, not something as volatile as volcano kisses and an obscure feeling of their souls joining. She and Spencer would never go through a terrible divorce, they would never leave each other because of a torrid affair. Their marriage would be sane and sensible.

Everything had been going along just fine until Luke appeared in her life again. She had to remember that she was not that little girl she once was, so besotted with him, so needy, that she couldn't live without him. Nor was he that little boy, in spite of his efforts to retrieve that relationship. They were adults now with no connection except through her father.

No connection except those adrenaline rushes you get every time he's near, the way his lips felt on yours, the way his heart beat in perfect rhythm with yours, the way you connect to him and feel complete.

145

The reminder of things she wanted to forget almost seemed to come from someone other than her, someone speaking directly into her thoughts.

She didn't need to think about any of that. Okay, she'd adored Luke when she was a child, but she was no longer a child, no longer at the mercy of reckless emotions and attachments, no longer dependent on anyone but herself.

She stood and turned off the lamp, then frowned. The lamp had been turned off when she and Luke were kissing, but she didn't recall switching it off, and Luke couldn't have done it without going past her to her end of the sofa. Maybe it had been an electrical fluctuation of some sort.

She turned resolutely toward her bedroom. She was doing the right thing. She needed a stable, dependable relationship. She needed Spencer. Well, actually, she didn't need him, which was why their relationship would work.

If you don't need him, why are you marrying him?

That detached voice in her head again.

She sank back onto the sofa.

Because they got along well, had the same interests. Because they could support each other and help each other in their careers. Their company was family-oriented, and most functions preferred they bring an escort. More married employees were promoted than single employees.

And because, if she were brutally honest with herself, she really didn't like being alone, and she'd felt alone since Luke had left her.

She couldn't remember her mother at all, at least not on a conscious level, but in some strange way, she'd really felt her mother's absence when Luke left. Although Papa had always been there and was the cornerstone of her life, nevertheless, she'd felt as if a piece of her soul had been

146

missing.

She'd replaced that piece on her own and she never intended to entrust it to anybody again.

When she married Spencer, she would have companionship without endangering that part of herself.

And if he should leave you, it wouldn't hurt the way losing your mother and Luke hurt.

Where were these thoughts coming from?

This was not the time for her to let her emotions get out of control. She needed to forget about Luke and focus on Papa. She needed to figure out how she could help him. Maybe she ought to talk to his doctor in Briar Creek, see if he'd noticed any mental problems, if he could suggest any drugs to help.

Papa's plight only emphasized the need to keep her feet on the ground. Papa had lost Mama, the love of his life, and now he missed her so badly, he imagined that she'd come back to him. How terrible that must be, to go through life wanting someone so badly his own life wasn't complete without that person, needing someone so badly it destroyed his mind.

Thank goodness she'd learned her lesson when she was young and could now proceed with her life in a safe, sane manner.

She walked down the dark hall to her bedroom.

Now if only she could forget the way her soul had connected with Luke's as they'd stood on the balcony talking, the way his lips had felt on hers, the extraordinary, soaring way he'd made her feel, the bonding she'd almost let herself fall into with him just before he yanked it away from her...for the second time.

Chapter Thirteen

Shortly after eleven the next morning Luke pulled in behind the jail with the requested legal documents and all the computer stuff. He'd dropped Katie off at her house. She'd promised to come by that afternoon and get everything set up, but she'd been blatantly anxious to get away from him.

The ride back to Briar Creek that morning had seemed twice as long as the ride to Dallas. From the time they had first got up, Katie had been courteous, polite and distant. In fact, she'd managed to take *distant* to new heights. All the way home, she'd again hugged the door handle as they drove, and he didn't protest this time.

He'd ruined their relationship again. He'd put an end to their friendship before it ever had the chance to get back on its feet.

He couldn't believe he'd done that...kissed Katie as if he wanted to possess her—which he did—as if he wanted to make wild, passionate love to her—which he did.

Didn't he have any sense of decency at all? Katie was his friend, for crying out loud, Sheriff's daughter, and he'd treated her like...well, like a woman. A woman he wanted to make love to.

That was bad enough, but hadn't he learned anything from his experience with Cindy? A friend was a friend and a lover was a lover. Friends were forever, but when the elements of sex and passion came into the picture, it was like a bad chemistry experiment. The compound was unstable and could blow at any minute. And he'd blown it with Katie last night. Big time.

He got out of his car and decided to leave all the computer stuff there. It would be safe in Briar Creek, behind the sheriff's office.

When Katie arrived, they could take it in. He picked

148

up the brown envelope containing a copy of Seth Flanders' divorce papers to take inside with him.

He didn't really understand why this document had been so important to Sheriff or why he'd needed it immediately rather than waiting for it to arrive in the mail. But he wouldn't ask, wouldn't question Sheriff's authority...not when he'd just spent the evening trying to seduce Sheriff's daughter.

"Hey, Luke!" Sheriff greeted him when he entered the older man's office. "Glad you got back safely. I really appreciate your doing this."

"No problem." Luke handed Sheriff the envelope while avoiding his gaze. He didn't want his mentor and friend to see in his eyes the guilt of what he'd tried to do—wanted to do—to that man's daughter.

"Katie called to say she'd be over here after lunch to get this computer contraption set up."

"Yeah, that's what she told me."

"I tried to talk her into coming over here right now so we could all go to lunch, but she wouldn't do it. You kids have a good time last night?"

Luke's head snapped up at that question, his guilty conscience wondering exactly what Sheriff meant. "We watched a little television then went to bed." Did that sound as suggestive to Sheriff as it did to him? "In separate bedrooms, of course." That probably made it sound worse.

Sheriff arched an eyebrow. "Luke, I reckon you and Katie are both adults. I'm not worried about what you do when you're alone together."

"We didn't do anything."

Sheriff's gaze was steady and unwavering.

Luke tried to smile, backed up and slapped the door facing. "Well, I guess I'd better get to work. I need to get caught up on whatever I missed yesterday."

"Not much happened to catch up on. I just hope yours and Katie's day wasn't as dull as it was here."

"Dull. Yeah, it was pretty dull. Running around, looking for computer stuff, going by the courthouse...dull."

Luke went into his office, sank into his chair and took a deep breath, trying to stop his guts from clenching.

Dull? That was sure the last word he'd use to describe yesterday.

True, he and Katie didn't *do anything* last night, at least not in the strictest sense of the term. They hadn't made love.

But in a different sense, he had done more yesterday than the other days of his life all put together. He'd kissed Katie, the most soul-searing, mind-blowing kiss he'd ever experienced in his entire life. Kissed her, held her body against his, wanted to make love to her, and then lost her.

If he'd been trying to screw up, he couldn't have done a better job of it.

***

Her purse clutched tightly in both hands, Kate sat stiffly erect in the plastic-covered chair in Dr. Stanley Kramer's waiting room. She'd called as soon as she got back to Briar Creek that morning and requested an appointment. She had to know if anything was physically wrong with Papa.

The waiting room was too warm, and the room deodorizer didn't quite cover the stale smell. A remnant of every illness that had come through the door over the years still seemed to linger.

She kept telling herself to relax, but to no avail. She hadn't slept much last night, had endured a tense drive back to Briar Creek with Luke this morning and now she was waiting to talk to Papa's doctor about his condition. Not one relaxing element in the lot.

Across the room Frank Jasper, clad in overalls and minus his teeth, sat singing to himself and keeping time with one muddy, work boot clad foot. Where the heck had he found mud in the middle of June in Texas?

Two chairs down from him Heather Richmond entertained her baby with a variety of toys and books.

Heather was a few years younger than Kate, but they knew each other by sight and family, well enough for Heather to fill their waiting time with tales of everything about her eight-month old daughter, Lydia, including details of Lydia's birth that Kate really hadn't wanted to hear. Not that she would ever go through that process, but she still didn't need to know the details.

Kate checked her watch. The nurse had said she could probably see Dr. Kramer around noon, and it was thirty-five minutes past. But that was life in Briar Creek. *Around noon* could mean anywhere between eleven and one and nobody got too excited about the lack of preciseness.

Lydia climbed down from Heather's lap and started crawling around the room. Kate tensed as the child came closer to her. Lydia looked up with a toothless grin, gurgled and, clutching the hem of Kate's skirt with one chubby hand while balancing with the other on Kate's leg, began to pull herself onto her unsteady feet.

"She's going to be walking any day now!" Heather said proudly.

Kate froze, uncertain what to do with the small creature with big eyes, incredibly smooth skin and a smile that reached right inside her heart. Her arms strained with wanting to pick up the adorable baby, but her mind screamed at her not to. What if Lydia cried? What if Kate dropped her? What if she hurt her?

It was, she knew, illogical to be frightened of babies. But they were so tiny, so soft and fragile, that the thought

151

of holding one terrified her. If she hadn't rushed down to Briar Creek to check on Papa, she would be going in for her tubal ligation this week and wouldn't have to be concerned about ever bringing a child into the world, a child she knew she couldn't possibly care for.

"Kate, the doctor's ready to see you."

"I have to go." Kate dared to touch the smooth soft cheek. Lydia made a noise of some sort, Kate jerked back and then Lydia started to cry.

Kate cast a frantic look across the room to Heather. "I'm sorry. I didn't mean to upset her."

Heather laughed. "You didn't do anything. She startled you and you startled her, that's all." She came over and retrieved her child. Lydia immediately ceased crying.

Kate stood, feeling a little shaky. "Whatever I did, you undid it."

"I didn't do anything, either. They're bonded to mommy at this age. You'll get the hang of it when you have one of your own."

Kate smiled weakly as she followed the nurse into Dr. Kramer's office.

She would not be having any of her own. The thought of failing someone so dependent and helpless was too scary, and she had not one shred of doubt that she would fail.

Dr. Kramer, who must be as old if not older than Papa, leaned back in his high-backed, creaky chair and ran a hand over his bald head. "Have a seat, Katie. What brings you here today? I haven't seen you in years. I figured you probably went to those big city doctors for what ails you."

Kate sat on the edge of another chair identical to the ones in the waiting room. In fact, she realized, her posture was identical to the one she'd maintained in the waiting room. This area, however, was cooler and smelled more of old paper and leather instead of illnesses. She ought to be able to relax a little more.

She licked her dry lips and tried to sit back. "It's not me I want to talk to you about. It's Papa."

Kramer's bushy white brows knit over his large nose. "Sheriff? Is he sick?"

"That's what I want you to tell me. He's been acting...strange."

"Strange in what way?"

"Anything I say to you is confidential, right? Doctor-patient privilege. Right?"

Kramer looked confused. "I reckon so. But if that's the way of it, I can't tell you anything about Sheriff."

"Oh." They stared at each for a moment, at an impasse. "I just want to know if he's all right," she said finally.

"Sheriff's in great shape. I gave him a complete physical before he ran for reelection last year. He's got the constitution of a man half his age."

"What about—" She swallowed hard, lifted her hands then dropped them to her purse in her lap.

Kramer leaned forward expectantly. "What about what?"

She cleared her throat. "Early senility." A long pause, then the dreaded word. "Alzheimer's."

Kramer frowned, his shaggy brows knitting again. "What in the world would make you think of something like that? Sheriff's mind's probably clearer than yours or mine."

Kate shifted uncomfortably in the chair and realized she was perched on the edge again. "He, uh, talks to Mama."

"Uh huh."

"He dances with her."

"Uh huh."

"She answers questions about cooking for him."

Kramer laughed and leaned back. "Well, that's a new one." He sobered. "Katie, you're young. You don't know what it's like to lose somebody you love with all your heart and all your soul. Well, I guess that's not quite true. You did lose your mama, but you were too little then to remember much about it. My wife died four years ago, and I still talk to her, dance with her, ask her advice, and, yes, sometimes she answers."

Kate fidgeted. "He put her on the phone to talk to me."

"Did she say anything to you?"

"No, of course not. Doctor Kramer, do you think Papa ought to be on Prozac or something?"

"Sheriff? Lord, no! Katie, trust me. There's nothing wrong with your daddy. You know that old expression, *joined at the hip?* Well, your mama and daddy were joined at the heart. She was a part of him, and he'll never lose that. Her body may not be here, but her spirit is. Don't you worry if he talks to her. He always has and he always will. Now tell me about you. When are you gonna get married and give Sheriff a grandbaby to spoil? I've got four myself and one great-grandson."

The discussion was over. Kramer wasn't going to tell her anything else about Papa, and she wasn't going to tell him anything about her plans not to have grandchildren.

Kate rose and extended her hand. "Thank you so much for talking to me, Doctor Kramer. You've taken a real load off my mind." He hadn't, but he had lightened it a little.

"Come by any time, Katie."

Kate left the doctor's office, got in her car and drove aimlessly around town, her mind replaying what Kramer had said, what Papa had said, what she and Luke had talked about, trying to make it fit into something coherent.

She wanted to believe Papa was all right, that talking to Mama was normal. Maybe she had overreacted. Maybe what Papa was doing was normal for any man whose wife had died.

She could kind of accept the dancing but putting Mama on the phone and getting culinary advice from her just did not seem normal.

Even so, his delusion didn't seem to be causing Papa or anyone else any harm.

Kate blinked away the fog from her brain, looked around and found herself down at the creek bank, a place she hadn't been in years. It was a spot where lovers used to park, but she and Luke had claimed the cave below as theirs. It was in the floor of that cave that they had buried the thorn with which they'd pricked their fingers and declared their eternal friendship. The thorn had undoubtedly decomposed by now, just as their friendship had.

What on earth had possessed her to drive down here?

She got out of the car, walked to the edge of the bank and looked down. When Luke had first left town, she'd gone to that cave often to feel closer to him...to talk to him the way Papa talked to Mama.

But Luke had never answered her.

She'd quit going to the cave when it became obvious that Luke was really gone. In fact, she hadn't been near it in years and had only come here today accidentally, a series of random turns while her mind was occupied with thoughts of Papa.

And Luke.

Not really, she told herself. Only as her conversation with Luke the previous evening related to Papa.

Yes, really.

That little voice inside her head was getting annoying. Last night it had made her question her

155

engagement to Spencer and now it was arguing with her
about Luke. Must be stress.

Okay, she told the little voice, so maybe she did have
an irrational urge to talk to Luke about everything,
including what Doc Kramer had said. In the past, Luke
had a way of helping her sort things out, put things in their
proper order and perspective, just as he had last night with
his comment about a thirsty man hallucinating water and
about the movie and how sad it would have been for
Elwood P. Dowd to stop seeing Harvey.

She gazed down at the creek below. Was it true what
Luke had said, that she'd chosen her condo in Dallas
because the view reminded her of this one? Had she been
trying to recapture something that was lost forever? Surely
not. She knew better than that. As she'd told Luke, a creek
is a creek and a tree is a tree. Coincidence.

*Just like the coincidence that you came to this place
in your confusion, looking for answers.*

She turned and went back to the car.

Whatever games her subconscious mind might be
playing with her, she was still in control. She didn't have
to listen to it.

She was no longer eleven years old, and she didn't
need Luke's friendship. That was over and done, and if
she'd required any further proof, she certainly got it last
night and this morning. Luke had kissed her, something
she knew they had both wanted, and then he'd run from
her and remained as distant as possible the next morning.

She got back in her car and started the engine. She
had promised Papa she'd get that computer equipment
installed and running.

Her hand hesitated on the steering wheel as she
backed out onto the road. Luke would be there. She was
still faced with training Luke on the computer.

No, she could train Papa on the computer and he

could train Luke.

If Papa was all right, then she needed to go back to Dallas.

Not that the thought of being around Luke again bothered her.

But she had things to do in Dallas.

She thought of that kiss, of the way his touch made her giddy.

Okay, maybe the thought of being around him did bother her just a little bit. All she needed was a short time away from him, long enough to get this chaos in her brain straightened out. Then she'd be fine.

Never mind that the thought of never kissing Luke again made her feel the way Elwood P. Dowd must have felt when faced with the injection of drugs that would get rid of Harvey forever.

Well, she could just get over it, and that would be a lot easier to do when she got back to Dallas, away from Briar Creek and Luke's presence.

***

Once Kate finished looking at the pictures of Evelyn's grandchildren and started working on the computers, getting the system set up and installing software, she became completely absorbed in what she was doing. Even so, Luke's presence somewhere in the office was like a shadow that constantly hovered at the corners of her mind.

She was working at the terminal in Papa's office when the phone rang. It had rung several times but Kate barely heard the sound over her concentration.

However, she heard as if with preternatural hearing Papa's soft words at Luke's door, "Luke, I may need you on this one."

She went out into the reception area. Papa and Luke were already rushing out the back door. "Papa? What's

157

going on?"

He turned back and smiled without the slightest sign of tension. "Just a routine call, Katie-girl. Hurry and finish those computers so Luke can use it for the paperwork on this one when we get back."

In contradiction to his casual words, he and Luke hurried out.

"Evelyn, where are they going?"

"Hank's Liquor Store out on the highway. The security company just called. His silent alarm went off." Evelyn shook her head, *tsked* a couple of times then went back to her paperwork. "Crime's getting almost as bad down here as it is in the city."

Kate could feel her heart rate increase. "Crime? You mean Hank's being robbed or something?"

Evelyn looked up. "It's all right, Katie. It's probably a false alarm anyway, but if it's not, Sheriff can take care of it. He does it all the time. That's what a sheriff does, you know."

A thousand images tumbled through Kate's mind...images of robbers and guns and Papa, of a ghostly Mama whispering in Papa's ear at just the wrong time, distracting him, advising him to shoot or not to shoot— who knew which?

Papa had told her nothing ever happened in Briar Creek!

Kate grabbed her purse and keys and ran out the door to her own car.

Hank's was only a couple of miles down the highway. When Kate squealed into the parking lot, she saw that the official Sheriff's car with colored lights whirling was already there.

Probably a false alarm, she told herself. Her heart was in her throat, and her hands were trembling so badly she could hardly get out of the car.

She dashed to the glass door of the small building, grabbed the handle and froze.

Inside the store Luke, no longer the little boy playing with cap pistols, shoved a big man with a stocking over his head against the counter and slapped handcuffs on him. Papa, as cool as if he'd been home pointing the remote control, stood back holding his gun leveled on the second man. An obviously terrified clerk stood behind the counter, as far back as he could get. The robbers looked other-worldly and evil with their features contorted by the stockings, but Papa and Luke had things under control.

They could not have been there more than a few seconds before she arrived, but that's all it had taken for them to subdue the bad guys.

Her terror turned to pride at the two men in their roles as something more than men...peace keepers for the town, protectors and guardians.

Your father and your friend.

But she barely had time to take a single breath of relief when a third man emerged from the back room with a gun in his hand, behind Papa.

Kate shoved the door open and started to scream, but any sound she might have made was drowned by an explosion. Time seemed to stop with the bullet in mid-air and Kate poised with her mouth and the door half open. For what seemed like an eternity, though it couldn't have been more than a fraction of a second, she didn't know who had fired, where the bullet was headed, if Papa or Luke had been hit.

Then she saw the third man's gun spinning from his hand as his eyes and mouth widened in shock. Papa straightened from a crouch and turned his attention back to the second robber while Luke charged over to grab the third man.

Kate eased the door closed and leaned against the

window, sucking in deep breaths and ordering her heart to slow down.

It was all right.

Papa and Luke could handle things. Papa's reflexes were good. He could still shoot accurately. Luke was strong and brave, very much a man with nothing left of the young boy who'd been her friend.

And she'd better get away from there before they came out and caught her. She didn't want Papa to know she'd doubted him.

And she didn't want Luke to know she'd been worried about him.

As she raced out of the parking lot and headed home, the phrase danced through her head, *Papa's all right*. Maybe he talked to Mama, but Dr. Kramer had vouched for his physical soundness, and the scene she'd just witnessed vouched for his mental stability and quick reflexes. Like Elwood P. Dowd, his idiosyncrasy was actually kind of charming.

She giggled to herself, giddy in her relief as her heart finally slowed from the scene she'd just witnessed.

So what if Papa wanted to set a plate for Mama. They could have tea the way they'd done when she was a little girl, using her toy dishes. A cup for Papa, one for Luke, one for Katie and one for Mama.

She pulled into the parking lot behind the jail but she didn't get out of her car immediately.

They'd invited Mama to those tea parties, now that she thought about it. Papa had always told her that Mama was still with them. When she'd brought home a good report card, he'd praised her and assured her that Mama would be proud of her, too.

Maybe this wasn't a sudden aberration at all. Maybe Papa had always communed with Mama.

As she'd grown up, the tea parties had stopped, of

course, along with many of the references to Mama.

Kate sat in the parking lot in back of the jail and drummed her fingers on the steering wheel, trying to recall exactly how Papa had acted when she was young, if he'd talked *to* or *about* Mama then.

When had everything changed? When had the references to Mama become fewer and less direct? When had her own vivid dreams about her mother faded?

She couldn't recall that exactly, either, but it almost seemed that her childhood memories were in color and her later ones in black and white.

She'd always associated that phenomenon with the natural process of growing up.

Coincidentally, it had come about around the time when Luke left. But that was, age-wise and experience-wise, when she'd begun to grow up.

She'd put her past behind her long ago, deliberately forgotten many of the details. Luke hadn't been the only one who'd been depressed by the major lifestyle change caused by his father's death and his subsequent move to Houston. The difference was she hadn't wanted to recall any of it...until now.

Not that she really wanted to now, but she needed to remember some parts. She needed to be able to remember specific details about Papa's references to Mama while editing out specific details about her friendship with Luke. There was no point in dredging up the pieces of the past that were painful.

But Luke had been such an integral part of her life, she wasn't sure she could separate the two.

With a sigh, she got out of the car and went into the building.

She'd just seen Papa handle himself quite well in a life and death situation. Doc Kramer had assured her that he was physically healthy. Papa didn't want to move to

161

Dallas with her. Short of having him declared incompetent, something she would never do, nor, she suspected, something any judge would agree to, there was nothing she could do.

As soon as she got the computer up and running and Papa and Evelyn trained, she would return to Dallas and get on with her life.

She barely made it back inside the office before Papa and Luke came in with their prisoners. While they dealt with the legalities of getting the three men installed in jail, Kate stayed out of the way, in Luke's office, working on his terminal. He came in once to get something and glared at her.

Well, he probably wasn't really glaring at her, just glaring about the situation in general. She shouldn't take it personally. Especially not when she didn't care what he thought of her and was planning to leave town soon anyway.

So why did she keep looking up from her work every time he passed the door, hoping to catch his eye so she could smile at him?

She focused on her work, fiercely ignoring that leftover urge from her youth.

***

Luke was furious. He could barely wait until he and Sheriff got the perps booked and into jail so he could confront Katie.

She was still in his office, working on that blasted computer.

He strode in and leaned over the desk, then spoke quietly so Sheriff wouldn't hear. "Outside. I want to talk to you."

She looked up, and for an instant something human and vulnerable, something of the old Katie, flickered, but then it disappeared, and he could see a sheen around her

162

like glass that was transparent and thin yet kept him from getting too close. "We can talk here," she said.

"No, we can't. I don't want Sheriff to hear this."

Fear brushed across her features. He ought to reassure her that nothing was wrong with Sheriff, but he didn't. He turned and walked away, knowing she would follow him.

When they were out back in the parking lot, he whirled on her. "What in the hell were you doing following us, trying to come in the door when we were in the middle of an arrest, when there were guns everywhere?"

She flinched. "I didn't realize you saw me."

"I saw you! Sheriff saw you! You almost distracted him from that other guy! You almost got him killed!"

Katie paled, her eyes becoming large and silvery in their lightness. She backed up until she bumped into a car, stopped and leaned against it, balancing with both hands. Her throat moved convulsively as she swallowed. "I'm sorry. I only wanted to help," she whispered.

"No, you wanted to spy! You didn't trust Sheriff or me to take care of the situation. Katie, I know you're worried about your father, and I know it's because you love him, but you've got to stop it. He's an adult. He may be older, but you've got to leave him his dignity."

Katie pushed herself erect. "You don't understand," she said quietly, then turned and walked back into the office, her head high.

Luke shoved his hands into his back pockets. Standing alone in the parking lot, the heat beating down from above and surging up from the concrete below, he watched her go.

No, he damned sure didn't understand. He didn't understand what was going on with Katie and he really didn't understand why, in spite of everything...her engagement, her distance, how different she had become over the years...he still wanted to go after her, pull her into his arms and comfort her, then kiss her breathless.

Maybe that last wasn't such a bad idea after all. He'd already lost her. The Katie he'd been friends with a lifetime ago had vanished into the mists of time. She was a different person.

He'd been furious when he caught a peripheral glimpse of her at the door of the liquor store just before that third man came up behind Sheriff. The distraction could have cost either him or Sheriff that critical millisecond of timing, could have cost them their lives.

But, he realized, he wasn't just mad at her for her foolish actions. He was mad at her for not being the little girl he grew up with. He was mad at himself for expecting the impossible. He was mad at the world because it kept right on moving along, changing with every heartbeat.

He'd been foolish to think he could pick up where they'd left off seventeen years ago. Neither of them was that same person. They'd been apart more years than they'd been together.

He'd found a good life in Briar Creek. Maybe some things had changed, but that was just what happened. He was back where he belonged, a few years older, a few lifetimes wiser...

And he had no idea what he was going to do about Katie.

***

The universe stretches into infinity,
filled with moons and stars and planets
and streaking comets. Rainbows decorate
the heavens above the earth after a storm,
and every day begins with the miracle of a
sunrise. But loving you, Jerome, and
watching our little Katie grow, is still the

best of all miracles and wonders.

Jerome smiled as he read the computer screen. "Emma, you never stop surprising me. You don't know anything about computers. How did you do that?"

Emma laughed softly somewhere in the vicinity of his left ear. "Why, Jerome Fallon, I know just as much about computers as you do! I listened to Katie explain it, too. Anyway, it doesn't matter. It's all energy, just like the television."

He studied the keyboard, then, his big fingers clumsy on the small keys, painstakingly tapped onto the screen *I love youu Emma Fallon. You and Katie are teh only miracles I neeed. Lets go home sweetheart.*

Her lips tingled against the skin of his cheek. "I have one more thing I want to do with your new computer system. Would you bring up that e-mail program?"

Jerome studied the screen, the keyboard, the mouse and scratched his chin. "Now how the heck do I make this program go away?"

"I can do it," Emma offered.

"Just give me a minute. I remember now. It's the X up there in the corner." He touched the mouse, sending the arrow skittering all around the screen, then finally centered it on the X and clicked.

Do you want to save the changes you made to Document 5? the ghost in the computer asked.

Of course he wanted to save Emma's wonderful note.
Save as
The universe stretches into infinity.

Jerome chose *yes* then brought up the e-mail program as Emma had requested.

Chapter Fifteen

Papa didn't complain the next morning when Kate told him she was going home early, probably the following day. In fact, he didn't even seem surprised.

She waited until around ten o'clock to go into the office, hoping Luke would be out on some sort of deputy-type assignment. After the way he'd yelled at her yesterday, she had absolutely no desire to see him. When they'd been together in Dallas, especially that night in her condo, she'd lost her mind completely and begun to relax around him, even kissed him. And things had gone steadily downhill from there.

You're a slow learner, Kathleen Fallon, she told herself.

No, you're not, Katie. You just have a soft heart that gets bruised easily.

Kate paused with her hand on the door of the Sheriff's office. Is this the way it started with Papa? Odd thoughts floating around in his head that seemed to come from somebody else? Would she soon be talking to Mama and maybe even seeing that big rabbit, Harvey?

She set her jaw and opened the front door of the Sheriff's office. "Good morning, Evelyn. Is Papa here?"

"No, he got a call to go out to the Granger place. I think Wayne Granger's just lonesome again. But Luke's here."

The way Evelyn smiled when she imparted that last bit of information made Kate cringe. Could everybody in the whole town see that electrical current that sparked between Luke and her? Even after he'd chewed her out yesterday, even while she was so angry with him she could have punched him and so hurt she could have cried, she'd felt that current as she brushed against him while going over some of the computer instructions.

166

Well, one more day and she'd be out of there. A hundred and twenty miles was a long way for electrical sparks to fly.

She went straight to Papa's office to finish up a few things on the computer system.

She barely had time to get the computer booted up when Luke charged in and slammed the door behind him.

Kate looked up. His jaw was set, his eyes dark with rage. Kate straightened automatically, ready to defend herself against another outburst like the one yesterday.

"You come down here to meddle in Sheriff's life, you nearly get him killed, then you start on my life."

Thank goodness she hadn't allowed herself to become too emotionally entangled with Luke again, or his attitude would really hurt.

Actually, it still hurt. A little. Not much. Okay, a lot. It was her own damn fault for letting him get through her defenses.

"I said I'm sorry. What else do you want me to do?"

He paced the width of the small office then back again, running his fingers through his dark hair that somehow seemed even darker this morning as if to match his mood. "Do you have any idea what kind of a problem you've caused?"

Had her spying somehow messed up their legal case against the would-be robbers? She couldn't stand it if she'd caused problems for Papa. She shook her head. "No, I don't have any idea. Luke, what's wrong? What did I do?"

He stopped in front of the desk and glared at her. "You really don't know, do you?"

She stood up with such force that the chair slammed back against the wall. "No, damn it, I don't know! I just said that! If you'll tell me, I'll try to put it right, but if all you're going to do is shout at me, I can't do anything!" Kate was humiliated to hear her voice crack. She wasn't going to cry in front of Luke. She hadn't cried in years, and she certainly wasn't going to start now.

For an instant Luke's gaze softened. He'd heard the crack, too.

"Back off," she snapped, reclaiming her pride. "If you have something to say to me, say it and get out of here. I have work to do."

"Yeah, right." He slammed his hands onto the desk top and leaned on his arms. "Work like sending e-mails under other people's names, stirring up things that have nothing to do with you. You may be the computer expert, but I'm the law, and in my book, what you did is just plain illegal!"

At least Papa's delusions were charming. Luke's were rude. "Illegal?" She slammed her hands onto the desk, too, and leaned toward him, her face inches from his, then ground out her words. "I don't have any idea what you're talking about. We didn't send any e-mail messages yet, so I certainly don't think any of those nonexistent messages could be illegal. E-mail and the internet are on my training agenda for later today. Unless you just time-traveled back from the future, it hasn't happened yet!"

For a long moment they glared at each other.

The room was small, the air conditioning inadequate. With the door closed and Luke's temper blazing so close to her, the atmosphere was stifling. Every breath Kate sucked in was an effort. Every breath brought her the earthy, familiar scent of a man she'd known all her life, a man now furious with her. If she still cared about him, if she still considered him her friend, this would be extremely painful. Fortunately, she didn't. Not really, anyway.

Finally he pulled back and so did she.

"You didn't send an e-mail to my mother's husband?" he asked quietly.

Kate shook her head to try to clear it. There must be something in the water in Briar Creek that made people act strange and have delusions. So far it had affected Papa, her and now Luke.

"Even if I had something to say to your step father, I don't know his name, much less his e-mail address. You can't just address something to *Luke's mother's new husband* and expect it to get there. You have to have an address that's exact down to every letter and every dot."

"You don't need to take that tone with me. I'm not completely ignorant about computers. I've lived in the big city, too."

Kate threw up her hands. "Fine. Then you should know that I didn't and *couldn't* send any e-mail to your step father, so what is this discussion all about?"

Luke collapsed into the chair in front of Papa's desk and again tunneled his fingers through his hair. His distress was obvious.

Well, he ought to be distressed, acting like a jerk two days in a row.

"Somebody sent an e-mail message to Jeffrey Hudelson at his address at the college. He's a professor. School's out, and if he hadn't had some kind of meeting to go to this morning, he wouldn't have even gone in and picked it up, but he did. The message is signed with my name and it came from this office."

Kate frowned. "What did it say?"

Luke leaned his head back and blew out a long breath. "It was an invitation for them to come visit me," he said quietly. "It said I'd missed them both and wanted them to see what I'd done with the old house."

"What's so horrible about that?"

"For one thing, I don't have any furniture in the house! Remember I told you I only have a bed. But Mom called a few minutes ago. She's thrilled, and they're coming to spend a few days."

"Well, you'd better start shopping for furniture."

"That's not the point. I don't like the idea of somebody interfering in my personal business."

"I don't understand this. The only people with the password to get onto these computers are you, me, Evelyn and Papa."

Their gazes locked, and Kate knew Luke was thinking the same thing she was.

"He doesn't know how to use the program," Kate defended.

"He's smart. He could figure it out. I never told him I wasn't thrilled about this marriage, but he's pretty sharp about reading between the lines. It would be just like him to try to get Mom and Jeff down here."

"Yes, but it's not like Papa to be deceitful. If he sent a message, he'd sign his own name."

She pulled the chair back to the desk and sat again, then booted up the internet program while Luke came around the desk to look over her shoulder.

"I don't see any copy of a sent message but that would be easy enough to delete. Let me check the log."

Even though she knew on a logical level what she had to find, Kate was still amazed to see the indication that a message had gone out at two minutes past six the evening before.

"After I left," Luke said.

"I was gone by then, too." She stared at the screen. "I know Papa can be manipulative, but he's usually pretty straight forward even in his manipulations."

Nevertheless, the proof was staring her in the face.

At least that was the only message that had gone out. At least he hadn't sent a message to Mama.

She supposed she ought to be proud of him, that he'd figured out the e-mail thing all by himself. She'd left him in the word processing program.

Without thinking, she booted up that program and checked the list of most recent files to see what else her creative father might have done.

The universe stretches into infinity? She didn't remember that one.

She pulled it up.

> *The universe stretches into infinity,*
> *filled with moons and stars and planets*
> *and streaking comets. Rainbows decorate*
> *the heavens above the earth after a storm*
> *and every day begins with the miracle of a*
> *sunrise. But loving you, Jerome, and*
> *watching our little Katie grow, is still the*
> *best of all miracles and wonders.*
>
> *I love youu Emma Fallon. You and*
> *Katie are teh only miracles I neeed. Lets*
> *go home sweetheart.*

Kate stared uncomprehendingly at the file that most certainly had not been there yesterday. Her first absurd thought was a wistful yearning to know the kind of love these people had.

But even as she told herself what a stupid reaction that was, it hit her that Jerome was Papa and Emma Fallon was Mama.

Though she couldn't imagine Papa composing such flowery language, he must have. The second part of the message sounded more like him...short and to the point with three typos and two punctuation errors. But that first part had her completely stumped.

Evelyn?

No way.

That left Luke and her with access to the system.

Belatedly she remembered that Luke was standing right behind her.

171

"Katie?"

The one word held a thousand questions, and suddenly she was relieved that she had to tell him, that she was forced to share her secret with somebody else, somebody who wouldn't condemn Papa. On a subconscious level she must have known all the time that Luke was there.

She sagged back in Papa's big chair and gazed into the eyes of the stranger who'd abandoned her all those years ago, who'd hurt her again as soon as she'd let down her guard even a little, but who had once been her friend. Maybe he no longer ranked in that category, but she had no doubt that he loved Papa almost as much as she did. She could count on him for that.

Maybe he'd even be able to help her remember exactly how Papa had talked about Mama when they were young, if this aberration was new or something he'd always done.

"I need to talk to you," she said quietly. "About Papa."

"I'm listening. I have been since you came to town."

"Not here. I don't want to take the chance of anybody overhearing."

"We'll go somewhere."

Kate closed down the program and walked out back, her entire body stiff and numb. As much as she'd held back from telling Luke, just so much she wanted to tell him now, to release the tension of carrying this secret alone. He'd always had an answer when they were younger, and a part of her wanted to believe he would now. It was probably a foolish hope, but it was her only hope at the moment.

This wasn't like she was becoming emotionally dependent on him again, she assured herself. Certainly after the last few days, she wouldn't have any trouble maintaining her distance from him. She just knew she could count on him to want the best for Papa. She simply needed his input and his knowledge, and if he failed her with that, well, she'd be no worse off than she was right now.

Chapter Sixteen

Luke supposed he ought to feel good as he drove with Katie beside him, out to the creek where they'd spent so many hours as children, a place where they'd be guaranteed the privacy she'd requested. This was what he'd wanted, for her to trust him, to tell him her problems, to resume their friendship.

But it wasn't the same thing. He and Katie weren't the same people they'd been all those years ago. If he had to put a name to what he felt right now, he wasn't sure he could. A little bit of anxiety about this new twist in events, a little curiosity about what Katie had to tell him and a little bit of fear that she was going to tell him something bad about Sheriff's health.

When he'd first read that message over her shoulder on Sheriff's computer, he'd thought Sheriff had a lover. He still wasn't sure. Could that be Katie's problem? Would she get this upset if her father had found somebody else after all these years?

He hadn't handled it very well when his mother remarried, though he'd had enough sense to keep his mouth shut, to know it was his problem, not his mother's. And it wasn't so much that she'd remarried, just *who* she'd married.

He had the top down on his car, and Katie rode beside him silently, facing forward, seeming not to notice as the wind whipped her bright curls into her face.

When he finally parked, she got out and looked around. He'd deliberately chosen the opposite side of the creek from their cave, but there was no way to avoid all the places they'd played as children, all the places that might hold unhappy memories for Katie. The two of them had pretty well covered the entire creek area...the entire town, for that matter.

174

He watched her as she surveyed the rocky bank tufted with grass and weeds, the trees and field behind them. The sun bounced sparks off her hair just like it used to, and after that ride, her curls had the same tangled wildness. If she stayed in this sun very long, she'd have freckles across the bridge of her nose again.

Seeing her in this familiar setting recalled the reality that his friend, Katie, was gone forever. The slender woman who stood a few feet away, her legs long in the tight blue jeans she wore today, her bottom rounded enticingly, was a stranger, a woman with a body he longed for and lips that could drive him crazy, but a woman he didn't know.

She looked at him and he saw that her eyes were bright with that same intensity she'd always had. Katie never did anything halfway.

A grasshopper whirred past them, and she jumped as if startled, then laughed. "Remember when we'd catch them and make them *spit tobacco*? Yuck!"

"I remember. Poor grasshoppers!"

"That old, burned-out house we used to make up stories about, it's just over that rise, isn't it?"

"Yeah, I think so."

She started to walk, and he followed. What the heck? He was too antsy to sit still anyway.

They almost missed the house. The remnants of charred wood had fallen or rotted away, and weeds had overtaken the stone foundations.

"There's the chimney," Katie said softly, almost reverently, parting the tall weeds to expose the last few crumbling inches of the structure. "It's still here after all, just hiding." She stepped closer, pushed down the weeds and began making stirring motions over an invisible fire. "Abigail Bonner was making soup from the last longhorn steer the day the Indians came. Remember that?"

Luke grinned. "I left my bow and arrow at home. Sorry. I can't kill you today."

Katie turned to him, smiling into the sun, and for a brief instant Luke thought he saw the little girl who'd caught crawdads with him, gotten covered with mud when they'd gone sliding down the big hill after a rain, dug for buried treasure along this very creek bank.

But it wasn't really her. They weren't children anymore. Things weren't the same. He couldn't retrieve the past.

"I don't have my gun to shoot back at the Indians, either," she said. "I guess we can't play that game." She moved over to sit on a large rock under a nearby tree.

He followed and leaned against the tree trunk.

She plucked a blade of grass and twirled it in her fingers, watching the motion as if it were something really important.

"Can you recall, when we were kids, if Papa ever talked about Mama in the present tense, as if she wasn't really dead? I don't mean that thing he always did with *your mother would...* I mean something like, *your mother said five minutes ago.*"

It was an odd question, and before he could answer, she began to speak again, the words pouring out like a flood gate had been opened.

Leaning against the rough bark of the oak tree he and Katie had once climbed, Luke listened while Katie, her gaze on the piece of grass that was disintegrating into fragments from her twirling, told him a rambling, disjointed story about Papa getting cooking advice from Mama, putting her on the phone, dancing with her and the note she'd found on the computer that morning.

Finally she tossed away the shredded blade of grass and looked at him. "I don't see how Papa could have written the first part of that note. You know him. Even besides the fact that the grammar and punctuation were perfect, that doesn't sound like him at all, does it?"

"No, it doesn't." Luke walked a few feet away, folded his arms and turned to look at her. "So what are you saying? You think Sheriff's senile? You think he should be committed or put on drugs or something?"

"No! Of course not! I think—" She spread her hands in a helpless gesture. "I don't know what to think. At first I was worried that he was losing his mind. That's why I followed you all to the liquor store. I was afraid he might see imaginary robbers or something. But he was great. You were great. And then I started trying to remember if maybe he'd always talked about Mama as if she was still alive. I mean, I know he did, but not in the same sense he does now. And he doesn't do it when you're around. I'm the only one who gets to hear what Mama's been up to in recent years."

She looked completely defenseless and vulnerable as she sat there on that rock, her eyes the same color as the sky overhead, the barriers he usually saw in them gone. He wanted to go to her, take her into his arms, assure her that everything was going to be just fine.

He shoved his hands into his pockets instead. He didn't have that right. They weren't friends. They certainly weren't lovers. She was nobody he knew anymore.

"I haven't seen any evidence of your father having problems. When I came back to town, it was kind of a shock to realize how old he is, but he doesn't act it. He never forgets things. His reflexes are unbelievable, as you saw at the liquor store. Katie, I don't know what to tell you. Have you talked to him about going to a shrink?"

She shook her head. "Can you imagine Papa going to a psychiatrist? He'd just chuckle and pooh-pooh the whole idea. If I did make him go, he'd soon have the doctor talking to Mama, too. You know how persuasive he can be."

Luke smiled. "I do know all about that."

He reached overhead and wrapped his fingers around a

tree limb. Katie expected answers from him. It had been a lot easier to give them when he was seven and she was six and the toughest question she came up with was why there was no *f* in *elephant* or how to explain to her father about the rip in her new shorts from that nail in the tree house they tried to build.

"Katie, I think you have to stop worrying about it. I promise to keep a close eye on Sheriff. If he starts doing anything funny, I'll let you know immediately. In the meantime, if he gets comfort from talking to your mother and even if he thinks she answers him, it doesn't hurt anything."

She nodded and folded her arms under her breasts. "I told myself that. Last night I was all ready to go back home tomorrow, as soon as I had a chance to do a few final things on that computer system. Then this morning I went in, and you jumped me about an e-mail I didn't send, and I found that note. Suddenly it was just all too much."

I was all ready to go back home. She was leaving...this town and his life.

Well, he'd lost her seventeen years ago when he'd left Briar Creek. Hadn't he just told himself that he and Katie were strangers? The thought of her leaving shouldn't make him feel like that time in Houston when a perp had landed a lucky punch to his gut and knocked the breath out of him.

"I'm sorry about jumping you. Both times. As far as the note—" He shook his head. "I don't know. Maybe Sheriff found it in a book somewhere and copied it. He's okay, Katie, really. You were thinking about him when we watched *Harvey* the other night, weren't you?"

She nodded.

"Maybe he is like Elwood P. Dowd. Maybe he just has one little defect in his reality, and it's a harmless one. It makes him happy. Go on back to Dallas whenever you have to, and I promise to let you know if anything happens."

178

She smiled up at him. He thought he could see those freckles across her nose, but maybe it was just the way the leaves dappled the sunlight on her face. "I'd really appreciate that, Luke."

"So you're leaving tomorrow?"

"I don't have to. I'd like to stay and see your mom. When are they coming?"

"Day after tomorrow." And suddenly a visit he'd dreaded began to take on a whole new light. It meant Katie would be around that much longer.

Like that made any difference in the long run.

"Why don't you want them to come? Other than your lack of furniture, I mean. What's wrong with her new husband?"

Luke hooked his thumbs in his front pockets and leaned his head back, stretching the kinks out of his neck, kinks he hadn't realized were there. Yesterday he wouldn't have answered that question, not for Katie or anybody else. But today, this morning, things had changed. He couldn't say how. He and Katie hadn't resumed their friendship. He realized that was impossible. They couldn't recapture what was dead and gone. They weren't lovers, either, though they'd come awfully close the other night.

But it was kind of like when the farmers burned off their fields at the end of the season, killing all the weed seeds and letting the earth absorb the ashes of crops and weeds alike. In the spring, fresh crops grew on the revitalized soil.

Just so, something new was growing between Katie and him. He wasn't sure what it was, but he was sure he wanted it. He'd be sorry when she left him and went back to Dallas to marry Spencer, but for right now, he wouldn't do anything to nip this new feeling that had sprung up between them.

"There's nothing wrong with Jeff," he answered.

179

"Actually, he's a great guy. I just worry about Mom. For one thing, he's a little younger than she is."

"How much is a little? A year? Two years? Big deal."

"Ten years younger."

She shrugged. "Big deal."

"He's a history teacher. He was *my* history teacher!"

"Ah!" Katie smiled knowingly.

"Don't give me that *ah!* business." Luke paced a couple of steps away then back again. "That's not the problem. Not all of it anyway. Yeah, it feels a little peculiar to have my former history teacher married to my mom. But we've all three been friends for some time. Well, since I've been out of school, and that's been a lot of years."

"Good. That means they didn't do anything hasty."

"That's one way of looking at it. But Jeff's been like a part of the family for those years. He lived in the same neighborhood, and he's always been there. When I was married to Cindy, we'd all four go out together, and I don't know why I never thought of it as dating, but I didn't. She was my mother, and he was my history teacher. Jeff's been such a big part of Mom's life for so long, what happens if they split up?"

"Good grief, Luke! You can't start planning their divorce just because they got married!"

"Divorce happens. Living with somebody isn't like just being friends with that person."

"No, I don't suppose it is."

"You remember what Dad was like. Well, Jeff's the complete opposite in every way. He's laid-back, likes to go to the theater and operas, he wears glasses, never been fishing or camping in his life. I guess part of what worries me is, if Mom was happy married to my father, how can she expect to be happy married to his opposite?"

"Maybe—probably—because she's changed over the years."

"Yes, she has. We all have. For one thing, I'm worrying about her now instead of her worrying about me. If she and Jeff get divorced, she loses it all. You can be friends and get married, but you can't get unmarried, fall out of love, and expect to be friends again. It just doesn't work that way."

Katie looked up at him in silence for a long moment. In fact, the entire world seemed to go silent as if it had ceased to exist, and the only reality was in her eyes.

"Luke," she finally said, "I understand you're concerned about your mother's happiness, but I know you too well to believe that's all that's bothering you.

Luke looked away and drew in a deep breath. Katie never let him get away with anything. "When she married Jeff, I guess because he's so totally different, it was like my last tie with Dad was broken, like everything about him disappeared, like he died all over again. You said once it was a good thing to block painful memories, but when you do that, they have a way of coming back at you with a sucker punch. Every time I see Jeff, I feel like I don't have a past anymore, kinda like I'm the invisible man, I don't even exist."

Katie nodded and chewed her lower lip thoughtfully. She didn't tell him he was being silly. She didn't have to. He already knew that. "Have you seen them since you moved back here?"

"No."

"Maybe now that you have your dad's old job and you live in your old house, you won't feel that way."

"Maybe."

"Where are they going to stay? Do you want me to ask Papa if they can use our guest room? I'm sure he'd be happy to have them. I'll even shovel out the dust and put on clean sheets."

"Thanks, but they'll stay at my place."

"Then you'd better get busy buying furniture."

"I've got two days."

Katie blinked and rose to her feet. "Two days? You think you're going to furnish your house in two days?"

"Well, yeah. I figured I'd go to McClain's on my lunch hour and pick out a sofa and a bed and a kitchen table. That ought to do it."

Katie rolled her eyes. "Why am I not surprised? How much money have you got?"

"How much money? Why do you want to know?"

She sighed. "I don't need your financial statement. I just need to know your furniture budget, how much we can spend."

We?

"I've got a little money. I bought some investment property in Houston when it was cheap. We can spend whatever we want."

"Good. I'll go to Tyler—"

"Tyler? What's wrong with McClain's right here in Briar Creek?"

"All right, we'll look there first, but they don't have a very big selection. If we don't find what you need, we'll go on to Tyler, pick it out and you can borrow a truck and get it this evening. We don't have time for them to deliver it. I don't suppose you have any extra sheets and towels?"

"I told you I've been busy restoring the house. I haven't had time for all that stuff. I've got one set of sheets and two towels."

"Okay, we'll have to get those, too. And then there's dishes and pictures..." She started walking back toward the car, but he took her arm and turned her gently toward him.

"Katie, you don't have to do this."

"Sure I do. I owe you something for not shooting me back there."

"Shooting you?"

"Oh, sure, you said you left your bow and arrow at

home, but I can see you've adopted the white man's ways. You've got your own fire stick." She looked down at the gun at his waist.

Luke laughed. No, he couldn't recapture the past and have his old friend back, but whatever new thing was developing between them was good.

Now, he thought, watching her bottom in those tight jeans as she walked away, if he could just keep his hands off her and not ruin things this time.

"Katie," he called after her, "no white furniture!"

She looked back and grinned. "I knew you didn't like my place!"

"I said it was nice, didn't I?"

She laughed, and his heart swelled with happiness. Yes, whatever was growing between them was definitely good.

***

That night Emma cuddled up to Jerome, her head on his arm.

"Emma, you continue to amaze me," he said. "I was getting a little worried especially after you told me Katie talked to Doc Kramer and then she said she was leaving tomorrow."

"I'm just glad the e-mail worked. I was afraid Francine and Jeffrey wouldn't come or they'd wait too long and she'd be gone. I could tell by the scared way she acted around Heather's baby that she was thinking of that awful tubal ligation thing again, and it's all my fault for leaving her when she was so young. She thinks she doesn't remember it, but she does, and she's afraid she'd end up hurting her baby like that. If only she could remember all the times afterward that I visited her, I know that would make a difference."

Jerome patted her shoulder. "It's not your fault. You didn't plan to die in that car wreck."

Emma sighed. "Things were pretty good between Katie

183

and me for a while after that. Of course I couldn't talk to her the way I do to you because I didn't want her going to school and telling all her little friends and then having them laugh at her. But we talked...in her dreams and sometimes in what she thought were her dreams. We communicated. But when Luke left and she shut off all her hopes and dreams, I couldn't get through to her. Until now, that is. She's starting to hear me again. That's a good sign."

"It's a real good sign. Did you know she'd be buying furniture for Luke when you set this up?"

"No, that had to be the idea of someone a lot higher in authority than I am, and it's a brilliant touch. Surely with a new bed in the picture, we can plant all sorts of ideas in their heads. They're having a hard time keeping their hands off each other already. They're so close to finding their hearts again. They just need a little more guidance."

Jerome chuckled. "Emma, you're the best guide I've ever known. And the prettiest."

She laughed softly and cuddled closer.

Chapter Seventeen

"Luke!" Evelyn shouted. "It's that crazy Homer Grimes again on line two!"

"Thanks! I'll get it in a second." Luke sighed then went back to his phone call on another line. "Sorry, Katie. I gotta run. The sofa sounds fine. I don't need to see it. I trust your judgment. Tell them Rusty Bob and I will be there in his truck to pick it up around six this evening."

"Great! See you then."

Luke clicked off Katie's call to take Homer Grimes'.

"Deputy Sheriff Luke Rodgers."

"Where's Sheriff?"

"He's out on another call." Actually he was at a late lunch, but Luke wasn't going to interrupt him for something like this. "Can I help you?"

"You could, but you won't. That dad blamed fool has gone and burned down my barn."

"Did you call the fire department?"

"Wudn't you listening to anything I said? Damned thing's already burned down. Why would I call the fire department now?"

Luke wasn't surprised. The building had been so old and dry when he'd been out there, he'd thought then that a hot day would set it on fire. "All right. I'll come out and file a report."

"You tell Sheriff to get his ass out here and arrest that crazy old coot before he decides to burn down my house and shoot me when I run out!"

"Did you see Seth set fire to your barn?"

"No, but I know he done it. Who else would have wanted to?"

"Good question. Who would have?"

"Nobody but Seth Flanders."

"And why would he want to?" If the man had wanted

the old barn destroyed, all he'd have had to do was wait for a strong wind, and it would have blown down.

"Cause he's crazy, that's why."

Luke had his own opinion about *Homer's* sanity. "I'll be out there in a few minutes."

He hung up, grabbed his gun and started out the door.

"What now?" Evelyn asked.

"Homer's barn burned down."

She snorted. "Probably one of those environmentalist groups. I bet he hadn't cleaned that place out in years. Probably ought to've burned down his house, too." She picked up a form and turned back to her computer to begin laboriously entering the data.

Luke settled his hat on his head. "I think you're right about that. It wouldn't surprise me if some of the rats and mice living in that barn got together and decided to burn it down as a community service."

Evelyn laughed. "Those two old men ought to be ashamed of themselves, fighting and carrying on like that when they used to be best friends."

"Any idea what happened to end their friendship?"

She shook her head. "Not really. I always thought it was jealousy. Seems to me like the trouble started when Seth got married. I was just a kid then, but I remember my mama and daddy talking about it, and Mama said she thought Homer was jealous of Seth's wife coming into the middle of their friendship. If that was right, though, you'd've thought after that woman left, they'd make up, but they didn't. They still hate each other. Beats the heck out of me."

"Me, too. When Sheriff gets back, tell him I'll be at Homer's place listening to him complain."

It was the last place he wanted to be. He'd hoped to get off early today and see what else Katie had found for his house. He'd been amazed at the progress she'd made yesterday in only half a day. It was really taking shape, starting to feel like a home.

And everything she chose was warm and comfortable and fit right into the old house, completely unlike her ultra-contemporary condo that seemed to have come straight out of the pages of a magazine but had no warmth or personality to it.

Katie had been more like her old self last night, too. The two of them and Sheriff had worked hard getting things hauled inside and moved into place. By nine o'clock, they'd been starving and too tired to go out for food, so Katie had made peanut butter and jelly sandwiches served with potato chips...the only things he had in his kitchen besides sardines and coffee.

Tonight, as much to keep Sheriff from overexerting himself as anything else, he and Katie assigned him to pick up a pizza on his way over while they did the furniture moving.

That would, of course, mean he and Katie would be alone in the house for a while even after Rusty Bob Wahr helped him unload whatever she'd found to buy today. Fortunately, they'd be too busy and too tired for him to spend much time lusting after her, to ruin the tenuous bond that was growing between them.

He went out the back door of the Sheriff's office whistling *Tonight* from *West Side Story*.

***

"Move it a little to the left," Kate instructed as Luke held the landscape painting above the sofa in his living room. "Right there." She stepped over the coffee table and knelt beside Luke on the hunter green sofa to hold the picture while he marked the spot for a nail.

She had surprised herself by the speed with which she'd been able to furnish his house in a day and a half. Of course, the furnishings weren't elaborate. She'd tried to match the overall tone of the way she remembered the house. That was, she thought, what Luke would want.

He seemed pleased with the result and, she had to admit, she was too.

He finished hanging the painting and stood back to look. "You did good, Katie."

"Thanks." She brushed a strand of hair back from her face and blew out a long breath. "You can say what you like about the good old days, but I sure am glad you put in some modern air conditioning. This furniture moving business is hard work."

He laughed then squinted at her face. "Hold still a minute. You've got something right there."

He drew one finger along her cheekbone, halting near her chin as his pupils dilated. She could feel her own breathing accelerate at his touch.

Abruptly he jerked his finger away.

"What was it?" she asked, hoping her voice didn't sound as husky to him as it did to her. "What was on my face?"

He grinned. "A clean spot, but now it's covered with dust from my finger."

Kate rolled her eyes. "I can't believe I fell for that again. You must have done that to me a hundred times when we were kids."

Still fighting the remnants of the desire he generated every time he touched her, she turned away and made unnecessary adjustments to the lamp table beside the sofa.

Spending so much time with Luke, working together to get his house furnished before his parents arrived, had been fun. They'd fallen into a comfortable routine—a comfortable, undemanding relationship—but in spite of working hard and staying busy, the inappropriate attraction seemed always to be lurking just around the corner, ready to leap out at unexpected moments. They were doing a good job of ignoring it, however, and she felt sure it would soon go away. If it didn't, she would be gone in a few days, and that would effectively shut it down.

A knock sounded at the door, and Luke went to answer it.

"Dinner's here!" Papa announced, brandishing a large pizza box.

"Great!" Luke said, taking the box from him. "I'm starved."

Papa came in and looked around, inspecting the room closely. "You kids sure did a good job. I can't believe you got so much done in such a short time."

"Katie did most of it. I just furnished the strong back and the hammer and nails." Luke carried the pizza into his large kitchen.

As they passed the door of the dining room, Papa looked in. "That is purely amazing. That table is almost identical to the one Francine and George had."

Kate cast a quick glance at Luke to see if the reference to his father would upset him, but he showed no sign if it did.

"Katie has a good memory," Luke said. "She got a lot of similar things. Mom's going to be really pleased."

Kate took down plates from the cabinet...plates she'd purchased just that morning...and set them on the smaller café table in the kitchen. "The wire back chairs aren't the same as the originals that were in here when we were kids, but they're really close to the ones that used to be in the drug store before it closed."

They sat around the table and opened the box.

Kate experienced a brief pang of guilt for letting her father have such a high-cholesterol, artery-clogging dinner, but she knew when she returned to Dallas, he'd be eating the same or worse.

For a few moments they ate in companionable

silence.

Luke reached for his second piece. "Sheriff, you make a mean pizza."

Papa chuckled. "It's not as good as the meal Katie made Saturday night, but it'll do."

Kate shuddered. "I don't even want to talk about that meal. I've made presentations to major corporations that involved high dollar deals, but I don't think I've ever been so frazzled in my life as trying to cook that meal."

And she still wasn't at all sure about how Papa had decided on the menu or come up with answers to her questions about cooking it.

"Just takes a little practice," he assured her.

"Don't count on me ever getting that practice, Papa. That's why we have restaurants and pizza delivery."

"You're being too modest, Katie," Luke said. "Those peanut butter and jelly sandwiches you made for dinner yesterday were definitely gourmet quality. And that side dish of potato chips? Well, I'd be willing to bet you can't get that kind of food in any of those expensive restaurants in Dallas."

Kate tossed a stray bit of black olive at him. "You'd better cool it or I won't make my special Marshmallows Flambeau when your mom gets here."

That occasioned a round of easy laughter from everybody.

Papa shook his head and reached for another piece of pizza. "I'd almost forgotten about the time you tried to burn down the woods."

"Yeah, well, some things are better forgotten."

"That's okay, Katie," Luke said. "You can come over here and cook any time you want to. I've got a fire extinguisher and good insurance."

The familiar voices and laughter floated around the room, and Kate drank it in, feeling the most relaxed she'd been since she'd come down here.

Even though Luke hadn't been able to give her any answers about Papa's peculiar behavior, in sharing it with him, she'd seemed to share the burden, and it lay much lighter when supported by two sets of shoulders.

Perhaps she'd overreacted to Luke's reappearance in her life. Neither she nor Luke bore any resemblance to the children they'd once been. She was no longer the dependent little girl who idolized the little boy she'd grown up with. She was an independent woman, and Luke was a man she didn't know and wouldn't have the time to get to know.

He was also a man who sent her pulse racing and her hormones off the chart, but that was incidental, something she, as an adult in control of her own destiny, could choose not to act on.

When the last piece of pizza had been consumed, Papa pushed back his chair and stood. "That was good. And now if you kids want to give me a quick tour of what you've done upstairs, I'll take it on home and get to bed early."

Kate looked at her watch. "Papa, it's not quite eight o'clock. Are you feeling all right?"

"Is it that late already?" He snapped his fingers. "Darn! My favorite show comes on at eight. We better make that tour really fast."

"Sheriff, you can watch television here. Try out the new set."

"Not the same as watching it at home in bed. When you get to my age..." He shrugged and smiled.

Something wasn't ringing quite true. His voice had an odd quality, almost too sincere or something. Kind of like the day he'd asked her to cook the dinner of foods he claimed were his favorites when he'd never eaten them before.

She suspected, for whatever reason, Papa wasn't telling the complete truth again.

"Papa, what's the name of your favorite show? I don't recall your mentioning something on Thursday nights that you just had to watch."

"You're not usually here on Thursday nights."

She'd give him that, though she had phoned him on Thursday nights before. "So what's the name of the show? Luke and I might like to see it, too."

Papa sighed. "Oh, Katie, when you get to my age, you can't remember little details like the names of all the television shows you enjoy." He checked his watch. "We'd better hurry if I'm going to get to see the bedrooms and still make it home in time to catch that show." He turned and walked away.

Kate and Luke exchanged a puzzled glance then followed him up the stairs.

Contrary to his assertion of a need to hurry, when they got to the door of Luke's room, Papa lingered. "I like it," he said.

Again Kate and Luke exchanged a puzzled glance.

"We didn't do a lot in here, Papa." She'd been reluctant to do much beyond finding a solid color spread for Luke's bed and a small dresser and night stand to get his underwear out of cardboard boxes and his phone off the floor.

Papa walked in, and they followed him. "It's a good room, a real good room."

"It was mine when I was a kid." Luke looked at her and shrugged, apparently as mystified as she at Papa's odd fascination.

"It's a small, square room."

Papa stood near the bed and scanned the place. "Good lighting, too. Windows on two sides. Good vibes, as you kids would say. Come over here by me and see if you can feel it."

Good vibes? Had her father really said that? He must be watching a lot of television reruns to pick up a phrase like that.

Mystified, she and Luke moved over to stand, one on each side of him. The three of them stood quietly for a few seconds.

She supposed if Papa saw ghosts, tuning into *good vibes* was to be expected.

"Feel anything?" he asked.

"It's, uh, pretty warm up here," Luke ventured. "I knew I should have put in a separate thermostat for upstairs."

"I'll turn on the ceiling fan." Papa moved across the room to the doorway and flipped the switch. "Both of you get closer together. Try to both get in the exact spot where I was standing."

Reluctantly, Kate moved closer to Luke, and he moved closer to her. Their shoulders touched. She held herself rigid, trying not to experience the sensations being near Luke always generated, but it didn't help. No matter how hard she tried, she was exquisitely aware of him beside her.

"Better?" Papa asked.

Oh, yeah. Better...and worse.

"It's, uh, cooler," Luke said.

He was lying. It was no cooler for him than for her. The breeze of the ceiling fan couldn't offset the heat of their bodies.

"Definitely cooler." She confirmed his lie.

"Well, stand there for a little while and see if you feel anything." He checked his watch. "Look at the time! I'd better hurry home. I'll see you kids tomorrow." Papa started from the room.

Kate went after him. "Wait for me. I'm staying with

193

you, remember?" She ended on a short laugh that came from tension rather than from humor.

Papa stopped. "I thought you were going to stay here and help Luke finish up with the house."

"It's pretty much finished."

"Katie, you should at least stay and help with the dishes."

"Oh, well, sure, I intend to do that."

She looked more closely at Papa. He was the last person in the world to worry about dirty dishes...especially when those dishes were only three plates. Was he—

A thought occurred to her.

No, surely he wasn't trying to—

He'd arranged for her first meeting with Luke to be just the two of them.

He'd asked her to cook Luke's favorite foods for dinner.

He'd engineered their night together in her condo in Dallas.

He'd managed to keep Luke and her together pretty much constantly since she got in town.

She gave a mental sigh.

Of course. She should have seen it sooner.

Papa was matchmaking. He wanted her to stand beside Luke in his bedroom, alone in the house, in the hopes that a physical attraction would develop.

If he only had any idea how successful he'd been!

For an instant, she was outraged, but she supposed it was only natural he'd want Luke, who'd always been like a son to him, to be his son-in-law. She really couldn't be angry at him for trying. Heck, she couldn't be angry at Papa for anything.

But she would have to set him straight so he wouldn't be disappointed.

This explained a lot of things, like why he'd sounded

so unhappy when she told him about her engagement to Spencer and why he'd been so eager to get her to come to Briar Creek right away.

Did it also explain why he'd suddenly started talking to Mama, why he'd put her on the telephone? Had he counted on her concern for his sanity bringing her straight to Briar Creek?

No, Papa might be manipulative and sly as an old fox, but he would never be deceitful. At least, not more than a small fib about his favorite foods or his favorite television show coming on.

She kissed him on the cheek. "I'll help Luke with the dishes and then I'll be home."

Papa smiled. "I'll show myself out."

"We'll walk down with you. The dirty dishes are in the kitchen."

When Luke closed the front door behind Papa, he turned to Kate. "What was that all about?"

Kate hesitated, torn between telling him, inviting him to laugh with her at the absurdity of the idea and being too embarrassed to talk about it.

But there was no real reason to be embarrassed.

"I'm not positive but I think—" She gave a short laugh to show how silly she thought the whole idea was. "I think he may be trying to get you and me, uh, together."

"Together?"

"You know. Matchmaking. Leaving you alone in the office when he knew I was coming to town, the trip to Dallas for papers they could have mailed to him, then conning us into spending the night there." She laughed again, ending on an exaggerated sigh and shaking her head. "He means well. He loves us both."

Luke didn't laugh. He smiled, but it was a sad smile. He rubbed his hand over the back of his neck. "It's not really all that strange. For Sheriff to want that, I mean.

195

Right after my dad died, I used to think that maybe one day Sheriff and my mom would get married and you'd be my sister. That was when I was still a kid, of course."

Kate's discomfort faded. Luke understood. Where Papa was concerned, she could always count on him to understand. "Guess that couldn't happen since it seems that death did not part Papa from Mama."

Luke smiled. "Yeah, that would make it kind of tough."

"Well, let's get those dishes done and I'll go home and check on him."

Luke waved a negligent hand. "Don't worry about the dishes. I think I can handle three plates."

The dishwashing episode at Papa's on Saturday night suddenly flooded Kate's memory…how sensual it had been to stand so close to Luke, to feel his fingers touching hers as she handed him the hot, slick dishes. She was relieved they would forego that delicious torture tonight.

Relieved and disappointed.

But she'd go with *relieved.*

"Then I'll say good night."

He walked out on the porch with her. Luke's porch was very different from Papa's. For one thing, Luke had trimmed the shrubbery and vines to the point it was possible to see the street. But also it wrapped around one side of his house where a second door led to the mother-in-law room. It had been their play room when Luke was small, and now she'd helped him set it up as a TV room.

She strolled around to the side, admiring the repairs and the exterior paint job that Luke had done.

The lazy summer evening was still light though the sun was low and the shadows long. Kate knew she needed to leave, but somehow she couldn't work up any urgency. A few years ago there had been a popular country song about front porches. Until this trip home, she'd forgotten how peaceful and languid they could make a person feel, especially in the summertime.

"I'd like to turn that room into a library one day." Luke's voice, close behind her, broke into Kate's reverie.

She whirled...and found herself in his arms as he reached reflexively to balance her.

Immediately he released her.

"You startled me," she explained with a nervous laugh.

"Sorry. I thought you heard me come up behind you." He was still much too close for comfort, close enough for those currents to flow between them.

She stepped around him. "No, I didn't hear you. I guess I was woolgathering."

He folded his arms and nodded, looking out over his yard. "Do you remember that book *Door into Summer* by Robert Heinlein?"

"Sure. Great book."

"I feel like I've found that door, coming back here. I was so busy running around the city, doing all the things I needed to do and wanted to do, every year when summer was over, I always felt like I wasn't through using it. Like I hadn't used it at all."

"I know what you mean." And it scared her, because she did know.

They walked back to the other end of the porch where a new, unfinished wooden glider sat.

"I need to get that stained before winter," he said, then sat down in it and looked at her. "You've been working all day, mostly inside the house or a car or a furniture showroom. Don't leave yet. Sit down and share some summer with me."

If he'd asked her to stay and make love with him or even to stay and talk to him, she could have said no, but she couldn't refuse to share some summer.

197

She sat beside him. Not touching, of course. The glider was wide enough for both of them.

Except the whole porch wasn't wide enough to keep her from experiencing that damned attraction.

For a few moments they sat without talking, listening to the music of nature...the sweet evening songs of the robins, the strident calls of the blue jays, the liquid trill of purple martins, the crickets, katydids and tree frogs just getting tuned up for the evening, an occasional car passing in the street. The scents of honeysuckle and four o'clocks drifted in on alternating breezes.

"Look," Luke whispered, pointing toward a large four o'clock bush with bright pink flowers.

Kate followed the direction of his finger and saw a vivid green hummingbird darting from blossom to blossom.

Neither of them spoke until the fairy creature darted away.

"I think I'll get a feeder," Luke said.

"What was Cindy like?" Luke was probably not one bit more surprised than she was at her abrupt, out-of-context, question.

He blinked then laughed. "Talk about a non sequitur."

"Sorry. I have no idea where that came from. You don't have to answer. It's none of my business."

"Cindy was a lot like you in some ways. Slim, red hair, darker than yours and straight. She was fun to be with. A nice person."

"Why did you get divorced?" After his description of Cindy, Kate felt as if Luke had divorced her rather than Cindy.

And he had, in a manner of speaking, hadn't he, when he left her?

Luke's jaw squared and thrust outward. He looked away from her, over the yard again. He didn't want to talk about his divorce, but she knew he would...because she'd asked.

"Actually the real question isn't why we got divorced but why we got married in the first place. I met Cindy right after we moved to Houston. She lived three doors down from me. We became friends but we were both right at the age where we were starting to notice the opposite sex. So our friendship always had an edge. I guess you'd say it was more like a game than a real friendship, like we were striving for the same goal, but we were on opposite sides." He shrugged. "I know that doesn't make any sense."

"It does," she assured him.

"We went through the stages...friends to dating to going steady to getting engaged to marriage to total indifference and divorce. She had an affair. I caught her. She told me she didn't think I'd ever loved her."

"Did you?"

Had she really asked the question or only thought it?

Luke was silent for several heartbeats. Finally he looked at her, his eyes searching her face as if for answers she was sure she wouldn't have even if she knew the question.

"I don't know. I know losing her didn't hurt nearly as much as losing you did, losing my best friend."

It was her turn to look away, toward the yard, the serenity of the trees and flowers. She felt as if Luke was probing her mind, as if he was silently asking how she felt about Spencer, if she'd ever loved him. She didn't want to think about that right now.

"Is that why you're so worried about your mother, because you married Cindy and lost her friendship when you got a divorce, so you think that could happen to your mother?"

"You have no idea what it feels like to go through a

divorce, to end up with a big, fat zero where you once had a relationship."

Yes, she had a real good idea. That's what had happened to her when Luke left.

She rose abruptly. "It's getting late. I know it's safe to be out after dark in Briar Creek, but I'm pretty night blind. I'd better go home."

He stood beside her. "I'll walk with you."

Her heartbeat quickened as she looked up at him. The shadows had deepened, and his eyes were dark and unreadable. His ebony hair was even more tousled than usual. He wore a tank top that showed every muscle in his magnificent arms and chest and most of the dark, curly hairs on those arms and that chest.

Yes, the insane thought ran through her head, *walk me home like we're sixteen and you never left me, and when we get to my door, come up and wrap me in those arms and kiss me until we both lose all common sense.*

Well, they weren't sixteen and he had left her. He'd even left her replacement, Cindy.

"That's not necessary. I'd rather go by myself. Give me some time to think."

She left the porch and started down the walk.

"Good night." His deep voice crossed the evening air and caressed her. "I'll call to be sure you get home all right."

She turned around to see him standing at the top of the steps, one sculpted arm extended with his hand resting on a column. His faded blue jeans wrapped snugly around his long legs, exposing those muscles as clearly as the shirt exposed his bare arms. He was every inch a man, and it would be impossible for any woman not to notice. She couldn't upbraid herself just for noticing.

"I'll be fine. You don't need to call." She slipped her cell phone from her purse and flinched. "I forgot to charge my phone last night. It's dead." She'd been too interested in thinking about Luke, about furnishing his house.

"I know your dad's phone number. It hasn't changed." He grinned.

She laughed. "No, it hasn't." She turned and walked away.

"Thanks for sharing some summer with me." His words were soft as the evening breezes.

She hesitated. But if she turned and looked one more time, she might lose the smidgen of control she had left. She might very well run back up those steps and throw herself into those arms.

Something she couldn't do because she was engaged to Spencer.

Something she couldn't do because she wasn't at all sure how Luke would react...at least, ultimately. She was pretty sure about his immediate reaction. She knew he wanted to kiss her. She'd be willing to bet that the thought of making love had crossed his mind.

But if they ever went that far, she would be irretrievably lost...and he could be gone again.

Chapter Eighteen

When Kate arrived home, she heard the sounds of waltz music, a little scratchy as if from an old vinyl record, drifting through the summer evening. Looking up toward Papa's window, she saw that he was once again dancing by himself.

She stopped halfway up the walk in front of the house, concealed by the gathering dusk and the overhanging branches of a catalpa tree, and watched him.

He hadn't turned on the light in his room, but it wasn't completely dark in there either. Maybe he had some sort of night light she'd never noticed.

Even from this distance she could see how tenderly he gazed at his partner, the protective way he held her. She could feel, as if it were palpable, the love emanating from them.

Him, not *them.*

There was no partner. Papa was dancing with and looking at empty air.

Her imagination was getting away from her again.

As she watched him, her heart swelled with love and a touch of wistfulness. Papa had such an amazing capacity for love.

But there was no point in her getting all wistful over that. Papa's capacity had taken him over the edge. Unable to deal with Mama's loss, he'd imagined her back with him.

If she were honest with herself, she'd have to admit that she had inherited from him that capacity to love with all her heart. However, she'd dealt with her losses differently than Papa had. Instead of losing her grip on reality, she'd put it all behind her and turned away from giving her whole heart ever again.

As she watched him move about the room, a vision

flashed through her mind of Mama and Papa dancing before Mama was killed. She frowned. Was it a real memory or just something she'd conjured up from Papa's stories and the scene before her?

It was a real memory.

Maybe she'd been too young to recall many details of life before Mama left, but she suddenly realized that she did remember that wonderful feeling of being totally secure and loved, and the agony of having that feeling yanked away.

Luke hadn't been her first lost love. Having already lost Mama had made losing him that much worse.

She shuddered in the warm summer evening and tried to shove those memories back where they'd been stored all these years.

But then—

For just an instant as Papa turned slowly in the dance, she thought she saw the outline of a woman...not flesh and blood, but more like an outline of light.

He turned again.

She'd been mistaken, of course.

It was only Papa.

Her imagination, filled with thoughts of Mama, had almost fooled her.

The way Papa's did him.

Yes, she had inherited from him that ability to love too much and be hurt too deeply.

She lowered her eyes, walked briskly up the steps and into the house.

She was just starting up the stairs when the phone rang, the noise shrill and invasive in the quiet house with the only sound Papa's old-fashioned music.

She ran to answer the phone, to stop it from disrupting his dance. It had to be Luke. She'd told him it wasn't necessary to call, but he'd always been overly protective.

She snatched up the receiver before it could ring again. "Luke?" she asked breathlessly. Damn it, she was thrilled that he'd called, she couldn't wait to hear his voice.

A moment of silence. Then— "Kate?"

It took her another moment to recognize the voice. Not Luke.

"Spencer! Hello! I didn't expect to hear from you until you got back from your trip."

"I'm back. It's Thursday."

"Oh. Yes, it is, isn't it? I've been so busy, I lost track of time."

"I understand. I'm only too well aware of how easily that can happen."

"I've just been up at Luke's house. That's why I called you *Luke* when I answered the phone. He was calling...I mean, I thought he was calling to see if I'd made it home safely." Why was she explaining when he hadn't even asked?

"Luke? Isn't that the deputy who spent the night with you at your place in Dallas?"

Coming from anybody else, the comment might have sounded like a sarcastic taunt, but Spencer's voice was so even and emotionless, she knew he was simply stating a fact. She'd always admired that about Spencer, his lack of jealousy, his calm, rational approach to everything. She'd just called him by another man's name, the same man who'd spent the night alone in her condo with her, and he wasn't upset in the slightest. Spencer was reason and logic personified.

Tonight, for some reason, that annoyed her rather than comforted her.

"Yes, that's Luke," she said. "I've been helping him pick out furniture for his house. His mother and step-father are coming to visit tomorrow."

"I see. When are you returning to Dallas? I really need you back up here by Sunday night. Can you be here by then?"

That would give her plenty of time to visit with Luke's mom, and she'd planned to leave Sunday morning anyway. She needed to be back at work on Monday. There was no reason the word *yes* should stick in her throat like that.

"Probably," she finally said.

"Probably? Kate, I need you here on Sunday evening. We've got a potential client flying in from Japan. The word is, he's very big on family. Brewer, Carmichael, Britton and I are meeting with him over dinner, and they're all bringing their wives. I need you to be with me. I thought that's why we agreed to get married, to help each other."

Kate considered Spencer's words for a moment. That had been part of their agreement, but she didn't recall that it had been stated so baldly.

"Kate?"

"I'm here. Of course I'll be there for the dinner on Sunday evening." Suddenly that was the last thing in the world she wanted to do.

She didn't want to stay here, couldn't stay here much longer. She was already getting in over her head, sharing summer with Luke, expecting him to call. If she hadn't been a strong-willed person with years of practice at maintaining a level head, she could already have become emotionally entangled with him. The physical part, that tugging of her hormones, would disappear when she got away from him, so she should get away as quickly as possible.

But the thought of going back to Dallas, to a business dinner with Spencer, had about as much appeal as a cold, greasy pork chop.

205

After she hung up the phone, she stood looking at it for several moments. Something was wrong with her. Something was very wrong. She'd worked so hard to get all areas of her life in order, and now everything in the personal area seemed to be shifting, falling into unrecognizable patterns, like the random patterns of a kaleidoscope.

Her head and her emotions were playing tug-of-war with her. She knew which side she was pulling for.

Or at least she used to know. She knew which side she *ought* to be pulling for.

She climbed the stairs then hesitated at Papa's door. No music came from within. She thought about knocking softly to wish him a good night, see him for a moment and absorb some of the unquestioning love and peace that always emanated from him. But she didn't want to disturb him with her problems.

Before she could walk away, the door opened. Papa stood there, his face overflowing with compassion and love, as if he knew exactly what had happened to her since he'd left her at Luke's, exactly what was going on in her muddled brain and heart.

Without a word, he took her into his arms and held her the way he'd held her as a child...only now they were both standing rather than him squatting to her height.

She wrapped her arms around him, and even though she'd grown, Papa's middle had, too. Her hands met at just the same place on his back they always did.

She pressed her cheek against the soft cotton of his shirt, the metal brad on his pocket forming a cool spot near her chin, and sank into the comfort of his constant love. Papa's essence, a gentle scent that evoked images of mountains and trees and this house, surrounded her as surely as his arms. An intermittent thread of lilacs drifted in and out.

"Papa, I'm so confused."

He patted her back. "You think you are, but you're really not." He was silent for a moment, and she had the odd notion that he was listening. "Mama says if you listen to your heart and ignore all that other crap, you'll find the answers."

Kate drew back from him and laughed. "Papa! Mama would never say *crap*!"

He grinned mischievously. "Okay, I may have edited a little bit."

She kissed his leathery cheek. "Good night, Papa. I love you."

"I love you, too, Katie-girl."

In her room, she fell immediately into a deep sleep, lulled by that scent of lilacs. Her last conscious thought was that she really should do some research in the field of aroma therapy and find out the exact effect of the fragrance of lilacs. It must be a potent one.

Mama sat on the edge of Kate's bed.

Kate knew it was only a dream, but she was pleased to see her mother again. She smiled sleepily up at her. "You didn't really say crap, did you?"

Mama rolled her eyes. "Your father. He's incorrigible. I said you should ignore all that extraneous clutter. After all these years, I should know better than to use one of what he calls my six-bit words."

"All these years?" Katie tried to think. Something wasn't quite right, and she needed to ask Mama about it, but her mind shied away from whatever it was. Mama was here. That's all that mattered. The rest was extraneous clutter.

"Yes, your father and I have been married forty-five years, you know." Leo jumped onto the bed and Mama began to stroke him, head to tail, as he did his invisible hand routine...except Kate could quite clearly see Mama's hand moving along Leo's back. Well, actually, Mama's hand wasn't all that clear. In fact, Leo's hair where she stroked

207

him seemed to rise into Mama's hand a fraction of an inch.

"I almost didn't marry your father," Mama said, and Kate's attention swung from the cat back to her.

"Not marry Papa? How could you not marry Papa?"

"I was young and scared. I hadn't known him long, not nearly as long as you've known Luke, and I'd never been more than twenty miles away from home." She brushed a hand over Kate's eyes, making her skin tingle and her vision become slightly unfocused. "My high school class took its senior trip to Dallas. I was living in Willoughby then, and even though it's only fifty miles south of Dallas, most of us had never been there. One of the places we went was the Dallas County Courthouse. A handsome young deputy sheriff from Briar Creek County was hurrying out the door and ran into me. He put his arms around me to keep me from falling, and I did fall then, head over heels in love with your father." She smiled. "He admitted to me later he ran into me on purpose so he could get to meet me. He didn't have to admit it. I had no trouble figuring that one out. He had a note already written, and he tucked it into one of my gloves. Young ladies weren't properly dressed on a trip without gloves and hats in those days."

"What did the note say?" Kate asked. At least, she thought she asked the question. She wasn't positive that her mouth moved, however.

"It said, 'Will you marry me?' And then his phone number and the words 'Call collect.' I did, of course. We talked every night, but never for long. He said he had to save money to buy us a house. I'd laugh and tell him he was being silly every time he talked about marriage. We'd only met the one time. But we both knew that was enough. After a month, he came to Willoughby to stay a week and get my family's permission to marry me. They gave it, of course. They knew how much I loved him. And who could ever say no to your father? But then after he left, I became terrified of

leaving my home and family, going away to a strange city. I thought about it for several days. The fear didn't go away, and I didn't see how I could leave them. I considered breaking off the engagement, but I couldn't imagine not being with your father. A month later we were married."

The dark room—how had she been able to see Mama if the room was dark? But dreams didn't have to make sense. The dark room faded into trees and grass and sunshine and people in retro-sixties clothes. It was like a black and white movie that had been colorized, except these colors were vivid and real.

Mama, young and beautiful, her red curls only partially subdued by the white veil, came out of the small church on Papa's arm. He was young and handsome and beaming in spite of the obvious discomfort of wearing a tuxedo. Mama wore the gown Kate had seen so many times in pictures and in the attic. The couple stopped at the top of the steps, and Mama tossed her small bouquet, then they ran to the street amidst a shower of rice.

Papa opened the door of a very used car Kate had seen in pictures, but the pictures hadn't captured the shine to which he'd buffed the faded brown paint. Before getting in Mama turned back to hug her mother, father, grandmother, brothers and sisters over and over. She smiled and laughed at their teasing even as tears streamed down her face, and her happiness was every bit as blatant as her sadness at leaving them.

Papa stood beside his new bride, shaking hands and beaming with love and pride but sadness that Mama should ever have to know any degree of sadness.

"Go on now," her mother urged, though she was crying, too. "It's not like you're going off to New York or something. This Briar Creek's only half a day's drive away from Willoughby. It's not like it was during the war when gas was rationed. We'll be up to see you real soon. Go on

now, Emma. Go with your husband."

The newly-weds drove away amidst much shouting. Noisy cans dangled from the back of the car.

"I cried all the way to Briar Creek," Mama said, once more sitting beside Kate in the darkened room that wasn't dark. "I was so frightened of going off to a new place, leaving everything and everybody I knew behind, but I knew I was doing the right thing. When you find the one who completes your heart and your soul, you know, and you know that person is all you'll ever need."

Kate closed her eyes. She didn't want to think about what her mother was saying.

Through her eyelids, she could still see Mama sitting beside her, stroking Leo. Well, that's the way it went in dreams. They made no sense at all, no more sense than what Mama had been saying.

"It makes perfect sense, Katie. You're not confused. You have been for years, but you're coming out of it now. Your heart is opening, blooming like my lilac bush blooms after a harsh winter. If it wasn't, you wouldn't be able to hear me again after all these years. Listen to what your heart tells you. Your fears will lead you astray every time. Only your heart will tell you the truth."

***

Kate woke the next morning to the sounds of birds singing outside her open window and Leo purring in her ear. Her first inclination was to pull the pillow over her head and go back to sleep, back to the safe, happy realms she'd traveled in her dreams.

But that was totally unlike her. She wasn't going to start hiding now.

She stretched, reached up to stroke the cat's soft fur, and her strange dream returned to her.

Not all that strange, she supposed, considering how confused she'd felt when she went to bed. In her dream, she'd created an all-knowing mother to help her through that confusion.

Though Mama hadn't been of very much help.

Listen to what your heart tells you. Your fears will lead you astray every time. Only your heart will tell you the truth.

Well, her heart was telling her it didn't want to ever feel the pain of loss again. Her heart was telling her to trust her mind.

She got up, grabbed a robe and headed for the shower. When she reached the door of her bedroom, she noticed it was slightly ajar though she was positive she had closed it last night. She turned and looked back at Leo who still lay curled in a ball on her pillow. He hadn't been in her room when she'd gone to sleep.

"Did you wake Papa and make him let you in here or do you have a secret passageway?" Leo opened one eye halfway then closed it again, keeping his feline secrets.

At least he wasn't doing that invisible hand routine. After her dream, Kate wasn't sure she'd ever be able to watch that again without expecting Mama to materialize.

And what was that business about the lilac bush opening up?

Okay, it was true that she'd stopped dreaming of Mama when Luke left and started again now that he was back in her life. But she'd stopped because she was growing up, setting aside childish things, and now the dreams had started because Luke reminded her of those childish things. Maybe she hadn't paid a lot of attention in psych class, but even she could figure that one out.

She'd be fine once she got away from his influence.

Mama was right. She wasn't confused. She'd been tired last night, and that had put her in an easily suggestible state, enabling Luke's presence to recall events and feelings of the past.

Today she was wide awake and in control again.

211

Ghost of Summer

* * *

Friday dragged by for Luke as he anticipated and dreaded seeing his mother and her husband, anticipated and dreaded seeing Katie again.

The entire week had been so crowded with events, especially the last two days when he and Katie had spent every spare minute getting the house ready, that an ordinary day seemed quiet and uneventful.

Well, wasn't that what he'd wanted when he'd run back to Briar Creek, a succession of peaceful, quiet and uneventful days?

He wasn't sure anymore exactly what he wanted.

His father's old job, his family's old house, Sheriff's friendship, and Katie's friendship. He had all those. Okay, maybe the last wasn't quite the same, but it was close. Last night had been really close. If he discounted the fact that he had not, in his youth, been half-crazed with lust, it was really close.

He pretty much had what he'd wanted, but it didn't seem to be what he'd wanted after all. At least, not quite everything he wanted.

He was in his office jacking with the computer creature when he heard Evelyn squeal. "Francine! Is that really you?"

He went into the reception area to see Evelyn hugging his mother.

Jeff was standing just inside the door, looking a little uncomfortable and out of place. In the classroom, the man was totally competent, dynamic even, but take him away from his books, and he always seemed slightly lost. Luke's father, on the other hand, had never met a stranger and, like Sheriff, was in control of any situation.

His father had never been rude or let anybody feel left out, either, Luke reminded himself, and he'd taught his son those traits.

212

He strode over to Jeff and held out his hand. "Glad you could come," he said.

Jeff smiled and shook Luke's hand. "Good to see you again, Luke."

His mother, released from Evelyn's grasp, turned and wrapped him in an embrace.

When she finally pulled back, he was surprised to note that she looked younger than when he'd last seen her.

She was a small woman, the top of her head barely reaching his chin, so she'd always seemed youthful. Her hair was different, though. The predominantly white color that had started developing after his father died was now streaked with dark blond and styled in a short, casual cut.

"What do you think?" she asked tentatively, lifting a hand to fluff out her bangs as he stared at her. "The color and the cut?"

"It looks great. You look great."

She smiled, and her eyes misted. "So do you. You look so much like your father in that uniform."

An uncomfortable silence ensued.

Or maybe it was only uncomfortable for him.

"Have you all been by the house yet?" he asked.

"No, we came straight here."

"The door's unlocked if you want to go on in and get unpacked. Your old room's ready for you. I'll be through here in a couple of hours."

"Take the rest of the day off," Sheriff said. Luke turned to see him coming in the back door. "Nothing ever happens in Briar Creek."

"Jerome!" His mother ran to hug Sheriff.

"How are you, Francine? You look great. Not a day older than the last time I saw you."

"Oh, you always were full of malarky, Jerome Fallon. I'm fine. How about you?"

"Good. Real good."

213

"Jerome and Evelyn, I want you to meet Jeff Quinton, my husband."

Everyone shook hands and welcomed Jeff. Luke knew he should stop worrying and be happy that his mother seemed so happy...and so young.

But the contrast between Jeff and Sheriff only emphasized how different the man was from his father, how different this marriage was from his mother's first.

Still, Katie was right. He couldn't worry about them getting divorced just because they got married. At least, he *shouldn't* worry. If he couldn't help it, he could keep his concerns to himself.

And as for his own selfish feelings about his father disappearing because Jeff had appeared, well, that was his problem. No one else's.

"Mom, what would you think about inviting Sheriff and Katie over for dinner tonight?" He knew his mother would want to spent time with Sheriff, and he himself would probably deal better with things if other people were around...especially if one of those people was Katie.

How easily he'd settled back into the routine of needing her.

"We can get a pizza or Chinese food," he continued.

"I think that's a wonderful idea, except I'll cook dinner."

"Mom, I don't want you to start working again the minute you get here."

"Nonsense. Jeff and I are taking gourmet cooking classes, and we'd love the chance to try out some of our recipes on real people."

"Katie and I will bring the dessert," Sheriff volunteered.

"Great. Then it's all settled," Francine said.

Luke smiled. "I guess it is."

It was all settled except for his peace of mind.

And he could tell that had major problems when he was anticipating Katie's presence as a soothing element.

Chapter Nineteen

Sheriff pushed away from the table and laid his napkin beside his plate. "That was mighty fine food. Francine, you and Jeff did good, and Katie-girl, that cake was delicious even if it was a little flat."

Katie gave her father a mock scowl. "Brownies, Papa, they were brownies and they're supposed to be flat."

Luke's mother reached over and clasped Sheriff's hand in both of hers. "Thanks, Jerome. It was strange to be back in that kitchen after all these years. Not that it's very much like it was then. The old place never looked this good. You kids have done a great job fixing it up and furnishing it."

Luke exchanged a smile with Katie sitting across the table from him. "When we're fifty, your dad and my mom will still be calling us *you kids*."

Sheriff chuckled. "That's right. You'll always be our kids. How about you, Jeff? Got any kids you can torment in your old age?"

They'd been doing that all evening, suddenly realizing they'd been excluding Jeff and making an effort to include him. Not, Luke thought in all fairness to Jeff, because he didn't fit in but simply because the four of them had so much history together that Jeff wasn't a part of.

"No," Jeff said. "I've never been married before. I'm waiting for Luke to produce grandchildren and skip straight to that part. I hear that's the most fun, anyway."

"Hmm." Luke ducked his head and scratched one eyebrow thoughtfully. "Have you and Mom thought about getting a dog?"

That elicited laughter, and everybody scooted their chairs back and rose.

"I'll do the dishes," Luke offered, "since everybody

216

else did the cooking."

"I'll help," Katie volunteered. "Those brownies came from a box. You can't really count that as cooking."

"Leave the dishes, Luke," his mother said. "They'll still be there tomorrow."

Luke looked at Katie who shrugged.

"The food'll get stuck on them, Mom. You always used to say that."

"Did I? Well, if it sticks on tonight, we'll soak it off tomorrow. Come sit and visit. That's more important."

His fastidious mother was willing to leave dirty dishes overnight. Amazing.

Jeff laid an arm across her shoulders. "If we can't soak it off, we'll throw away those dishes and buy new ones."

His mother laughed and gazed up into Jeff's eyes as if they were lovers.

Well, weren't they? However weird it was to think about his history teacher and his mother as lovers, they were married.

Luke followed the others into the living room where Sheriff, Jeff and his mom sat on the sofa and Katie took the arm chair leaving him the big recliner. He'd bought the recliner for himself but somehow it didn't feel like his as he sank into it. It didn't feel right.

His father had always had a recliner while his mother had her favorite arm chair next to a floor lamp so she could read or crochet at night. This felt weird, to be in his father's place.

"Luke," Jeff said, "I'm looking forward to your showing me around this weekend. I've been doing some research on your little town since you moved back here, and it has quite a fascinating history."

"Briar Creek fascinating?" Katie asked in disbelief.

"Then I assume you haven't heard the story about the

217

cave," Jeff said.

"The cave?" Katie echoed and looked at Luke.

"No," Luke said. "We haven't heard any story about a cave, but we do know where it is. At least, where one cave is. Katie and I used to play there. Tell us the story."

"Then the cave still exists! I was afraid it would have been filled in by now."

"As of last week, it's still there, if this is the same one."

"Well, the story goes, that back around 1850 a couple of robbers held up the bank in Tyler. They made it to the Angelina River where they had a boat hidden. They went down the Angelina to where it branched off to Briar Creek. Apparently Briar Creek had more water in those days. Anyway, a few miles down, they found a big cave set in the bank. I don't know how big it is now, but at the time it was, according to the story, big enough for the two men to walk in."

"It's still that big," Luke affirmed.

"They planned to hide the money on the theory that, if they were caught and didn't have the evidence on them, they couldn't be sent to jail. Later, they'd go back and reclaim their loot. But when they went back, it was as if the earth had swallowed the cave. They couldn't find it again. They thought it was magic, that the cave was cursed or something. In reality, the creek had probably risen, and it was underwater. Nevertheless, the men gave up, went on to rob other banks and eventually got caught."

Jeff's hand rested casually on his wife's knee, and she gazed at him adoringly.

"A few years later," he continued, "a young cowboy and the woman he loved, who happened to be an Indian princess, were running away from the world. In those days, it wasn't acceptable for an Indian and a white man to marry. They came down that same river, and a terrible

218

storm arose. They thought they were doomed until they saw a cave open up as if by magic. They took shelter to wait out the storm and were, well, um, doing what young lovers do, and, in the process, jolted some rocks loose, exposing the hidden money. They returned it to the bank, collected the reward and, with that money, established the town of Briar Creek."

"What a wonderful story," Katie said. "Gosh, Luke, if we'd known that, we could have dug around to see if there was any of that money they overlooked."

"Isn't that something?" Sheriff said. "All these years I've lived here and never heard that."

"I suspect the early town fathers wanted to hush up the Indian involvement."

Sheriff nodded. "Likely. Luke, you have Indian ancestry. Maybe you're a descendant of that princess."

"Actually," Jeff said before Luke could laugh it off, "that's possible. The records are sketchy, but, from what I've been able to determine, that's actually very much a possibility."

Luke folded his arms and smiled. "Well, it makes a good story."

As the evening progressed, Luke was surprised to find himself becoming increasingly more comfortable with Jeff, as if they had resumed their old relationship when Jeff had been a friend of the family, his teacher and mentor, someone a little older than him and a little younger than his mother.

Finally Sheriff stood and stretched. "Time to take these old bones home to bed."

Katie rose, too. "I know you both probably have lots of plans, but I'd love to see you again before I leave Sunday."

Francine stood and hugged Katie and Sheriff. "Our plans include spending as much time with all of you as we can."

Everyone went out on the front porch, and Katie and Sheriff started down the walk, but then Sheriff stopped. "Luke, could you come with me and bring back a book I have that I know Jeff would enjoy reading. It's about some of the old families around town."

"You don't have to do that tonight," Jeff protested. "I can get it from you tomorrow."

"When you're as old as I am, you never put things off until tomorrow. Luke won't mind. It's only a couple of blocks, and it's a beautiful night for a walk."

"Of course I don't mind." Luke stepped off the porch and moved up beside Sheriff. He had a hunch the man was matchmaking again, but he hated to refuse his request. He could handle being thrown together with Katie. If they were going to maintain their friendship, he had to learn to handle it. "You're right. It is a beautiful night. I was thinking about taking a walk, anyway." Actually, he'd been thinking about going down to the cave.

When they got to Sheriff's house, the older man paused on the steps. "Why don't you kids wait out here and enjoy all these stars and that big Texas sky while I go in and find that book?"

Katie gave Luke a knowing smile. "All right, Papa."

Sheriff went inside, and Luke could hear his heavy footsteps going up the stairs.

"He's doing it again, isn't he?" Luke asked.

"He means well." Katie leaned against a porch column and looked out at the sky her father had touted. For a few moments, they were both quiet, listening to the sounds of the night. "Do you suppose that story Jeff told about the cave is true, or did he make it up?" she asked, her quiet voice barely making a ripple in the night air.

"It may not be true, but he didn't make it up. Jeff sticks strictly to the facts as he finds them in books."

"Well, it's a great story. I don't think the cave was underwater at all when those men came back. I think it was magic that hid the cave until the cowboy and his Indian princess came along."

Luke blinked, looked at Katie and blinked again. This sounded like the fanciful Katie he'd known all those years ago instead of the practical Kate, the systems analyst who lived in a condo in Dallas.

"Anything's possible," he said, replying to her question as well as his own thoughts. Both seemed pretty unlikely...but possible.

"I like Jeff."

"I do, too. I always have. Whatever problems I have are with me, not him. But didn't you feel a little funny tonight, you and me sitting where my parents used to sit, and the others on the sofa where you and I sat when we were kids?"

"Maybe a little," she admitted. "But it's not the same chair or the same sofa, Luke. Everything changes. Our parents get old, and we take care of them like they used to take care of us."

"Ever wonder what it would be like if Sheriff remarried?"

At that moment strains of a waltz tune came from Papa's bedroom window overhead.

Katie walked slowly into the middle of the yard and looked up. Luke went with her. Sheriff's window was dark. He didn't seem to be dancing tonight.

"I don't think Mama would let Papa get remarried."

For a moment Luke couldn't tell whether she was being facetious, and he suspected she wasn't sure, either.

Then she smiled.

And he smiled. "No," he said. "She wouldn't."

"We've changed, Luke. We've grown up. Your mother has remarried somebody totally different from

221

your father. Everything changes except for one constant."
She looked up at the window. "Mama."

"Ghosts are like that."

She turned her face to the sky and spun around in a
slow circle. "Papa's right. It is beautiful tonight. Look at
all those stars. You can't see that many stars in the city.
Too much light." She drew in a deep breath.
"Honeysuckle. Nothing says, *summer's here!* like the scent
of honeysuckle."

"I smell lilacs, too. Don't they just bloom in the
spring?"

Katie's eyes shone as if she'd captured some of that
starlight just by looking at it. "Lilacs only bloom in the
spring in the real world. Briar Creek has magic. Caves that
appear and disappear, ghosts...I guess lilacs can bloom
here any time they want to."

Briar Creek must have magic. That was the only
explanation for why he pulled Katie into his arms, and
together they began to whirl around the yard, waltzing to
the music coming from Sheriff's window.

Either it was magic or he had lost his mind. Maybe
both.

Her body in his arms was soft and warm and real.
Her steps matched his as though they'd been dancing
together all their lives, and the ground beneath, which he
knew for a fact was uneven and stubbled with clumps of
grass, seemed smooth as any dance floor.

Katie's face turned up to his, her gaze holding his as
surely as his arms held her body.

"We never danced before," he said, full of the wonder
of it.

"We did the Hokey Pokey in grade school."

"We did, didn't we? And you could never remember
which was your right foot and which was your left."

"But I made up for my lack of expertise with my

222

enthusiasm."

"You did everything with enthusiasm."

She tossed her head back, and smiled. "I think I had too much wine with dinner."

"We didn't have wine with dinner."

"Then why do I feel this way?"

"What way is that?"

"Drunk. High. Like we're dancing on air. Like there's magic everywhere."

"I don't know. What did you put in those brownies?"

She laughed softly. "Milk and eggs."

The music ended and they stopped dancing.

"I've had milk and eggs before," he said, "and they never made me feel like this. I think you may be right about that magic."

They'd stopped dancing, but he hadn't taken his arms from around her. In fact, he pulled her closer, craving more of the magic of her body against his.

This really was insane. Katie was becoming his friend again, she was returning to the Katie she used to be. He was going to spoil it all, and he couldn't stop himself.

His lips touched hers lightly as the night air touched his face. She responded, her lips clinging to his, and he was hopelessly lost, all common sense scattered to those stars millions of miles overhead. For the first time in his life, he understood the meaning of *crazy in love*...and he was too filled with the wonder of it all to think about how crazy it was.

We shouldn't be doing this, Kate thought as Luke's kiss sent her senses reeling, as if she were flying so high she could touch those stars she'd just been admiring. They shouldn't be doing this, but right now she couldn't remember just why. Right now nothing mattered but the feel of his hard body against hers, his mouth on hers...soft and firm, giving and taking, and the magic of the night surged through her. She'd never wanted anyone or anything so much in her life.

The music started again, a slower tune this time, and she and Luke moved with it, their bodies swaying together as one, his lips hovering above hers, dipping for light, fairy kisses while his arms held her tightly, securely against him.

After all these years, she'd come home, reclaimed her soul mate. The world had shifted back to upright.

Somewhere in the back of her mind, an alarm bell was clanging loudly, but the music surrounding them, coming from Papa's window and from inside their hearts, muffled the noise. She didn't want to hear it. She just wanted to go on forever, dancing in Luke's arms.

He pulled her closer, deepening the kiss, and she knew that wasn't all she wanted. Their dance should include the final, ultimate merging of their souls and bodies.

That alarm bell clanged more loudly, finally getting her attention.

She couldn't be doing this!

Reluctantly, her mind straining against her heart, she pushed away from Luke.

For a moment, he stood looking at her, his eyelids heavy with passion, his eyes clouded with the spell they'd both been under. Then his eyes cleared, and he stepped back and drew a shaky hand across his forehead. "Oh, God, Katie, I'm sorry." He sucked in a deep breath and faced her. "I know you're marrying Spencer. I know we can't be anything but friends. I swear it'll never happen again."

Marrying Spencer?

She'd forgotten again.

She wrapped her arms around herself and backed farther away from Luke, from the magnetic pull that he still had over her. "I don't know if I can marry Spencer."

"You don't know?"

She hadn't meant to say it aloud. "I'm very confused. I don't know what I'm saying or doing right now."

"Are you in love with him?" His dark eyes bored into her, and she knew she would have to tell him the truth...whatever the truth was.

"I don't know. I don't know what love is. I thought I had everything all figured out, but I don't know anymore." She spun away from him and walked toward the house.

"Katie, I want to be your friend. I need you in my life. I love you." She froze with one foot on the top step of the porch.

"I've loved you since we wore matching diapers," he continued, completely changing the meaning of what he'd just said. "Whatever I have to do or not do, I don't want to ever lose you again."

Spencer wasn't the only one who had her confused.

A few minutes ago she'd wanted nothing more than to waltz off into the sunset with Luke, to be happy in his arms forevermore. Sure, that was a fantasy, part of the magic the night had somehow woven about them. But it had been a beautiful fantasy.

Then Luke had apologized and cancelled out everything.

Even if she decided she couldn't marry Spencer, that wasn't why she had to pull away from Luke. Luke wasn't safe. He'd let her down once and he'd do it again...and he'd just proved it. How could he apologize for the most wonderful experience she'd ever had in her life?

***

Watching from the window, Emma shook her head. "Jerome, those two are absolutely the most stubborn people I've ever met in my life."

"They are that, Emma." He didn't remind her that this

225

wasn't exactly in her life. That was a technicality, after all. "But they're on the right track. Katie's starting to realize that Spencer is wrong for her. If we're patient, they'll get there."

"You be patient, and I'll guide them a bit more."

Jerome chuckled. "There are those that might call what you and I are doing *meddling* rather than *guiding*."

"Oh, no. Meddling is...well, it's different. Remember, I was granted a special dispensation to come back and help raise our daughter. Whatever I have to do is officially sanctioned."

"Your methods are a little unusual, but they do seem to be working." Jerome smiled and pulled his wife into his arms. "Let's don't waste the music."

As they danced across the floor of his bedroom, Jerome had to resist the urge to pull Emma against him more tightly. He couldn't do that, of course. His arms would slip right through her.

But he wanted to. He wanted to hold her as close as possible and dance until dawn.

The time was getting closer when Katie and Luke would realize their destiny lay with each other. And when that time came, Emma's special dispensation would be up.

Jerome couldn't complain. The bonus years with her had been wonderful. He was the most grateful man on earth and he'd never complain.

But he sure hated to think about her leaving.

Chapter Twenty

When Luke got back to his house, Jeff was sitting on the top step of the porch.

The book Sheriff had wanted Jeff to have. Luke had forgotten about it. Sheriff had been so busy playing music to weave a spell about Katie and him that he hadn't brought it out to them...and Luke had been so enthralled by that spell, the reason he was at Sheriff's house had completely slipped his mind.

"I forgot your book," Luke said, anxious to get past Jeff to the safety of his room so he could try to figure out just what the hell had happened and what he was going to do about it. "I'm sorry. We can get it tomorrow."

"That's not why I waited up for you. I wanted the chance to talk to you alone."

"Can we do this tomorrow? I've got a lot on my mind."

"I know you do. Please sit down."

Luke scowled...fiercely, he thought. "*You know I do*? What do you think you know?"

Jeff was not intimidated by his fierce scowl. "It would be hard to miss the fact that something's going on with Katie and you, and you aren't certain what to do about it."

"Katie and I are...friends. She's engaged to some guy from Dallas. That's all there is to that story." Luke started across the porch to the door.

"All right. Then we'll talk about something else. Do you want to tell me why you and I can't be friends anymore since your mother and I got married?"

Luke backed up. This was inevitable. He might as well get it over with. He sat down next to Jeff.

"As far as I'm concerned, we are still friends," he said.

"Not like before."

"Of course not. Nothing's like it was before. Everything's changed."

"Not everything," Jeff replied calmly. He was using his professor voice now. "The way I feel about your mother, the way I feel about being your friend, none of that has changed."

Luke reached down for a dead leaf that had fallen from the tree overhead, crumpled it into a wad and tossed it into the darkness. What the hell. He might as well tell Jeff how totally deranged he'd become, dancing in the yard with Katie, kissing her, worrying about his mother and her new husband getting a divorce when they'd only recently got married. He and Jeff had always been able to talk about anything.

"I worry about Mom. She's a strong lady, but it hit her hard when Dad died. She put up a good front, but even when I was a kid, I knew she was having a tough time. Not that it stopped her from being a great mother. She took care of me. Now it's my turn to take care of her. I guess I feel pretty protective."

"You want to protect her from me?"

Luke stared into the night. "No, of course not. I guess I just want to protect her from ever being hurt again."

"You think I'm going to hurt her?"

"All right, this may not make a lot of sense, but the way I figure it, as long as you and Mom were friends, she was married to Dad, sort of."

"And you think I'm trying to take your Dad's place."

"Damn it, don't put words in my mouth. As long as she was still married to Dad, in spirit, so to speak, we had a link to him. Then she married you, and that link disappeared. Now, I know what you're going to say. Dad died a long time ago, and Mom's still alive and entitled to a life of her own. I agree. And she had one. She had you and she had me and we all had each other, and everything was fine. But then it changed, and now it's not that anything's wrong, it's just that everything's unstable."

Even in the dark, he could see that Jeff was mystified. Luke blew out a long breath. Hell, he didn't completely understand it all himself. "The way I see it, friends are forever, but married people get divorced. You can climb the ladder from friendship to marriage, but going back and being friends after a divorce doesn't happen very often. So if you and Mom get a divorce—" He spread his hands. "It's all gone...you, Dad, everything. Mom's at ground zero." Luke rested his elbows on his knees. "I don't guess I realized how crazy it sounds until I put it into words."

"It's a good thing I'm your friend because friends stand by each other even when one of them goes nuts."

Luke laughed, and the sound that went out on the quiet summer night bordered somewhere between amusement and hysteria. "You think I'm nuts?"

"Could be. Did you just do something really dumb with your Katie?"

"Could be. I kissed her. Told her I loved her."

"That doesn't sound so dumb."

"As a friend."

"That was dumb."

"She's engaged."

"That could be a problem."

"She said she didn't know if she could marry the guy. So you see, that proves it. You fall in love, you fall out of love. You become friends, you're stuck with each other, crazy or not."

"At one time you loved Cindy."

"I remember."

"How did it feel tonight when you kissed Katie?"

A thrill darted through Luke at the memory. "I don't

know if I can describe it. It was like stepping out of an airplane and actually being able to walk on the clouds."

"You feel that way when you kissed Cindy?"

"Not exactly. To be honest, it wasn't even close. It was more like..." He hesitated, suddenly reluctant to talk to his mother's husband.

"Desire?"

"Sure."

"Lust?"

"Oh, yeah."

"You liked her."

"Of course."

"But no walking on clouds?"

"Nope."

"Then it wasn't enough for marriage."

For a few moments the two men sat on the porch steps. He hated to admit it, but Jeff might have a point. He hadn't thought about it that way. He'd questioned whether he'd ever loved Cindy, something that would have made their entire marriage a sham and a waste. He hadn't considered that there were different kinds of love, and that not all kinds were the stuff of which marriages were made.

But wasn't that sort of what he'd just implied to Katie...that he loved her in a different way than a man loved a woman, in a friendship way?

Yeah, he'd just told her that outrageous lie.

Well, what the hell was he supposed to do when she was engaged to that Spencer guy in Dallas? Friendship was the only way he could keep her in his life.

Though she had expressed doubts about marrying Spencer.

Which had only confirmed his fears about the temporary state of romantic love. She wasn't even married to Spencer, and already she was falling out of love.

So what would he do if Katie called off her

engagement, became a free woman?

Look her in the eye and tell her he only wanted to be friends?

Yeah, right.

"You feel like that about my mother?" Luke finally asked.

"Walking on clouds, you mean?"

"Yeah."

"Yeah."

"You hurt her, I'll break your face."

"Are you kidding? I hurt her, *she'll* break my face."

Luke laughed. "She would." He rose. "I think I'll take it up to bed. See you in the morning."

"Luke, I'm glad we finally talked."

"Yeah, me, too." They hadn't really resolved anything, but it felt different. Better. He still had those weird feelings of losing his dad forever along with his own identity, but that really didn't have anything to do with Jeff. That was his own problem, something only he could resolve.

He still worried about his mother's future, that she might get hurt. But he felt a little more confident about it, knowing that Jeff and his mother had that same wild and crazy attraction he and Katie had.

If Katie decided not to marry Spencer, then Luke would have to make a decision. As it stood now, he wasn't sure he could ever be *just friends* with her. He wasn't sure there would ever come a day when he could see her and be near her and not want to hold her, kiss her, make love to her.

He was afraid he'd already crossed the line, that things had already changed between them, and now they had to figure out where they were going next. The answer to that might be *apart*. He might have already lost Katie again. And this time, just as before, through doing really

231

stupid things, things he seemed to have no control over, like holding her and kissing her.

But this time those really stupid things had sure felt right and wonderful at the time.

***

The next day Kate begged off going with Luke, his mother and Jeff to examine the cave. She had spent too many hours down there after Luke left, hoping in some way to reach him, and then finally she'd cut off that part of her life. After last night, she certainly wasn't ready to go there again.

She met the three of them and Papa at Dodie's Diner for lunch, then they took Jeff on a tour of downtown Briar Creek. Though, as it turned out, Jeff actually took them on a tour. Kate saw what Luke meant when he said Jeff was dynamic in the classroom. The quiet man had done his research, knew the history of every building in Briar Creek, and told it in the detailed but captivating way he'd told them the story about the cave the night before.

"Greene's Department Store used to be Shipley's Grocery Store," he told them, "although in those days the grocery stores were more like a department store and a grocery store combined. Shipley came here from Louisiana in 1866, right after the Civil War ended. He fought for the South, even though he didn't believe in their cause. After the War, he decided to come to Texas where a man's worth was judged by what he could do, not his family or his money. He built the first store with his own hands, a pretty simple shack. Then as the town grew and he prospered, he hired someone to build him a decent place." Jeff ran a hand over the wooden clapboards. "The current owners have made improvements, but I wouldn't be surprised if this is the original structure."

"Could be," Papa confirmed. "That building hasn't changed since I was a boy, and that was a long time ago."

As they made their way through town, Papa greeted everyone they met, and they had to stop every few feet when someone recognized Luke's mother and had to greet her, be introduced to Jeff and hear how she'd been doing for the past seventeen years.

"This is another place that hasn't changed much over the years," Papa said when they reached Billy Ed's Bar and Grill. "Grill's been out since sixty-eight. Billy Ed's just too cheap to get a new sign."

"This was once the Briar Rose Saloon and Dance Hall," Jeff said, "owned and managed by a woman named Rose Swanson. And two doors down, on the corner, was the Briar Rose Brothel. Rose was a smart businesswoman. She believed in diversification."

Luke laughed. "So Windsor's Fine Jewelry was once a brothel. That jerk has his nose in the air so high he'd drown if he went outside in a rain storm. I'll never be able to look at him again without smirking."

They reached the building in question, and Kate stepped back a few paces to study it in this new light. "It's so elegant with all those bevels and leaded glass in the door and windows. Somebody must have redone it somewhere along the line."

Jeff studied the tall oak door with the glass insets and the intricate designs that made the windows virtually opaque, then smiled. "I don't think so. This is pretty much the way it looks in old pictures. This was a high-class place where the wealthy men of the town could go. The poor farmers and cowboys were stuck with the saloon." He moved back beside Kate and pointed to the balcony. "She had that wrought iron railing shipped in from New Orleans. She wanted the perfect showcase for her girls. They'd stand or sit up there in their elaborate dresses and entice customers, though Rose never let them shout or get vulgar. They were supposed to conduct themselves at all

233

times as ladies."

As Jeff talked, Kate noticed the way Luke's mom watched him...her eyes full of love and pride. Luke was right about one thing. Jeff did make her happy.

It was the way she'd imagined Papa looking at Mama the other evening when he'd been dancing by himself.

It was the way Kate knew she would never look at someone, the way she didn't dare look at someone. Jeff and Francine were happy now, but who knew how long it would last? And Papa's intense love for Mama had crashed his mind just the way an overload could crash her computer.

A loud *boom* shattered the quiet afternoon air of Briar Creek.

"What—" Kate started to ask.

"That direction," Papa said, and he and Luke ran back the way they'd just come.

"I believe it was a gun shot," Jeff said.

"A gun shot?" Kate whirled to run after Luke and her father, her heart pounding in her ears.

Francine grabbed her arm. "Katie, they're trained to deal with things like that. We're not. We need to stay out of the way."

"Papa keeps saying nothing happens in Briar Creek!" She remembered how angry Luke had been at her for spying on them at the liquor store, but she had to risk it. She couldn't stay there quietly while the two people who meant the most to her in the whole world risked their lives.

She whirled away from Francine and ran to the saloon. Three people had already congregated at the door and were holding it open. She pushed through to the front just as another shot rang out.

Her eyes adjusted to the dimness and she saw Luke standing at one end with his gun drawn while Papa stomped across the room, shoving tables and chairs out of his way as he went.

Papa was mad, and Kate was terrified. He was marching straight toward an elderly, bald-headed man wearing faded overalls, sitting on a bar stool and pointing a gun at him.

"Don't come any closer, Sheriff!" the man ordered, and Kate repeated the command in a whispered prayer.

"Why? You gonna shoot me, Homer? Give me that gun before you hurt somebody besides the cockroaches on Billy Ed's floor." He stopped in front of the man, reached over and snatched the gun away from him then emptied the bullets onto the floor and stuck the gun in his belt. "Damned old fool! What the hell did you think you were doing? I oughta run you in, make you spend a few nights in jail. A man your age! Are you drunk? I don't care if you are. That's no excuse!"

Homer's face crumpled. For a minute Kate thought he was going to cry. He turned on his stool, picked up his beer and downed a sizeable portion of the almost-full mug.

"He threatened to kill me." Another elderly man appeared at the opposite end of the bar where he'd apparently been crouching out of sight. The second man was similarly dressed in overalls and faded denim shirt but had a few strands of white hair across his head.

"Is that right, Homer?" Papa asked. "Did you threaten to kill Seth?"

Homer ducked his head and nodded.

Papa heaved an enormous sigh, shook his head and slid onto the stool next to Homer. "Fay, bring us all a cup of coffee. Luke, get rid of the gawkers in the doorway. Seth, get over here. We're going to stop this nonsense right now. I've had enough from you two."

Kate knew the exact instant Luke spotted her in the

235

crowd of *gawkers*. His brow lowered, and his face darkened.

"All right, everybody," he said, striding across the floor toward them. "Let's move on outside and let Sheriff do his job."

The other people backed out, and Kate, satisfied that Luke and Papa were all right, tried to go with the crowd, but Luke caught her arm, restraining her from leaving.

"What are you doing here?" he grated as the door closed behind her.

She jerked her arm out of his grasp. "You and Papa ran into a place where somebody was shooting. What did you expect me to do? Wait and see if you survived?"

"That's exactly what I expected you to do. Your father's not senile, and I'm not a little boy. We're grown men. We're the law. We can deal with liquor store robbers and drunk old men. I thought you understood that."

"I do understand, but that doesn't mean I don't worry." About Papa and about Luke. Like it or not, he'd edged his way back into her heart.

She whirled to leave but was stopped by the sound of Papa's voice. "It's okay, Katie-girl. Come on over here. Might help you to hear this."

"Papa, I'm sorry. I didn't mean to—"

"It's okay," he repeated, extending an arm toward her.

She crossed the room and stood beside him, in the shelter of his arm.

"Katie, you remember Homer Grimes, don't you?"

"Yes, I do. How are you, Mr. Grimes?" She cringed as the polite but completely inappropriate response came out of her mouth.

"And Seth Flanders." Papa indicated the man seated two stools away from Homer.

"Hello, Mr. Flanders," she said.

"And all of you know my deputy, Luke Rodgers."

Good grief! Papa was acting as if this was an afternoon social.

"All right, now that everybody's good friends," he said, his voice still leisurely though Kate could hear the underlying steel, "I want to know just what the hell is going on between you two. And don't lie to me because I already know more than you think I do."

"Then you know more than me." Seth crossed his arms, his jaw set stubbornly. "This old coot used to be my best friend, and one day he turned into my worst enemy. Wouldn't talk to me, snarled at me every time he saw me and now he's done tried to kill me!"

"If I'd been trying, you'd be dead now!" Homer snapped.

"Why, you haven't been able to hit the side of a barn with that gun in twenty years now, not since your rheumatiz got so bad."

Kate jumped as Papa slammed Homer's gun onto the bar. "That's enough! I said I want to know how this feud started. I don't want to hear it going on and on. Homer? What happened to turn you against Seth?"

Homer thrust out his chin. Even in the dim light, Kate could tell he needed a shave.

Papa turned slowly on his bar stool, picked up his coffee and sipped then set it back down and shook his head. "You two have pushed me past my limits. Luke," he said quietly, "take out your gun and blow this old fool's head off. He's getting on my nerves."

Kate gasped.

Luke's hand dropped to his gun, but he didn't take it out.

"You can't do that!" Homer protested, his eyes wide. Apparently he wasn't one hundred percent sure Papa couldn't do that.

"You thought it was all right a few minutes ago for

you to blow Seth's head off because he got on your nerves. What's the difference?"

"I didn't do nothing to you, Sheriff! Seth Flanders stole my woman!"

Kate hadn't been aware of any background noises in the bar before, but she was certainly aware of the silence now. As if her senses had all become acute in the absence of sound, the scents of beer and stale cigarette smoke seemed suddenly overpowering in their intensity...and woven in and out like a delicate thread in an intricate tapestry was the scent of lilacs.

"You never had no woman to steal!" Seth protested.

Homer spun around on the stool to face Seth. "And you know why? Because you stole her! I loved Glenda from the first minute I saw that trim little filly."

"What? You never told me you had any interest in Glenda!"

"I don't have to tell you everything! I had a helluva lot more'n an interest. I was plumb crazy about her. Then just when I was fixing to make my move, you up and married her!" Homer reached for his beer glass, ignoring the cup of coffee, and gulped the last few drops.

"Well, if that ain't the craziest thing I've ever heard in all my life!"

Homer turned back to him. "Sure, go ahead and make fun of me."

"I ain't making fun of you. I'm just saying it's crazy to get mad at me for stealing a woman you never had."

"I might'a had her if you hadn't jumped up and swept her right off her feet. I never stood a chance. You was a good-looking devil in them days. You're an ugly old coot now. Time's made us even."

Seth shook his head in disbelief. "I can't hardly believe you've been mad at me all this time when you know that woman run off and left me back in 1966 for

some salesman in a convertible coming through here on
his way to California! You ought to be glad you didn't get
her!"

"But you had her for close to two years," Homer said,
his gravelly voice so soft Kate had to strain to hear.

"Yeah," Seth admitted, "I reckon I did. Them was
good years."

"You see? That's better than never having nothing,
and that's what I got. A big, fat nothing."

"You had me as a friend till you run me off!"

The men sat quietly for a moment.

Kate looked at her father, but he shook his head and
lifted a finger toward his lips as if to tell her not to say
anything.

Finally Seth spoke again. "I painted that face on your
barn, but I never did any of that other stuff. I wouldn't ruin
your crops or cut your fences or even burn down that
worthless old barn."

Homer sighed. "I know you didn't. It was me. I did it.
When you put that face on my barn, it give me an idea
how I could punish you and get you put in jail."

Kate looked from Papa back to Luke. Only she and
Seth seemed surprised at this confession.

"I reckon I'm the one that ought to be shooting you."
Seth's tone was blustery, but Kate detected no real anger.

"Go ahead," Homer said. "You already killed me
once when you stole Glenda."

"If I stole her, and, mind you, I ain't admitting I did
'cause you didn't have her for me to steal from you, but if I
did, and you tried to get me thrown in jail and blackened
my name around town, then it seems to me we're even."

"Could be. Fay, bring us some more beers. We don't
need this muddy water you call coffee."

Fay looked to Sheriff who nodded.

She drew two beers and set them in front of Seth and

239

Homer. Both men lifted them and drank deeply.

Homer wiped his mouth on the sleeve of his denim shirt. "She a good cook?"

Seth moved a couple of barstools closer, only one away from Homer, and shook his head. "Nope. Couldn't boil water without it sticking to the pan."

Homer made the final move to sit next to Seth. "I was sorry to hear about your Ma dying."

"That's been twenty years ago."

"Yeah."

Papa eased off his stool, and he, Luke and Kate left the bar.

The bright sunlight was blinding when they pushed through the door to the outside world. Kate took a deep breath replacing the barroom smells with the scents of sunshine and dust...and lilacs? She must have the scent on her clothes from Papa's house. It couldn't be everywhere.

This time of the year, it shouldn't be anywhere.

"How did you know, Sheriff?" Luke asked.

"I wasn't sure. I was guessing. But it was the only thing that made any sense. If Homer had resented Glenda coming between them, he'd have been happy when she left. Seth even tried to mend fences, but Homer just got meaner."

"He resented the fact that Seth had the woman for two years, even though she left him, while he never had her at all." Luke shook his head. "I guess it's the old, *Better to have loved and lost than never to have loved at all*."

And why, Kate thought, had Papa wanted her to be there to hear?

So you could see the parallel between Seth and Homer with Luke and you. So you'd know that some people who've never had such great love in their lives would be jealous that you had your mother and a

240

wonderful friend all those years even though you lost them both for a little while.

So you'd know you should trust your heart the way you used to...the way you want to now.

The voice was so strong this time, Kate turned and looked behind her, half expecting to see someone there.

Half expecting to see Mama there.

Oh, boy! She was losing it for sure!

"Katie?"

"What?" She whirled at the sound of Luke's voice. Papa and Luke were looking at her strangely.

"Let's go. Jeff and Mom are waiting for us up the street."

"Okay." *No.* "No."

"*Okay, no*?" Luke repeated. "Is this multiple choice?"

Kate could feel the perspiration breaking out on her forehead. Well, it was a hot day.

But that wasn't it. This heat came from inside, from fear and confusion and the struggle to figure out what was going on in her own mind. "I've got to check on something."

"What?"

"I don't know." She spun away and ran the four blocks to where she'd parked her car.

Without a clue as to where she was going or why, but with an irresistible urge to be there, she got in her car and drove.

And wound up at the cave.

Chapter Twenty-One

Kate's palms were damp on the steering wheel as she sat looking out the windshield and wondering what on earth she was doing there.

You think your friendship thorn has disintegrated? Then go find out.

Kate's head swung toward the passenger seat. The voice was so strong it was almost audible.

For a moment, from the corner of her eye just as she turned, she thought she saw the outline of someone in the seat beside her. But it was only the sunlight glaring off the hood of her car. That's all it could have been.

She was stressed and tense and hot and carrying on conversations with herself, but she was *not* seeing ghosts.

She got out of the car and walked down the slope, taking the circuitous route to the cave where she and Luke had played and pledged their friendship a lifetime ago. Tufts of grass and weeds impeded her progress in her sandals, and her steps disturbed a few loose rocks that tumbled down to splash in the creek.

She was nuts to be doing this. What possible purpose could it serve? She was *not* going to dig in the dirt and try to find that silly thorn they'd buried no matter what some psychotic voice in her head told her to do.

The cave was just as she remembered it. When she stepped inside, the temperature immediately dropped as it always had when she and Luke had played there. Once when they'd heard about the concept of *earth homes,* she and Luke had proudly informed Papa that they already had an earth home.

Just as the temperature was cooler inside, so the outside sounds were muffled. The chirrup of a cicada seemed to come from far away. The whole world seemed far away.

For a moment, time itself seemed unstable, seemed to be slip backward as she smelled the damp earth and stones, a scent that seemed somehow to be laced with lilacs.

Kate frowned. She'd forgotten how the scent of lilacs had permeated everything even when she was a child. It had to be coming from her. Her clothing, her hair, her nostrils had to be carrying the scent from home. That was the only explanation of why a cave would smell like spring flowers.

She sat on one of the big rocks along the side, rested her elbows on her knees and her chin on her fists. The place had always had an eerie quality, had always inspired Luke and her to make up fanciful stories. Like the one about having a friendship that would never die.

Was Jeff's story about the Indian princess and her lover true? Probably not. But inside the cave, Kate could almost believe it.

Right in the middle of the dirt floor was the spot where she and Luke had buried their thorn. For a long time after Luke left, there had been a slight mound marking the spot.

But no more. The floor was uniformly flat. All evidence of that young boy and girl was gone.

She reached down and picked up an arrowhead, turned it over and studied it. Was this one of the arrowheads she and Luke had used to dig their hole?

Not likely. She laid it back down and stood.

What the heck was she doing there, anyway? She should get back to town before Papa, Francine, Jeff and Luke thought she'd lost her mind completely. Besides, she was being rude. This was the last day she'd have to visit with Francine and Jeff. Spending that day in a cave by herself was dumb.

She took a step toward the entrance, stopped, picked

up the arrowhead and started to dig in the middle of the floor.

Okay, she'd dig around a bit, but if she didn't find that old aspirin box really soon, she'd leave and go back to the real world.

She struck a hard object and, against her will, her heart rate accelerated, anticipating. She scraped away the dirt and found that it was only a rock.

What had she expected? That plastic aspirin box had probably splintered into a hundred pieces. She'd be lucky to find one splinter, especially since she had no idea if she was even digging in the right place.

Better to stop wasting her time and leave.

She kept digging as if her will was no longer her own.

Again she struck something solid. Again she scraped away the dirt, expecting to find another rock.

Instead she saw one end of the yellow and white aspirin box.

She sat for several moments staring at the faded plastic. Emotions...too many of them to identify...welled up inside. She shoved them down determinedly even as she ordered herself to get up, walk out of that cave and stop acting like an idiot.

Dizziness washed over her as she reached down to try to get the box out, and she realized she'd forgotten to breathe.

Using her arrowhead to pry up the other end, Kate extracted the small, rectangular item, stood and set it in her palm. It lay there, cool to the touch, dirty, faded...nothing special, nothing magic.

Wasn't that what she'd expected? No magic?

So why was she disappointed?

The sound of footsteps crunching outside, sending more rocks tumbling down the slope, drew her attention to

244

the mouth of the cave.

Luke walked in carrying a blanket draped over one arm. He had to stoop slightly. He was now too tall to stand upright very far back in their cave. Nothing was the same.

"I thought I'd find you here," he said.

"Why would you think that? I'm not even certain how I got here."

"It's where you always used to go when you were upset. I'm not sure what happened in that bar to upset you, but I could tell it did. What have you got there?" He peered more closely at her hand. "Oh, my God." His voice became hushed and reverential. Good grief. It was only an old plastic box. "Have you opened it yet?"

"No." To her dismay, her voice sounded the same as his.

He laid the blanket on the floor and motioned for her to sit. She did, and he sank down beside her.

"Open it," he said quietly.

She shook her head in slow motion, her gaze fixed on that absurd little box. Why couldn't she just open it and get this over with?

Because she didn't want to see tangible proof of the deterioration of her relationship with Luke, of the inevitable deterioration of all relationships.

Love never deteriorates. You never really lost Luke or me. We're right here and we love you. All you have to do is open your heart so you can see that love.

Kate's head snapped up. It was one thing to hold nonverbal conversations with herself, but to reassure herself that she loved herself was going one step too far.

"Katie?" Luke's audible voice drew her back to reality.

She looked down at the white and yellow plastic in her palm. With a swift motion, she grasped the end with her other hand and yanked it open.

245

The lid crumbled as it moved.

The thorn lay in the bottom of the box, intact.

She shrugged. "With the plastic and the dirt around it, it was sealed. That's why it didn't deteriorate."

"No, that's not why." In the dimness of the cave, Luke's eyes were dark and vast as the night sky.

"What? You think it's magic or something?" She tried to sound jaded and realistic, but even to her own ears, her words came out breathless.

"I don't think that thorn is magic. I do think what we have is magic."

Kate knew him so well, she knew what he was thinking, what he was going to say, and she didn't want to hear it, didn't want to go there. Nevertheless, she couldn't take her eyes from his, couldn't protest, could only wait.

He took the box with the thorn from her and set it on a rock beside them then lifted one hand to cup her cheek, her chin in his palm. "Are you going to marry Spencer?"

"No." The answer was out of her mouth before she could think about the question. When had she made that decision? When she'd danced with Luke on the lawn? When Spencer had called Thursday night? When Luke had kissed her at her condo? She wasn't sure, but she was sure she couldn't marry him. Too much had changed. She'd changed too much.

The corners of Luke's mouth turned up in the familiar smile she knew so well and didn't know at all. This smile was lazy yet alert, the smile of a man alone with a woman he desired and suddenly sure he was going to possess that woman. "I've loved you since we wore matching diapers. You know that, don't you?"

She'd known he was going to say those words.

"As a friend." She whispered the words, knowing that wasn't what he meant but needing him to contradict her.

He lifted his other hand to her other cheek and gazed

directly into her eyes. "Yes. As a friend. And more. I've been kidding myself, trying to believe we could just be friends. I was—I *am* so afraid if we cross the line and become lovers, I'll lose you. But hearing those crazy old men in the bar made me realize something. I have to take the chance. I don't want to end up eighty years old and thinking about all the might-have-beens."

He touched her lips with his, tenderly, the way best friends would kiss, then drew back and looked at her. As if he could tell...and he probably could; he'd always been able to read her mind...as if he could tell the way his touch thrilled her, sent her blood rushing and her heart pounding, his hands slipped to her waist and he pulled her to him and kissed her again. This time his lips on hers demanded far more than friendship. This was the way he'd kissed her in her condo and on the lawn, the way lovers kissed.

She responded, her arms reaching around him, pulling him closer against her, pressing her body to his, her breasts to his hard chest, her thighs to his, her heart to his.

This was crazy, completely insane, but incredibly right and wonderful.

She wasn't going to marry Spencer. She knew that for a certainty. She was free to kiss Luke, even to have an affair with him if she chose. She could satisfy these wild cravings, get them out of her system, give her body to Luke but keep her heart separate and safe. Once satisfied, maybe she'd be able to go on, free of this all-consuming passion for him.

She had a vague notion she was lying to herself, trying to justify her desires, but it didn't matter. The only thing that mattered right now was kissing Luke.

His lips on hers were familiar and new, bringing poignant memories and promises of unexplored, undreamed of delights. His arms around her were strong, the arms of a man, yet with the tenderness of the boy she'd once known.

Gently he eased her back on the blanket, his lips trailing kisses along her throat, his tongue teasing the sensitive hollow. The sound of his breathing in the quiet of the cave seemed an echo of her own.

His fingers fumbled with the buttons of her blouse, and she felt a rush of cool air on her stomach followed by Luke's warm breath as he kissed the tender flesh.

Her body was exposed to him. She ought to feel vulnerable, embarrassed, something besides comfortable and right, as if the world had shifted into place. The man bending over her was the same person she'd known all her life, and he was somebody entirely new and different.

He unfastened the front hook of her bra and pushed it aside, and even that felt as natural as breathing, as natural as his mouth on her breasts. Her back arched upward, pushing her bare breasts toward him, yearning for more of his touch, but he stopped, lifted his head and looked at her.

"Katie, I don't want us to do anything you're going to regret," he said, his voice husky with desire, his eyes narrow, smoky slits of passion. "You say the word and we stop right here."

She was barely coherent enough to wonder if she would regret this, if she really could keep her heart separate from her body. She wasn't coherent enough to know the answer, though. Her mind and body were consumed with the need for Luke's touch, his skin against hers, this bonding that was so long overdue. She couldn't say *no*, not even if she knew this would ultimately end in pain and loss. A part of her had been missing for a very long time, and having it back felt so good and so right.

For answer, she unbuttoned his shirt and ran her fingers through the mat of coarse hair then pulled him to her for a deep, sensuous kiss, her breasts pressed against his naked chest, their hearts pounding against each other in perfect rhythm, just as they must have been beating in rhythm all these years even while they were apart.

When he slid down again, his hands cupped her breasts and his lips closed around one nipple, sucking and teasing, sending jolts of electricity spiraling through her body, taking her to a place she'd never been before, increasing her urgent need for him until it was completely out of control. She moaned at the exquisite pleasure as his mouth moved to the other nipple.

With one hand, he found the button on her shorts, and she reached to help him, to rid herself of the barrier between their bodies. There had never been barriers between Luke and her. There should be none now.

He tugged down her shorts as she lifted her bottom to help him, then he yanked off his own clothes, and finally their bodies were together, skin to skin, nothing between them. With his hands and his mouth, he explored every inch of her, and she did the same to him.

"This scar—" His fingers on her thigh, tantalizingly close to her center, stopped their explorations and traced the scar she'd almost forgotten. "It's from the time we were stealing peaches from Leonard Goggans' tree and he caught us. You slipped and fell and caught your leg on a broken branch." He stroked the scar again, his fingers reaching higher. "I don't know who was more scared, you, me or Leonard Goggans." He kissed the scar, his lips and tongue stirring sensations she hadn't known—wouldn't have believed—existed.

On his body she found the old scars from bicycle wrecks and falls along with the new ones from football injuries and an appendectomy. Each one she kissed and recalled or learned about.

Finally when they had each covered every inch of the

other's body, he knelt between her legs, his hardness centered and pressing against her, then stopped again.

"Katie, are you sure?"

She groaned. "I'm sure. I want you. I love you." She bit her lip. She hadn't meant to say she loved him. She didn't. She only wanted him.

But as his flesh slid into hers and their bodies were joined in the ultimate union, she knew she'd been lying to herself. She did love him. With all her heart and her soul and her body. Later, she'd have to deal with that revelation, but right now her entire consciousness was filled with the sensation of Luke's hardness moving inside her.

"I love you, too, Katie," he whispered against her ear. "I've always loved you and I always will."

Together, the way they were meant to be, their bodies surged upward, spiraling to new heights, the sensation obliterating all thought until they reached the crescendo, peaking at the same moment...together.

***

For a few minutes or an hour...time had lost meaning and consistency...Kate lay cradled in Luke's arms, savoring the afterglow of their love making.

But slowly reality crept over her with a cold, déjà vu quality.

It wasn't quite the same as before, of course. She and Luke had certainly not made love before he moved away seventeen years ago. But they had sat in this same cave, holding each other and promising always to be friends.

The terror rose in her throat, threatening to choke her if she didn't get away from it.

What had she been thinking, opening herself up like that, letting him get close to her...again?

She hadn't been thinking, of course. That was the whole problem. She'd been *feeling*. That always caused problems.

Again today Luke had promised *always. I've always loved you and I always will.*

She couldn't plead youth and innocence this time. This time she'd gone in with her eyes wide open, completely aware of the situation. She'd thought she had herself under control, her life well-ordered. She'd thought she could give her body and withhold her heart.

Telling Luke she loved him was not part of that order.

Neither was realizing the words were true.

After all this time, how was it possible she hadn't learned to keep her heart safe? She'd been so pleased with the relationship she and Spencer had...safe, uninvolved. Yet she had thrown all that aside for a moment of wild passion and unbounded emotion with Luke, the man who'd taught her the foolishness of loving with her whole heart.

Sure, Luke had said he loved her, just the way he'd once said he'd always be her friend, always be there for her. His relationship with Cindy hadn't lasted, either. That alone should have been enough warning to keep her from getting emotionally entangled with him again.

Except she wasn't sure there was any *again* to it. Just as Luke had said about his love, her love had been there all along, even while they were apart, changing and evolving as they changed and evolved, shoved aside by both of them for different reasons, but remaining forever a part of them.

She sat up, her head spinning with the shock of that realization.

He touched her bare back, his fingers trailing a path along her spine, and even now her eyes closed as she sighed with the pleasure of that touch.

"I meant it, Katie," he said softly. "I love you."

251

She closed her ears to his words, stood and began retrieving her clothes. Funny how tossing them aside in the heat of passion had felt so warm and alive, and now gathering them up afterward felt empty and exposed. "We'd better go back. It's getting late. Everyone's going to wonder where we are."

"I told them I was coming here and expected to find you. Sit down and let's talk."

She avoided his gaze as she dressed. "I need to get back. I have a lot to do tonight." She needed to return to Dallas, to her well-ordered, safe life, away from Luke and Briar Creek and all the memories she couldn't deal with.

He caught her shoulders and spun her around to face him. "Look at me, Katie. Look at me and talk to me. Something just happened between us, something important. You can't run away and ignore it."

She looked past him, over his shoulder, into the dark, hidden depths of the cave, anywhere but into his eyes. She wasn't sure what she'd see there or whether she was ready for it...whatever it was.

"What happened between us shouldn't have," she said. She shouldn't have let her emotions spill out, shouldn't have let Luke inside her heart again.

All the pain she'd shoved down so many years ago resurfaced, and suddenly she wanted to hit him, to punish him, make him feel what he'd made her feel.

"I'm still officially engaged to Spencer." She said it to make her position clear even though she wasn't engaged in her heart, even though Luke had made that sensible, nonthreatening marriage impossible. She couldn't stand before God and Sheriff and promise to love, honor and cherish one man when she loved another

He dropped his arms. "You said you weren't going to marry him." His voice had hardened, become that of a stranger. Luke had gone away. Again.

252

That made it easier for her to button her blouse with trembling fingers and leave.

At least, it should have made it easier.

***

Luke sat on the blanket and watched Katie leave, restraining himself from going after her. For a few minutes there, their souls had touched again, they'd found the closeness they once shared with the added depths that came from being adults.

At least, he'd thought they had. But then she became more distant than ever. Before they'd made love, she'd said she wasn't going to marry Spencer, but afterward she'd thrown her engagement in his face.

He rose, gathered up his clothes and yanked them on, cursing himself for seven kinds of an idiot. Okay, so he'd wanted her and she'd wanted him. He could have—should have—controlled himself. But the Katie he knew would never give herself to any man she didn't care for. She'd said she loved him, and he'd thought after making love, after their bodies and hearts were joined, the distance of years and heartaches would be closed.

But it hadn't happened that way. The distance had grown. She'd left without a backward glance, the way he'd always feared.

He'd wanted more than friendship, just as he had with Cindy, and, once again, he'd ended up with nothing.

Only losing Cindy hadn't hurt anything like this. When he'd lost her, he'd lost his wife, the woman who shared his bed and his home.

When Katie walked away, he'd lost half of himself. This journey back to Briar Creek, back to his past, was supposed to be healing, but instead he suddenly felt the way he had when his father's death was new and he'd been forced to leave Briar Creek and Katie...empty and alone.

He stooped and picked up the box that held their

253

intact thorn.

Damn it! He should have kept his libido under control, should have settled for having her friendship. They had come around to that, resumed the closeness they'd once shared.

What a crock! The feeling between Katie and him had been more than friendship from the first time she'd walked into his office on Friday. Hell, it had been more for as long as he could remember. Just because sex hadn't been a factor in the equation when they were young didn't mean love hadn't been there.

Sure she'd been his friend, but more than that. She'd been his partner, his soul mate.

He took the old thorn from the box and started to toss it away. Fat lot of good it had done.

But he couldn't do it. Instead, he put the thorn in his shirt pocket and left the cave. At the entrance, he stopped and looked back to the dark depths that stretched toward the rear, to the place he and Katie had once discovered ended not in a rainbow or golden treasure but simply with the roof and floor meeting. That was just the way he felt right now, only Katie wasn't with him to share the blackness.

Chapter Twenty-Two

The bright sunlight was muted by the approach of evening as Kate drove home. Maybe that was why the silver Mercedes parked in front of her father's house glared with an intensity that hurt her eyes.

Surely that wasn't Spencer's car. He wasn't supposed to be here!

She pulled in behind him and recognized the license plates. It was Spencer.

Damn! What was he doing here? She'd hoped to have at least the night and the drive home tomorrow to get her feelings for Luke sorted out and back in proper order, then decide what to tell Spencer...or at least *how* to tell him. Especially after what had just happened, there was no doubt about *what* she had to tell him.

Her first impulse was to keep driving, go right past Spencer's car, run back to Dallas, to the mature, satisfactory life she'd built there.

But Spencer was a part of that life. She had to face him.

And then you're going to have to face your feelings for Luke.

No!

She pushed that annoying little voice down, shoved it into a compartment along with her feelings for Luke, shut it away in the dark.

She got out and strode resolutely along the walk, across the porch and into the house.

Spencer, looking as tense as she'd ever seen him, shot up from the sofa. He was immaculate as always, every blond hair in place, the crease in his khaki slacks razor sharp, but something in his expression or his demeanor made him appear rumpled.

The old photo album was open on the coffee table.

Great! Papa had been showing Spencer her baby pictures!

Papa, lounging comfortably in his recliner, smiled. "Katie-girl! I'm glad you're home. Spencer's been waiting for you. Your mother and I were starting to get worried."

Your mother and I? Baby pictures and Mama. No wonder Spencer looked tense and rumpled.

Leo curled beside the empty arm chair, and a glass of tea sat on the lamp table next to it. Well, hadn't she known it would come to this eventually? Mama had finally joined them for tea.

Spencer moved toward her. "Kate, we need to talk." He took her arm to guide her out the door. She started to resist, just on general principles, but he was right. They did need to talk.

"We'll be back in a minute, Papa."

"Don't hurry. I'll go get us some more tea."

As she started out the door with Spencer, she heard Papa say, "Emma, let me get you a fresh glass, too. The ice has melted, and I know you don't like your tea when it gets all watery like that."

Spencer gave her a significant glance then hurried her on outside. He stopped once they were on the porch, but she urged him on.

"Let's sit in your car." Only the screen door separated her from Papa who would soon be returning with fresh tea for everybody, Mama included, and she had a feeling her conversation with Spencer wasn't going to be anything she wanted Papa to hear.

When they reached Spencer's car, Kate felt an odd reluctance to get inside, to leave the beautiful summer evening.

Or maybe she just dreaded talking to Spencer.

She forced herself to slide onto the leather seat and allow him to close the heavy door behind her. Thus trapped, she gazed out the windshield, suddenly wishing with all her might that she was out there instead.

He got in the other side and started the engine.

"I don't want to go anywhere," she protested.

"I understand. But we need some air conditioning. How do you manage to breathe in that hot house, especially with that lilac room deodorant?"

"Actually, I rather enjoy the scent." Room deodorant. Of course. That explained the fragrance.

"Kate, I realized when you first started talking about coming down here that something wasn't right. You seemed distressed, but it was none of my business, and I didn't want to interfere. Now I understand. You should have told me about your father. Surely you weren't worried I wouldn't want to marry you just because your father has mental problems."

"No, of course not. Well, maybe." Actually, she realized, that had played a part in her keeping Papa's secret from Spencer. In some dark spot of her mind, she had feared that her fiancé, always so perfect, wouldn't want to be associated with her if he knew her father consorted with her mother's ghost.

"It's not like we plan to have children who might inherit your father's defective gene," Spencer reassured her.

She looked at him, at his handsome, regular features, into his blue eyes that had always seemed calm and stable but now seemed a reflection of the artificially cooled air coming from the vents of his car.

"Papa's defective gene?" she repeated slowly. "There's nothing defective about my father."

Spencer smiled, and again she saw him in a different light. What had always appeared to be a confident smile now seemed smug. "Nothing except he thinks your mother's still alive."

"Okay, he's got one little glitch. That doesn't make

him detective. He's the most wonderful man on earth. Seeing Mama makes him happy. It doesn't hurt anything."

"Of course it doesn't. But we have to face reality. It doesn't look so good. After we get married, we'll find a nice home for your father."

"I've already talked to him about moving to Dallas. He doesn't want to. He wants to stay right here."

"Then we'll find a home for him here, get him the best of care. With counseling and drugs, he should be able to live out his remaining years quite comfortably."

It suddenly dawned on Kate what Spencer was suggesting. The *home* of which he spoke wasn't going to be a new house. "You want to have my father committed to some institution and drug him up until he can't see Mama anymore? Absolutely not! That would break his heart!"

An image flashed through her mind, the scene from the movie, *Harvey,* when Elwood P. Dowd, to please his sister, was waiting patiently for the doctor to give him the shot that would take Harvey away forever. She suspected Papa would do that if she insisted, give up his ghostly wife.

She wasn't going to insist.

She also recalled that the movie had left the viewer with a question as to whether Harvey might actually be real.

Of course, that was only a movie.

Spencer's forehead wrinkled in a scowl. "Are you saying you'd rather your father be mentally ill than get help? That's totally illogical."

"We're not talking logic! We're talking about a human being!"

"Kate, listen to yourself. You're not making any sense. You've always functioned on pure logic."

Ironic, she thought, that she had always prided

herself on being motivated by logic and reason rather than unstable emotions. Lately she'd forsaken that logic and seemed to be operating purely on emotions...with mixed results. Her encounter with Luke hadn't been the wisest choice, but she had to follow her heart where Papa was concerned.

"My father isn't hurting himself or anybody else with his harmless hallucinations."

"Not hurting—Kate! Good God, your father's the sheriff! He carries a gun! You can't have a man who talks to his dead wife running around with a gun!"

Kate's temper blazed even though Spencer was saying exactly what she'd thought at one time. But Spencer had no right to say those things about her father.

"I could defend Papa to you and tell you he's just as competent as he ever was and I know that because I've seen him in action, but I'm not going to because that's really none of your business. He's my father, he's the sheriff of Briar Creek County, and he's absolutely nothing to you, so you just stay out of it!"

"Kate, what's the matter with you? First you send me that crazy email, and now you—"

"What email? I didn't send you any email."

Spencer gave her a strange look, as if he thought she might be in need of some kind of drugs herself, as if perhaps she had inherited her father's *defective gene.*

He reached into the back seat and brought up his briefcase, opened it and withdrew a piece of paper. "I printed out a hard copy."

Kate took the sheet of paper and scanned the printed message. It appeared to have come from the Sheriff's Department of Briar Creek, from Papa's email address.

As she studied the paper, she recalled that Luke had sworn he had not sent a message to Jeff, but that message had supposedly originated at his terminal, and now a message had come from Papa's terminal under her name.

What the heck was going on?

She looked at the body of the note.

My dear Spencer—

"My dear Spencer? You think I'd start a letter like that?"

"I admit, it didn't sound like you, nor does the rest of it. However, you've not been acting like yourself recently."

She couldn't argue with that assessment.

She read the rest of the note.

I don't know if I can marry you. I'm very confused. I don't know what I'm saying or doing right now. I don't know what love is. I thought I had everything all figured out, but I don't know anymore. Please come to Briar Creek immediately.

Kate stared uncomprehendingly at the piece of paper in her hand then read the words again to be sure she'd read them right. Except for that last sentence, it was, almost verbatim, what she'd said to Luke the night they'd danced on Papa's lawn.

Had Luke sent the message to Spencer in a misguided effort to help her tell him the engagement was off? If he had, why would he add the last part, asking Spencer to come to Briar Creek? And where did he find Spencer's email address? Since it was through the company, even if Luke had been proficient at using the internet—and Kate was positive he hadn't lied about his lack of ability there—it would have been extremely difficult, if not impossible, to find Spencer's address.

Luke had accused her of sending the message to Jeff asking him and Francine to come to visit, and she knew she hadn't done that. They had decided the only person it could have been was Papa even though she hadn't been able to figure out how he could have. Jeff, being on the faculty of a college, would have an email address that was a little easier to find, but still Papa would have to know more about the internet than he did.

"Kate?"

She dropped the paper as if it had suddenly burned her fingers. "What?"

Spencer retrieved the message from the seat between them and stuck it back into his briefcase in the exact space from which he'd withdrawn it.

"Is it true?" he asked. "Do you want to call off the wedding?"

The automobile's engine purred softly while refrigerated air blew from the vents. If they were sitting on the porch, they'd be able to hear the sounds of nature—insects and birds and the wind in the leaves.

Kate no longer had any idea of what was right, but she did know this was all wrong.

"Yes, it's true. I didn't send that note. I was going to talk to you when I got back to Dallas, but it is true that I don't think we should get married."

Spencer compressed his lips and frowned. "Kate, do you realize how inconvenient this is going to be?"

"Inconvenient?" She hadn't expected Spencer to make an impassioned plea for her to change her mind. He wasn't an impassioned kind of guy. But...*inconvenient?*

"The plans we've made. Everything will have to be rearranged."

"We didn't make plans of any great consequence. This whole wedding thing was geared to disrupt and change our lives as little as possible. From the beginning it's been—" She swallowed hard and forced herself to admit it. "Nothing of any consequence."

"We both agreed it would be convenient to be married."

"I know we did, but one of us disagrees now."

"Why?"

Kate spread her hands. "Spencer, we don't love each other."

"Kate, I seem to recall that was one of the things you said we had in our favor, that we wouldn't get involved in all that messy emotional nonsense and cause ourselves a lot of problems."

"You're right. I said that. It seemed like a good idea at the time."

"So now you want all that messy emotional nonsense? Is that it?"

"No, I don't want it." But she had it, whether she wanted it or not, and now she had to decide what to do with it. "I just don't want us to be married."

"Kate, you're really not acting like yourself. I think this trip down here and having to deal with your crazy father has got you so stressed, you don't know what you're saying."

"My father is not crazy!" She wanted to slap Spencer, but at least his rude comment gave her something concrete to use against him. "That's it! No way would I ever marry somebody who has no respect for my father!"

She shoved open the car door, slid out and tried to slam it. The door was too heavy, the automobile too well sealed for any real effect. It closed quietly.

She whirled to leave, but Spencer's voice stopped her. She turned back to see that he'd rolled down the electric window. "Will you be back in time to go to that dinner with me tomorrow night?"

She hesitated on the brink of saying *yes,* of being cordial and accommodating and not disrupting Spencer's carefully structured life any more than she had already.

But he'd called her father crazy, said he had a defective gene.

"No. I'm sorry, Spencer. You'll have to find

somebody else to go with you to the dinner and to the wedding. It shouldn't be too difficult to plug another woman into my slot since being there is pretty much the only requirement."

"Fine. If that's what you want."

The window slid silently up to close the opening between them.

As Spencer drove away, she noticed he was already on his cell phone. He'd have someone for Sunday night before he got back to Dallas.

As far as her own life, well, that wasn't going to be quite so easy to fix.

She took mental inventory as she made her way back up the cracked walk to Papa's house.

In spite of knowing the consequences, she'd fallen in love with Luke all over again. That was a big, huge mess in the midst of her carefully-ordered life. If she let it, that could change everything. She could once again find herself drowning in a sea of emotions, terrified of being hurt or abandoned.

If they hadn't made love, she might have been able to continue to believe she didn't love him, but they had, and her defenses had come tumbling down.

She paused with one hand on the screen door as a chill went down her spine.

They had made love, and they hadn't used any protection. Luke had probably assumed if she was engaged, she was on the pill. He probably assumed she and Spencer were having sex! As if she'd let anyone get that close to her.

Anyone but Luke.

Or maybe he had been as swept away by their passion as she had been, and hadn't thought anything at all.

In any event, she could be pregnant.

A baby.

Cold terror washed over her in the heat of the summer evening. She couldn't raise a child. She had no idea how to be a mother. She couldn't take care of a helpless child.

Katie—

No! She shoved that annoying voice down again.

"Katie? Why are you standing on the porch with your hand on the door? Come on in. Is your friend gone?"

Kate opened the door and went in, each movement slow and heavy as in a nightmare when a monster pursued her and she couldn't get away.

She wanted to throw herself in Papa's arms, beg him to make everything all right. But even as much as Papa loved her, he couldn't do that. He hadn't been able to take away the hurt when Luke left or when her mother died.

No, that wasn't quite right. After her mother died—

She shook her head, unable to catch the evanescent memory.

After her mother died, Papa had talked about her so much, Kate almost felt as if her mother were still there.

Almost.

She crossed the room stiffly and noticed that instead of more iced tea, Papa had made hot chocolate, just the way he had when she was a little girl and needed comforting.

"So that's Spencer," he said, handing her a mug.

She sat on the sofa and sipped. Rich. Papa always used whole milk.

"Spencer's actually a very nice person," she replied. "He's just not very...emotional." And he'd called Papa crazy. "Or nice. He's not a very nice person. I was mistaken."

"I'm afraid I have to agree with your mother, Katie. He's definitely not the right one for you."

Kate considered correcting him about her mother, then

decided against it.

"At any rate," he continued, "I'm glad you're not going to marry him."

Kate nodded and lifted her cup to her lips for another drink of cocoa when it occurred to her that she'd told Spencer she wasn't going to marry him while sitting inside his well-insulated car. She hadn't mentioned it to Papa yet. She lowered the cup and looked at him.

"How did you know I'd called off the engagement?" His hearing couldn't possibly be that good.

"Your mother told me."

Oh, well, sure, why hadn't she thought of that? Ghosts probably had supernatural hearing abilities.

"After tonight, I can't believe I ever considered marrying him."

"In the setting of a big city and big business, he probably came across real different than he did down here."

"Yes, he certainly did."

"When you get married, your mother and I want you to have the kind of love we have. We don't want you to settle for anything less. Your mother knew from the beginning what a big mistake Spencer would have been. We want you to love somebody so much he's like a part of you, so much you can't remember what your life was like before that person came or what it would be like if he left."

Papa was describing the way she felt about Luke. But he didn't understand how painful that sort of love could be.

"Guess you've loved Luke since you were just little tykes," he said, evidently thinking she wasn't getting the point quickly enough.

"The love that children have for each other is a different kind of love," she protested.

"Love is love. You can add other elements to it, like sex, but the love part is pretty basic."

She could feel her face grow hot. "Papa! Are you

suggesting that Luke and I—"

He shrugged. "None of my business. You're both adults. You're young and healthy and you did spend the night together in Dallas."

"You set me up, didn't you? You didn't need those papers from the Dallas courthouse."

He focused his gaze on his cup of hot chocolate. "Of course I needed them. I wanted to find out the exact dates of Seth Flanders' marriage and divorce. Okay, maybe you could have got them the night before, but your mother thought if the two of you had a little time alone together—" He looked up at her, shrugged and smiled.

She ought to be angry. This whole situation with Luke was Papa's fault. But she loved him too much...and she knew he'd done it all out of love for her. On the positive side, it had saved her from marrying Spencer.

Which reminded her of the reason Spencer had come to Briar Creek.

"Did you send that email to Spencer asking him to come down here so I'd see what a jerk he can be?"

"Oh, Katie-girl, you know I don't know anything about that email stuff."

"You didn't send it?" Luke was the only other possibility.

"Of course I didn't. Your mother did."

Kate set her empty cup on the coffee table and went to kneel beside Papa's chair. "Mama didn't send that note," she said softly. "Mama's dead."

"I guess it depends on how you define dead. She isn't quite like she used to be, but she doesn't like to hear that."

Well, she supposed it was better than an outright denial.

"Mama didn't send the email. She didn't encourage you to play matchmaker between Luke and me. She died in the car wreck twenty-six years ago."

He nodded. "Twenty-six years. Hard to believe."

But he didn't say he didn't believe it. Encouraged, Kate plunged ahead. "So she can't be talking to you. Can she?"

A soft smile and a dreamy expression settled on his face. "You used to talk to her, too, when you were young, Katie-girl. But then after Luke left, you closed your heart to love, so you couldn't see or hear her anymore. Now your heart's opening up again. Mama said you can hear her again, and sometimes you almost see her."

Your heart's opening up? That was the same language her mother had used in her dream.

"I talked to her memory," Kate replied firmly, reminding herself as well as Papa of the reality. "You told me so much about her, you made her live for me, and that's something I'll always treasure. But, Papa, she isn't really alive. You haven't really been talking to her. It's not possible for someone who dies to return to this world."

"Not without a special dispensation. The good Lord knew I wouldn't be able to raise you alone, so He let her come back just for that purpose."

He even had the details figured out.

"Papa, listen to me. What you're saying is impossible."

"Impossible." He nodded thoughtfully. "On the surface, you'd think it was impossible for an act of love between two people to create life. You wait, sweetheart, until the first time you hold your own baby, and then you tell me if you think anything's impossible when it comes to taking care of your child."

She flinched. Even though she wasn't going to marry Spencer, she still didn't want to have children.

Unless, of course, she had no choice.

She swallowed hard and thrust that idea aside to deal with later.

Papa set his cup on the coffee table and picked up the photo album. He thumbed through, found what he was looking for and laid the album back on the table in front of her. "That's you and your mama when you were just a few weeks old. You were born with a full head of red, curly hair. You were one of those impossible miracles that happened anyway. We'd been married seventeen years when you came along. Your mother cried when you were born. Oh, not from the pain. She went through two days of labor and never complained. But when old Doc Stanton laid you in her arms, her whole face lit up and she cried."

For no discernible reason, Kate could feel the tears forming behind her own eyelids, could feel an old pain trying again to creep up and grip her heart.

She stood. "Papa, I've got to go back to Dallas tonight. Right now."

"Right now?" He looked up in shock. "Why?"

She shook her head. "I just do. I'll call you tomorrow and I'll be back next weekend for my clothes." She leaned over and hugged him, then grabbed her purse and ran out the door, fleeing as if for her life...certainly for her sanity. Surely when she got back to Dallas she'd be able to get her thoughts and her life in order once again.

***

Jerome stood at the door and watched Katie drive away.

"I don't understand, Emma. Everything seemed to be going so good."

"She's frightened, Jerome. I didn't stay to see what happened between Luke and her in the cave. Perhaps I should have, but I didn't want to intrude. Whatever it was, she's terrified, and she's shut me out again. I can't get through to her."

"What are we going to do?"

"I'm not sure. I need to have a chat with Luke and Francine and maybe even Jeff. They're all in pretty receptive moods right now, back in the old house and with

268

lots of love flowing around all of them."

Jerome went back into the house and returned to his recliner. "Come sit in my lap for a little while, Emma. Let me hold you while we talk about what to do with our wayward daughter."

Emma settled on his lap and smiled up at him. "Do you have any idea what the neighbors would think if they should look in the window and see you with your arms wrapped around thin air?"

"No worse than what Spencer thought when he saw you petting Leo."

Emma laughed. "He certainly wasn't worthy of our Katie. You were pretty hard on him, though. You know I can't drink tea anymore."

Jerome chuckled. "He wasn't real sure. He kept looking at that glass. It would've been a hoot if you'd been able to make that tea go down."

He kissed his wife's transparent, tingly cheek. The failure of their plans meant she'd be with him for a while longer, but it was a bittersweet thought. He hated the notion of her leaving, but he couldn't stand for their precious Katie to be unhappy.

Chapter Twenty-Three

Luke pulled up in front of his house and parked.

The first time he'd driven by Sheriff's place, he'd seen Katie sitting beside some slimy jerk with blond hair in a silver Mercedes with the engine running. A quick computer check of the license plate on that car revealed it was registered to Spencer Osborne of Dallas, Texas.

So that was Spencer.

Interesting that Katie hadn't mentioned Spencer was coming to Briar Creek.

Angry at her for deceiving him, at himself for being deceived, and at the whole world in general, Luke had driven by the house again a few minutes later just to check on the situation...and found both cars gone.

That told him all he needed to know, but being a law man, he'd checked his facts anyway. He stopped and knocked, and Sheriff verified that Katie had left for Dallas. She would, he assured Luke, be back next weekend.

Katie was gone. Not just physically, but all the way gone.

He got out of his car and went up to his house.

His car, his house, his job.

So much of the past he'd reclaimed.

But not his friend, his love. Not Katie.

He'd lied to himself about one thing. He hadn't wanted her back just as his friend. He'd wanted all of her. And she hadn't wanted to give any of herself to him.

After today, after her spoken words as well as the way she'd responded to his lovemaking, he didn't doubt that she loved him. But for whatever reason, she didn't want to.

"Luke, what's wrong?" His mother stood holding the screen door open, waiting for him.

He forced a smile. "Nothing's wrong. Why?"

"Don't give me that. I'm your mother. I know when something's wrong."

He shrugged. "Katie's gone back to Dallas. Sheriff begged off for dinner tonight. Said he'd see you and Jeff tomorrow."

"Oh. I rather thought you and Katie were—"

Luke pushed past her. "No. Katie and I aren't."

Jeff looked up from his seat in the recliner where Luke had sat the first night they were there. It was the same spot where Luke's father's old recliner had sat for many years.

Luke knew he was in a black mood, ready to find something or someone to take out his anger and despair on, and for a moment he expected to be angry at Jeff for being where his father wasn't.

But it didn't happen.

He was sorry his father wasn't there, but he was glad Jeff was. He was genuinely glad his mother had someone to make her happy. The fact that *someone* happened to be a friend of his actually made it even better.

Katie was the only part of his past he hadn't been able to come to terms with.

***

Jeff picked up two pieces of luggage and headed downstairs with them. It was Sunday afternoon, and their visit was over.

Luke picked up the remaining bag and started after him.

"Luke, could you come here for just a minute?" his mother, sitting on the bed, asked.

Luke set the luggage down and crossed the room.

She patted the bed beside her. "Sit."

Luke sighed. He really wasn't in the mood for a mother-son talk.

271

But he sat.

"I'm so glad you've accepted Jeff as my husband."

"I'm happy for you and him both, Mom. Really. You have a husband and I have a friend. It worked out pretty good."

"I love him in a different way than I loved your father, you know, which doesn't diminish either love. They're different, and each came in its own time."

"I understand." But he didn't understand why she felt it necessary to tell him something they'd already discussed.

"I fell in love with your father the first time I went out with him. We were married a couple of years, though, before we became best friends. It was nice to do it the reverse way with Jeff. I don't think you can truly love someone unless you are best friends."

Now they were getting to the heart of the matter. "Mom, if you don't mind, I'm twenty-nine years old. I think I can take care of my own love life."

"It doesn't appear to me that you're doing such a good job of it. I watched you all those years with Cindy, and I know how you felt about her. You're wrong when you think it was going from friendship to love that ruined it for you two. Neither the friendship nor the love was deep enough. It wasn't the kind that lasts forever, the kind that makes a marriage, the kind you have with Katie."

"Mom, Katie's engaged to that Spencer guy." *Who drives a silver Mercedes and has every blond hair in place and a smarmy smile on his face.*

"No, she's not. She broke it off with him."

"How do you know that?"

His mother frowned and looked momentarily confused. "I'm not sure how I know, but I do know. Someone told me. Sheriff, I imagine."

He rose indignantly and took a step backward. "You

272

talked about this with Sheriff? Damn it, Mom, I'm not a little kid anymore! You can't go around discussing my life with other people!"

"Calm down, Luke. Jerome and I weren't discussing your problems with Katie. We haven't had a chance. But I'm sure he must have been the one to tell me about Katie. I don't know who else it could have been."

Luke picked up the bag again. "I'd better get this downstairs. I'm sure Jeff's waiting with the trunk open."

He left before she could protest again.

When the suitcases were stowed in the trunk of their car, Jeff slammed the lid and turned to Luke. "Can we talk for just a minute?"

"Sure." He didn't really want to, but he could do one more session of reassuring Jeff that things were copacetic between them.

He followed Jeff to the shade of an elm tree in the front yard. Jeff leaned against the tree, folded his arms and assumed his professorial expression. "It took me a long time to convince your mother to marry me."

Luke smiled. "I'm glad you were persistent. I can't say that I'm ever going to think of you as my stepfather, but it's nice to have a friend in the family."

Jeff nodded. "Yes, I am your friend. That's why I need to tell you that it took me a while to convince your mother to marry me."

"You said that already."

"Then you didn't listen very good the first time." Jeff straightened. "You're a bright boy, Luke. You never really had to struggle for anything you wanted. You received good grades without trying. You got a job with the Houston Police the first time you applied. This position in Briar Creek opened up for you when you needed it. You even got married the first time without any real effort. You just sort of moved from one stage to another by unspoken agreement. It's time you worked for what you want, Luke."

"What are you talking about?"

Jeff drew in a deep breath. His features took on the expression he got when some student was being particularly dense about an important point he'd just made. "I'm talking about Katie. If you love her as much as I think you do, you must go after her. You lost her a lot of years ago by ignoring her. Don't do the same thing this time."

"She left me! She went back to Dallas to be with that Spencer."

"She and Spencer aren't getting married."

Was Luke the only one in the county who hadn't heard this bit of news? "Who told you that?"

Jeff stopped and frowned. "To be honest, I don't know. Maybe your mother. I'm sure someone did, I just can't quite remember who. Anyway, I'm sure you need to go after her. She's frightened because she spent so many years building up her defenses after losing you and her mother, and now you've broken through those defenses and she's running scared. You have to go to her and reassure her."

It was Luke's turn to frown. "How do you know all that? You sound more like a psych teacher than history."

Jeff looked slightly confused again. "I do, don't I? I'm not sure how I know that, but I'm positive it's accurate."

"Have you talked to Katie?"

"No, of course not. Your mother and I have discussed the issue, however."

Luke still wasn't sure where either of them had come up with all that business about Katie, but he did understand where they were coming from. His mother was still trying to take care of him, and now she had Jeff in on the program.

He clapped a hand on Jeff's shoulder. "I'll handle it.

You and Mom have a good trip back to Houston and come up again any time you get a chance. You're always welcome here."

They walked back to the house to find that Sheriff had arrived and was standing with Luke's mother on the porch.

Everyone hugged and shook hands, and finally Jeff and his mother were gone.

"Sure was good to see Francine again," Sheriff said.

"Yes, it was," Luke agreed.

"I like that Jeff. Nice fellow."

"Yes, he is."

Luke waited tensely for Sheriff to say something about Katie, hoping the older man wouldn't subject him to another *discussion* about Katie and him.

"Guess I'll mosey on home. See you in the morning." Sheriff stepped off the porch.

Sheriff was leaving without bringing up Katie? Suddenly Luke realized that wasn't what he wanted after all.

"Did you tell my mother that Katie wasn't going to marry Spencer?"

Sheriff stopped and turned back. "Nope, don't believe I did. But it's true. She's not. She'll be back in town next weekend. Reckon you can talk to her about it yourself then."

Luke watched Sheriff, whistling happily, *mosey* down the walk toward his house.

Jeff and his mother wanted him to storm the fortress of Katie's condo while Sheriff seemed totally unconcerned.

Luke went back inside and sat down by the phone. He could call her, but he had no idea what he'd say to her. He'd already told her he loved her, and she'd run away.

But he was going to take Jeff's advice. He wasn't

275

going to let her go this time.

Katie had been partially right about one thing. He couldn't recapture the past.

But she wasn't completely right. He couldn't recapture the past because it wasn't gone. It was still there, still all around him, an influence on everything he said and did, on all his actions. It blended with the present and gave it poignancy and richness.

His father had given him values along with his childhood memories and dark hair and a Roman nose. None of those things would ever go away.

The past he'd been so anxious to recapture was integrally tied to Katie. Without her in his present, he had neither past nor future.

***

Sunday evening Katie sat on her third-floor balcony enjoying her view of the creek.

Well, to be perfectly honest, she wasn't enjoying it all that much.

Running to Dallas to hide hadn't worked this time. Luke was everywhere she turned.

His scent was in the elevator. He was on this balcony, firing up the grill, standing beside the tree, looking down at the creek. He was in her condo, sitting at the table and on the sofa...kissing her on the sofa.

Her bedroom, which should have been free of his memories, wasn't. He'd invaded her dreams last night.

How had she allowed this to happen? She'd spent years getting her life in order, and now in one week Luke had sent everything crashing to the ground.

Okay, it was a good thing that she'd decided not to marry Spencer. But letting down her barriers and opening herself up to Luke again wasn't so good. How could she have done something so reckless?

And while she was on the subject of reckless, making

love with no protection certainly fell in that category for more than one reason. Her emotions as well as her body had been unprotected.

Again the fear of the possibility of trying to be a mother washed over her filling her with a nameless terror.

She couldn't think about that now...wouldn't think about it. In a couple of weeks, if she had cause to worry...well, she didn't really know how she could cope with it, but there was no point in worrying now when it might be needless.

Thank goodness she would be back at work tomorrow. She could go in early and stay late, throw herself into her work and purge her mind of Luke and all her problems.

She'd done it when she was a child. She could certainly do it as an adult.

***

Things were going reasonably well, she thought Monday afternoon. Even a morning meeting with Spencer had been uneventful. The two of them had conducted business as if there had never been anything personal between them.

Actually, there hadn't been.

But shortly before four o'clock her assistant came into her office with a special delivery package.

"Thanks," Kate said. "Just put it on my desk. I'll get to it in a minute."

Kate finished what she was doing, then saved her work on her computer and turned to check out the rectangular, brown paper wrapped package.

It was from Luke.

She bit her lip. Damn! She hated the way her heartbeat increased, and her hopes rose when she saw the return address.

This was just the way her heartbeat had increased and

her hopes had risen a hundred times all those years ago whenever the mailman had stopped to deliver a letter to their house or when the phone had rung and she'd gone racing in to answer it.

She picked up the package, swiveled in her chair and tossed it into her trash can without even opening it. She didn't want to know what was inside. She wasn't going to think about that part of her life again.

She went back to work on her computer.

The window behind her desk gradually darkened, and the cleaning woman came in while Kate continued to work.

"Can I get your trash?" the woman asked.

"Sure." Kate handed her the can...but then hesitated and, against her better judgment, took out the package.

She was curious. That's all.

When the woman was gone, she finally opened it and found a journal.

Her first thought was that it somehow related to one of the stories Jeff had told them about Briar Creek's history, maybe an old journal kept by one of those early residents.

But this book looked like it was brand new.

She opened it to the first page.

Two torn movie stubs lay between the pages. Luke had written a date in June, two years after he'd moved away. *Katie and I went to the movies, but I don't remember what we saw. We sat in the balcony and I held her hand and suddenly she wasn't that little kid with the messy hair anymore. She's growing up and so am I.*

What on earth? Nothing like that had happened! Luke had been in Houston two years by that time, not back in Briar Creek going to the movies with her.

What was he doing, trying to rewrite history?

She thumbed through the rest of the book, but the

pages were blank. Toward the end, several appeared to have been torn out.

Irritated with Luke for sending something so inane and irritated with herself because it touched something deep inside that she didn't want touched, she shoved the journal in a desk drawer and started to leave for home.

On second thought, she'd better take it with her. If somebody found it, they'd think she was nuts.

***

The next day's delivery was a larger package.

By that time, Kate couldn't help being intrigued. Her assistant had barely closed the door behind her when Kate ripped it open to find a high school letter jacket and one of the pages torn from the journal. The date was in October, four years after he'd left town.

I made the winning touchdown tonight but only because I could hear Katie cheering so hard. Later under the bleachers, I gave her my letter jacket and kissed her. It was like stepping out of an airplane onto a cloud.

Kate stood in her office staring at the stupid letter jacket with a stupid smile on her face and stupid tears in her eyes.

Damn him! He wasn't going to do this to her! He'd gone away and left her and she'd dealt with that. He wasn't going to bring up the past, try to rewrite history and make her get all emotional about it.

She picked up the phone and dialed the number for the sheriff's office. She'd put a stop to this right now.

But she got a computer voice telling her all circuits were busy and her call could not go through.

Just as well. She didn't want to talk to Luke.

She could send an email since the sheriff's office had that capability now.

She pulled up her email program and typed: "Luke— This is stupid. Stop it. I'll leave your journal and your

279

letter jacket at Papa's this weekend, and Papa can bring them to you on Monday." Then she hit the send button. So much for his nonsense.

The next day, Wednesday, her message was returned to her by the ubiquitous Daemon mailer...*server unknown*. Of course the server was known! What was going on?

Another call to Papa's office got the same computer voice telling her the circuits were busy. They must be having telephone problems in Briar Creek.

That afternoon a smaller package yielded a class ring on a gold chain and another page from the journal. The date was in May, five years after he'd moved away.

I asked Katie to go steady, and she said yes. I am the happiest man in the world!

She picked up the phone to call again and got the computer message again.

She put down the phone and slipped the chain around her neck before she realized what she was doing.

Angrily, she yanked it over her head, tangling the chain in her hair.

Rather the way Luke was continuing to tangle himself in her life.

Finally she got the thing off, though not without the loss of a few red hairs that remained permanently snared in the chain.

She'd take it along with the jacket and the journal to her father this weekend.

Thursday brought a wrist corsage and a date two weeks after the last one.

Took Katie to the senior prom and told her how much I love her and how I don't want things to end when we go off to college.

Damn it, what was this obsession of his with the past? He had to understand that events couldn't be changed. The past couldn't be retrieved or rewritten. The present might not be what someone wished it was, but no one had a choice. Everyone had to live in the now, make it as pleasant as possible, find compensations for what got lost in the past.

She'd done a good job of that.

Until now.

Friday's delivery brought a diamond ring.

No, she told herself. It wasn't a real diamond.

But she suspected it was.

The message had the current date and the words *I asked Katie to marry me. I'm waiting for her answer.*

She crumpled the paper and resolutely tossed it into the wastebasket.

This really had to stop.

She'd go to Briar Creek tonight, leave right after work, and tell Luke as soon as she got there.

But just before five o'clock, Kate's computer flashed an error message indicating her system had crashed.

In a panic, she worked for an hour to find the problem...which abruptly resolved itself for no apparent reason. She was relieved to find the original error message had been in error and that everything on her system was intact.

She finally left her office, exhausted, only to find she had no better success getting through the computer-controlled traffic lights out of Dallas than she had getting through the phone lines to Briar Creek. For some reason, all week the computers she normally considered her best friends had become her enemies.

By the time she got to Briar Creek it was dark and she was exhausted.

Papa greeted her at the door with a cup of hot chocolate.

Her tension began to fall away in layers.

She set down her suitcase, stroked Leo as he rubbed

against her leg then accepted the cup from Papa. "How did you know exactly when to make this so it would be hot when I got here?"

"Your mother told me."

Of course.

She sat down on the sofa to sip her chocolate. Leo curled in her lap, purred loudly and shoved his head under her hand, demanding to be petted.

Another layer of tension melted away.

"There's something so soothing about being here, Papa. When I came in, I was completely frazzled, and now, suddenly, I'm at least half relaxed."

"This old house is permeated with a lot of love, Katie-girl. That's always soothing to the soul."

"That lilac scent helps, too. I'm going to have to do some research into all this aroma therapy. Obviously there's something to it. Where do you get that room deodorizer?"

"I don't have any room deodorizer. Lilac has always been your mother's favorite scent. After a while, those things you love just start to become a part of you. It's nice, isn't it?"

Kate smiled. There was no point in arguing with him or trying to convince him that Mama's ghost wasn't drifting through the room, trailing the scent of lilacs.

By the time Kate went up to bed, she could barely keep her eyes open.

***

Jerome stood at the base of the stairs and watched Katie go up, then listened for the sound of her bedroom door closing.

"Well, my love, this could be it," Emma said. "I think I may be able to get through to her tonight."

Jerome wrapped an arm around his wife's waist. "I hope so. I sure hate to see our baby hurting." He hated the thought of his wife leaving, too, but that was the natural order of things. He'd already had her far longer than he'd ever dared hope.

"She's ready to give in. And how could she resist with what Luke's been doing this week? I've always liked that boy, but I never realized he was so clever. All of those things were his own idea. I had no hand in that, except getting Francine and Jeff to talk to him and putting in a few computer blocks."

Jerome nodded. "Luke is clever, and he knows our Katie so well. Just think how clever our grandchildren will be."

"That's one of the points she and I still have to talk about."

"I'll be waiting for you in our room." He leaned down and pecked Emma's tingly lips. "You give new meaning to the term *sizzling kisses*," he teased.

"Oh, Jerome!" She blushed and smiled.

Chapter Twenty-Four

Kate had just dozed off when she heard her name being called.

"Katie-girl."

Papa was the only one who called her that, but it didn't sound like Papa's voice.

She rolled over and there, in the moonlight that filtered through the branches of the cottonwood tree outside her window, she saw Mama sitting on her bed stroking Leo.

Well, not exactly Mama, like in a flesh-and-blood person, but sort of a transparent Mama...and she was glowing a little. Most people didn't glow.

Kate sat bolt upright, her heart pounding, then reminded herself she was asleep and dreaming. It was only natural that she should be dreaming about Mama after Papa had been talking about her so much. No big deal.

"We haven't been able to talk like this in years," Mama said. "I've missed that."

"Me, too." As Kate spoke the words, she realized they were true even though they made no sense. "We used to talk like this when I was little, didn't we?"

Good grief! What was she saying?

"Dream like this, I mean."

That wasn't a whole lot better.

Mama smiled and ran her hand over Leo's back while he did his invisible hand routine just as she'd done in the other dream Kate had had of her. "We did talk like this," Mama said. "I'd come in to see you almost every night, sometimes in your dreams and sometimes like now."

"This is a dream."

"If you need it to be."

"Why'd you stop? Why'd you leave me?" The questions came out before Kate could stop them. She frowned at her own absurdity. "Why am I asking these questions when it's *my* dream?"

"After Luke left, you stopped believing. I was able to come back to you and your father because I love you both so much and because you both love me. But that means you can only see and hear me with your heart. I couldn't reach you until you opened that door again, until you were able to let Luke past the barrier you put up."

"This dream isn't going the way I want it to. I'm going back to sleep now."

She laid her head on the pillow and resolutely closed her eyes. Leo walked over her stomach and rubbed his cheek against hers. Damn, he felt real!

"You can't go back to sleep now. You have to get up and get dressed. Luke's going to be over here in a few minutes, and you need to go down and tell him you'll marry him."

Kate sat up again. She'd never before had such a bossy dream!

"Luke's going to be over here in the middle of the night? Right."

"He is. I sort of suggested it to him."

"Right." She hugged Leo to her. It was normal to dream about her cat, she supposed. That part was okay.

"It's true," Mama said. "I'm not connected to Luke the way I am to you and Papa so he can't see me, but he loves you both so much, I've been able to make suggestions to him as well as to Francine and Jeff. The hearts of those two are very open to love." She smiled fondly. "I'm sure George approves of their marriage."

Kate pushed her hair back from her face as if that would somehow allow her to see more clearly. It didn't. Mama was still there. She was still dreaming.

"This is absolutely the last time I drink Papa's hot chocolate before I go to bed. If I didn't know better, I'd think he drugged it."

"Katie, you know in your heart that this isn't a dream. If you'll only look deep within, you'll remember how we used to talk. I need for you to remember and to realize that I never left you, and I never will, not even when I have to go on. When people love each other, they're never separated, not by miles or years or even death."

Kate closed her eyes, rubbed a hand over them, looked away and then back.

Mama was still there.

And with a shock, she did remember how she'd accepted this sort of thing as completely natural when she was a little girl. Then when Luke had left, her mother had, too, and the pain had been unendurable.

Her mother laid a transparent, faintly glowing, tingly hand on hers, and Kate's heart swelled with the amount of love that touch transferred, the amount of love that had brought her mother back for her.

"You have the love that grows between a man and a woman, Katie, if you'll just accept it," Mama said. "Luke is your soul-mate, just as your father is mine. You'll be as happy as we are. But I also want you to know the love between a mother and child, all the wonder of holding your baby in your arms. You're frightened of that because you don't want your children to experience the pain you went through when you lost me...twice...once in the car wreck and again when Luke left and you closed your heart so I couldn't reach you. But now you know there's nothing to fear. Even when you're all settled and I can go on, you'll have my love in your heart."

The last barrier fell. "Mama?" Kate asked in wonder. She realized tears were streaming down her face, though she didn't think she was crying.

"Yes, Katie-girl. I'm here. I always have been and I always will be even when you're not able to see me." She stood and planted a tingly kiss on Kate's forehead. "Get up and get dressed, sweetheart. Your best friend should be here any minute."

Mama left. She didn't disappear in a puff of smoke or a flash of light. She walked out in a fairly conventional manner...except the door was only open a few inches, just enough for Leo to come in.

Kate sat blinking in the moonlight. She was awake. But had she been awake a few minutes ago?

She touched her face and felt the dampness of her tears. Her heart was still warm with the love she'd felt in her dream.

Or her actual conversation with her mother.

Leo purred and demanded she pet him.

The way Mama had been petting him.

The way Mama had been petting him all those times Kate had laughed about his invisible hand routine?

She did remember now that her mother had visited her often in her dreams when she was a child unable to tell the difference between dreams and reality.

And even beyond that time.

Up until Luke had gone away, until she'd closed her heart to love.

Something thudded against the side of the house.

Was someone outside?

A flicker of fear shot through her, but this was Briar Creek. No one would break and enter Sheriff's house.

She got out of bed and went to the window.

A ladder sat against the house, and Luke was climbing that ladder.

"What are you doing?" she demanded. "Are you nuts?"

He looked up, smiled and sighed. "I think I must be. Katie, I love you a lot, but this is it. After you climb down from your window and we sneak out, we're through

287

reliving the past. Do you have any idea how many boxes I had to go through to find my football jacket and class ring?"

Kate laughed. She couldn't help it. She'd just been visited by her mother's ghost who'd left her feeling all warm and mushy inside, and now she discovered the deputy sheriff climbing up a ladder to her window. "What are you doing here in the middle of the night?"

"It's not the middle of the night. It's ten-thirty. But I have no idea what I'm doing here. I was watching the news when I had a sudden urge to come by and see if you'd arrived yet, just check to see if your car was here. Then when I saw this ladder lying beside the house, I thought, what the heck? Who's going to arrest me? So, are you ready to sneak out?"

It was completely absurd and ridiculous...but Kate wanted to do it. "We can't do that."

"Why not?"

"There's a screen on the window."

Luke sighed again. "Okay, I'll go get a hammer."

"I suppose you could do that, or I could I just come out the front door."

"I'd like that. I'd *really* like that. I feel *really* stupid right now."

"You don't look stupid."

"I don't?"

Kate drew in a deep breath. This was it, time to make a choice. She could choose to run away again. Not just to Dallas, but inside herself, lock her heart behind strong barricades and keep out the pain. But she'd also keep out the love and all the happiness that came with that love.

Or she could choose to open up...to Mama and Luke and even the possibility of children.

"No, you don't look stupid. You look wonderful. You look like the future, so let's stop with all this bringing back the past and talk about that instead. I'll meet you at the front door in five minutes."

Kate hurriedly yanked off her oversized T-shirt and jerked on the halter-top summer dress she'd driven down in. She'd chosen it for comfort, not style or beauty, but it would have to do for right now. Anyway, Luke had loved her when she was a scrawny kid with scabs on her knees and dirt on her face.

From her suitcase, she extracted the diamond ring then ran downstairs. Her bare feet made almost no sound on the steps, but several of them creaked from her weight. However, there was little likelihood that Papa was asleep with all the visitors...ghostly and otherwise.

She hesitated at the foot of the stairs for a moment and looked back toward her room.

Had she really been talking to Mama's ghost or had it all been a dream?

One thing she knew for certain, the love was real.

She opened the door to find Luke sitting in the porch swing.

She smiled. "Hi."

He smiled. "Hi."

She offered him the box, and he frowned. "I see. Does this mean your answer is *no*?"

She sat beside him and felt momentarily shy. But there was no need for that. She'd known Luke all her life. He was her best friend. "Of course not. It just means I want you to ask me in the present and in person."

He grinned. "Do I have to get down on one knee? I got this football injury in high school, and I've already stressed it tonight climbing a ladder after a woman who wouldn't climb down with me and—"

"Okay, you can forget the knee business!"

He opened the box and took out the ring. "Katie Fallon, I've loved you since—"

"And I'd appreciate it if you'd forget the matching diaper business, too."

"I was going to say, I've loved you since the first time I can remember."

"You were not. You can't lie to me, Luke Rodgers. I know you too well."

His dark eyes shone though they were on the porch, hidden away from the moon and the stars. "Yes, you do. And you know how much I love you."

A lump rose in her throat and she became as serious as he. "I do know," she whispered. "And I love you the same, with all my heart."

"Katie, if you'll marry me, I swear I'll never leave you again."

"I know that, too. And I will marry you if you promise we won't have to make love on that hard cave floor ever again."

She held out her hand, and he slipped the ring on her finger then grinned and wrapped his arms around her. "You didn't seem to mind. But I'm sure we can find plenty of other places."

He lowered his lips to hers and she gave herself up to a kiss that tasted of the past and the present and held a world full of wonderful dreams of the future.

When he finally, reluctantly, drew away, his eyes were heavy-lidded with desire and both of them were breathing hard. "How about if we set the date real soon?" he asked, his voice husky.

"Good idea. We can do that. I already have a dress in the attic." She lifted her hand to admire the ring, the promise of her life with Luke. "It fits perfectly. How did you know my ring size?"

Luke shrugged. "I'm not sure how I knew. I just did."

And suddenly Kate knew. Mama had said he'd been open to her suggestions.

She hadn't been dreaming.

From Papa's window, the strains of *Anniversary Waltz* drifted down.

Papa hadn't been sleeping.

She took Luke's hand. "Dance with me."

They moved out into the yard, and Luke pulled her into his arms.

"We'll have better dance floors in the future, too," he promised with a wink.

"No, we won't. It couldn't get any better than this."

As she danced with Luke in the front yard where once they'd played, she looked up to Papa's window and saw him dancing with Mama.

Epilogue

Jerome stood on the porch and waved as Katie and Luke drove away in Luke's big old convertible, off to Padre Island for their honeymoon. The happy couple waved back, and Katie blew him a kiss.

He turned, went into the house and climbed the stairs to his bedroom. From the window, he and Emma watched Katie and Luke round the corner.

"Our Katie looked so beautiful in your wedding dress. She's the prettiest bride I've seen since you."

Mama smiled and leaned her head on his shoulder. "She was beautiful. And Luke was almost as handsome as you."

"You were right, Emma. She and Luke just needed a gentle nudge in the right direction."

Emma nodded. "It makes me so happy to see her happy again."

Jerome put one arm around his wife and his other hand on the window sill, bracing himself. "She is happy. I guess we finally got her raised. I couldn't have done it without you. Now I reckon you'll be going on." He forced himself to smile a wobbly smile. "I know you have to, and I'm not complaining. I've had all these extra years with you, a chance most people never get. But I'm sure gonna miss you."

He looked out the window and swallowed hard, determined not to let her see his sadness.

Emma cuddled closer. "I've been here an awfully long time now. I don't think a few more years will make much difference on a cosmic level. I'd kind of like to stick around to see my grandchildren, especially that one that's about the size of a lady bug right now. And then maybe I'll wait around a little longer until you're ready to come with me."

Jerome looked at his wife and smiled. "I'd like that, Emma. I'd like that an awful lot."

THE END

About the Author:

I grew up in a small rural town in southeastern Oklahoma where our favorite entertainment on summer evenings was to sit outside under the stars and tell stories. When I went to bed at night, instead of a lullaby, I got a story. That could be due to the fact that everybody in my family has a singing voice like a bullfrog with laryngitis, but they sure could tell stories—ghost stories, funny stories, happy stories, scary stories.

For as long as I can remember I've been a storyteller. Thank goodness for computers so I can write down my stories. It's hard to make listeners sit still for the length of a book! Like my family's tales, my stories are funny, scary, dramatic, romantic, paranormal, magic.

Besides writing, my interests are reading, eating chocolate and riding my Harley.

Contact information is available on my website. I love to talk to readers! And writers. And riders. And computer programmers. Okay, I just plain love to talk!

http://www.sallyberneathy.com